Priory, Louisiana

A Novel

Priory, Louisiana

A Novel

Pat Kogos

BIG PORCH PRESS
St. Louis, Missouri
www.bigporchpress.com

Priory, Louisiana: *A Novel*. Copyright © 2013 Pat Kogos

All rights reserved. No part of this book may be used or reproduced in any manner whatsoever without written permission except in the case of brief quotations embodied in critical articles and reviews.

For information, contact Big Porch Press, www.bigporchpress.com.

This book is a work of fiction. Any references to historical events, real people, or real locales are used fictitiously. Other names, characters, places, and incidents are the product of the author's imagination, and any resemblance to actual events or locales or persons, living or dead, is entirely coincidental.

FIRST EDITION

Cover and interior art design by Ann Paidrick.

ISBN-13: 978-0-615-80693-8
ISBN-10: 0-615-80693-7

*for anyone who's been
lost in a storm*

*with special appreciation to
Sam, Teddy, Margaret,
my parents—Bill & Jean,
my big, supportive family,
and my brilliant community of writers*

PRIORY, LOUISIANA

CHAPTER ONE

"Mama, please? Can I *please* ride down the hill?"

"No, Lena. The levee's too big to go straight down. Too dangerous, mija. We'll take the ramp, like we always do."

"Papa?" Lena implored.

Raul Melendez smiled and shook his head. *At seven years old, she's already playing both sides.* "No, my love. Listen to Mama."

Ida reached over to hold her husband's hand. They walked behind Lena's purple bike, within a step or two of her bobbing frame. Raul raised his wife's hand to his lips and kissed it.

Two older kids rode past, kicking up a spinning cloud of shell dust. When it settled, Ida marveled at how small her daughter looked against the panoramic landscape. To her left, down a bumpy expanse of grass and weeds, past the River Road, lay a sprinkling of familiar houses, as luminous as multi-hued swamp irises. Houses constructed of hewn cypress, knotty pine, and baked bricks. Plantations surrounded by fields of cotton, sugar, and an oil refinery. Priory, Louisiana. Their home.

To her right, down a matching expanse of bumpy slope and an unspectacular bed of tumbled rocks and shells, rolled the Mississippi River. The Mississippi that wound its way past Priory and Baton Rouge, then through mystical New Orleans, before seeping into wetlands in Plaquemines Parish on its way to the Gulf.

Lena pulled ahead of them on the shell path then slowed. The reduction in speed made the purple bike waver underneath her small frame. Its front wheel pointed toward the river, then wobbled toward the equally steep descent leading to town. She looked down the hill, wanting so badly to give it a try.

Ida sped up to reach Lena so she wouldn't fall, but her daughter's course was already set. She could no longer withstand the magnetic lure of desire. It possessed her with such intensity.

Lena jerked the handlebars and ripped down the forbidden hill, away from her parents and the river, leaving the levee's high perch. The inevitability of this ride washed over her like the hot breeze against her face. Deep inside her thrilled young body, she knew she would one day do this. She'd been dwelling on it, fighting the urge, for as long as she could remember. Maybe since she'd been five.

She clenched the handlebars. The hill's every crevice tried to unseat her. Red and white streamers waved from her bike handles. Auburn pigtails fluttered in her wake. Lena heard her parents' frantic voices, growing fainter as she raced away from them, "No, Lena, no!"

When she finally reached the bottom of the levee, and safely braked to slow then stop, her heart thumped a tribal beat. She stared at her shaking hands and feared looking uphill to see her parents' reactions. Lena struggled to control her ragged breathing, tried to suppress a victorious grin, and glanced skyward.

She watched with curiosity as her father held her mother close to his chest, rubbing her wide back. Ida's shoulders rose and fell, and Lena wasn't sure whether her mother was laughing or crying. As an adult, Lena would suppose it had been both. She'd forever remember the silhouette of her parents clutching one another under the hazy pink smear of a late afternoon sky.

When Ida pulled back, and looked down the levee's slope at her brave but unpredictable daughter, she couldn't help but grin. Lena had reached the bottom safely only by the grace of God.

Ida's grin burst open into joyful laughter. An unexpected font of bliss. Its resounding exuberance rode the humid air down uneven terrain to Lena. Turning her brown eyes to the sky, Ida whispered, "Gracias, Padre. Muchas gracias."

Raul laughed, too. It was hard not to be joyful at the sight of wild little Lena, triumphant and gleaming, perched safely atop her bike at the bottom of the levee.

With her parents seeming to be as jubilant as she was, Lena reveled in the accomplishment. She wanted to do it again. The thrill of it was addicting. It grew within Lena's soul in a way she'd never be able to explain or deny. Lena was invincible. She'd disobeyed her parents and everything had turned out all right.

At age twenty-seven, Lena climbed the concrete steps of the levee once again, as she often did. Chirping swelled from the branches of trees beyond the River Road. Its crescendo pushed against Lena's back, attempting to propel her forward. But the steps multiplied before her, so she paused to massage her sore knee and study the approaching blue sky.

The early morning sky was wide and full of secrets. It was all-knowing, that sky. It had seen everything, floated above the earth's surface, witnessed city traffic and Native American dances, absorbed tears and laughter into its own complex essence. The sky liked to appear far away, but it was deceiving like that. It drew Lena's eyes away from the earth, as if it weren't at the same time touching her sweaty skin and circling her weary frame. As if it weren't at the same time drawing something from her.

Lena looked down to the jagged scar on her knee. It ached today. Some days, it felt like every scar on her body ached. At the apex of the levee, she inhaled moist river air and wiped her wet forehead with the back of her hand.

She eased herself down onto the earthen road and sat cross-legged on the highest point in Priory, in the spot of remembered joy. Lena closed her eyes and basked in the love she imagined was stored in the patch of earth below her. Her mother's orange-water perfume enveloped her. Her father's baritone voice played inside her head.

Opening her eyes, Lena searched the endless sky for a sign. Something to give her hope.

But the sky seemed so clear, so distant.

Please, God, I don't know how to get past this. If you can hear my prayers, let me know.

Thousands of miles away, above South Atlantic waters, a tropical depression brewed. Its presence shifted air patterns across the world's atmosphere, swirling dormant winds. It drove itself invisibly, quietly, toward Lena's all-knowing Priory sky.

PRIORY, LOUISIANA

Mornin', Y'all   Sunday, August 21, 2005

"*Mornin', Y'all.* This is Melody Melançon and you're listening to WPRY 90.5, bringing you and your mama up-to-date on the latest in Priory.

We got us some metery...meteor...some weathermen here in Priory, y'all. Bunch of smarties meeting over at the College of Priory tomorrow morning to yak about hurricanes and global warming. Lord, *I* could give *that* talk. Oh, rats, did I just take the Lord's name in vain? Father Abelli, if you're listening, strike that last sentence.

Anyway, after the weather people huddle up at the college, they'll be headed over to Mélange Plantation for some lunch. If y'all have nothing to do tomorrow or you just need to sweat out last night's Sazerac, they're inviting the public to join them in a jazz funeral. It'll really be something, y'all. They'll be second-lining behind Colonel Bishop's Brass Band to the Cemetery of Three Crosses, mourning folks who lost their lives to hurricanes.

It's got all the makings of a beautiful Loo-siana day: heat, food, and a raucous parade.

That's it for now. But remember, if you're not listening to *Mornin', Y'all,* you might as well be living in Oklahoma."

CHAPTER TWO

Priory, Louisiana

New Orleans was heavy with humidity, but not more than usual. August brought with it death and desire, but not in remarkable doses. There was one peculiarity, though. One nagging, off-the-shore oddity. The temperature in nearby Gulf waters had risen in recent years. It was only a degree or two. To Tom Vaughn, its gradual rise had gone unnoticed.

He walked out of his Lakeview double and went to his Jeep. After popping open the back door, he threw his navy duffle onto a mess of software manuals.

Every uneasy fiber in his body urged him to get into the car and not approach Mimi's door. He could call her from the road and tell her he'd be gone for a while. She was such an understanding old girl. Certainly, she wouldn't haze him for leaving without notice.

But he couldn't do it. Couldn't drive off without seeing her. So, in a black shirt he hoped Mimi wouldn't question, he walked back onto the front porch, shaking his head. After a hesitant knock on her door, Mimi appeared. When he saw her droopy blue eyes, the eyes of a lovable bloodhound, he knew he'd done the right thing. She was a tonic; her lipstick-smile eased his pain.

"Hey, Mimi." Tom planted a kiss on her squishy cheek. Mimi closed her large lids and basked in her grandson's affection.

"Hey, darlin', how you doin' today?" she asked.

"I'm aggravated as shit."

PRIORY, LOUISIANA

A raspy laugh spilled out of her. She led Tom over to a table set with sugared pecans, a retired deck of hole-punched casino playing cards, an Old Fashioned in a rocks glass, and a frigid bottle of beer.

"Now, Tom, you'll feel better after we play a little gin. You always do."

"I don't think I'm gonna play gin today."

She looked confused. "How 'bout boo-ray?"

Tom smiled. "No, darlin'. Not boo-ray either."

Mimi ignored him, sat down, and picked up the deck. She shuffled while Tom stood there.

How could he explain the unrest? The urgency?

His grandmother's manicured hands dealt the cards: one to Tom's beer, one to her Old Fashioned, rhythmically, and without hesitation. They fell onto a crocheted tablecloth fashioned by Mimi herself.

"I can't play cards today," Tom repeated.

"Nonsense. We always play cards on Sunday. We haven't missed a Sunday since you moved in." He sat down across from her and fanned his deck. While he configured his hand, she sipped her cocktail. "What the hell are you wearin', Thomas?"

"Nothin' special." He rearranged his cards and tugged at his shirt collar. "I thought I might wear black for a change. You know, to make me look handsome and a little mysterious. Like Johnny Cash." Tom winked at his grandmother.

Mimi's hanging jowls shook when she laughed, and she egged him on, "You look more like that jerk, Father McMann, than you do Johnny Cash. You didn't go see that sad excuse for a priest again this mornin', did you, hon?"

"Yeah, I saw him. That guy drives me nuts. Today, he told some woman, durin' the gospel, to remove her child from church because it was cryin'." Heat rose into Tom's face, and his eyebrows reached for each other. "Father McMann stared her down, Mass suspended, until she left."

Mimi's face sagged. "So typical."

"I can't go there anymore, Mimi."

"Now you're talkin'. I told you to stop goin' to that fool a year ago. There's a perfectly lovely priest over at St. Roch. It's a little further, but worth the drive."

Tom was fidgety, unable to focus on his game or his grandmother. His attention bounced all around her walls, first to the photos of Grandpa Dirk, then to pictures of Tom's mother as a young child. He looked at the portrait of Mimi above the fireplace. Even though she was bedecked in a ball gown, her young eyes sparkled with mischief.

With an expression he wore regularly as a ten-year-old, he looked at his grandmother and asked her seriously, "Mimi, do you think I'm goin' to hell if I start skippin' Mass? Think that'll land me in hell?" He swigged from his cold brew and waited for her answer. The trickle in his throat was soothing.

She put her cards facedown onto the table. "You are in quite the mood this mornin', aren't you, love? What's goin' on inside that beautiful brain? *Goin' to hell?* What kind of conversation is that? Of course you're not goin' to hell."

Tom had trouble believing her while he was playing gin in a priest's shirt.

Mimi continued, "Now why don't you tell me what you're doin' in that get-up? And what the hell did you do to your hair?"

He reached one hand up to his newly slicked-down ebony hair and grinned. He stood up, walked around the table, and kissed Mimi on top of her silky white curls.

"Mimi, you saucy old broad, you've got a filthy mouth." He paused. "Truth is, I'm goin' on a little road trip. You know, see the country."

"You are? Dressed like that?"

"Yep. Dressed like this."

"When you leavin'?"

"Right now."

"What for? Can't you wait 'til after gin?"

Tom didn't want to explain. He'd imagined several versions of his story but each was more inane than the last. He didn't have the heart to tell her the truth. The truth about his mounting failures, the way they were piling up, creating a stench so awful that he had to get out from underneath them. He could never find the right words for that. "Nope. Can't wait any longer."

"Where you goin'?"

"Not sure."

Mimi rose from her chair, shook her head, and hugged him around a waistline that had expanded a few inches in recent years. Tom held her with an embrace as routine as afternoon rain.

"I'll call you," he promised. Then he left, forcing Mimi to play solitaire all afternoon, pondering her grandson's strange behavior and his sudden need to travel.

As he backed out of the driveway, Tom became fixated upon their shared double. It was a one-story ranch with blonde bricks and rust-colored doors. Quaint. Comfortable. Boxwoods and impatiens softened the transition between lawn and house. A towering pine rose from thick grass near the street, its uneven shadow darkening Tom's doorway. *How typical*, he thought. Even though both sides of the house were physical mirrors of each other, the sun was only shining on Mimi's.

PRIORY, LOUISIANA

CHAPTER THREE

Mary Bell panted and walked up the painted wooden steps of her nineteenth century cottage. Her hands rested on her hips and her shoulders slumped. She'd run two miles every morning for a year, but the rolling hills of Priory, Louisiana, were still a challenge, particularly on humid days. At the front porch, she turned around under the wooden sign for The Retreat. Facing the stiff green lawn and the narrow street beyond it, Mary Bell exhaled.

Doc Wilson was driving by, easing through the morning fog, his Cadillac cutting deftly through haze like scissors through lace. He stopped, rolled down the window of his chocolate Caddy and yelled, "Hey, Mary Bell, how's your Sunday?"

Mary Bell smiled. "Great, Doc. Couldn't be better."

"Any sick guests today?"

"No, they all seem to be in good health." Between heavy breaths, she added, "But maybe *I* could use an oxygen tank."

"You look okay to me, missy, but call me if you need me." Doc peered over the top of his glasses. He waved and then rolled down the street, his left arm hanging out the window. The fog enveloped him until he disappeared.

A purple martin emerged from a gourd house in the glossy magnolia tree. It twitched then followed the good doctor's path into the mist, rising and falling like an amethyst wave.

Mary Bell pivoted. Inside the screen door stood Lafitte, smiling his uneven grin and wiping his hands on the front of a Tabasco apron. His smile was an infectious, one-sided, triangular affair. One corner of his mouth, directly below a patched eye, was immobile. The warm smell of bacon grease drifted out from behind him.

"Morning, Lafitte. Breakfast smells awesome."

"Morning, Mary Bell." He pushed the creaking screen door open, and the door shook, as Lafitte's hands always did. She grinned and stepped past him.

They walked through the dining room where the table was adorned with an antique lace tablecloth, eight settings of Depression glass water goblets, crystal juice cups, mismatched pieces of sterling silver, and an Audubon-inspired china set Mary Bell's parents had purchased at an estate sale.

She walked through the swinging door of the kitchen, delighted by the piquant, distinguishable scents of chicory coffee and buttered grits. Muted sunlight streamed in through the windows, washing the room in gold.

"Everything looks great, Lafitte." Mary Bell picked up a piece of bacon and bit into it. "I'm starving."

She loaded up a plate and sat down at the small maple table against the window. Lafitte was on duty, and he exited the kitchen several times through the swinging door, his tall body a commanding presence. Guests came downstairs, and their conversations buzzed in the nearby dining room.

Mary Bell gazed out the window, sipping from her cool orange juice, raising the glass to her forehead. She couldn't believe she'd been lucky enough to run into Henry Shane in the park. The mailman had said Henry was back in town, but she hadn't given him much thought. As a kid, Henry had been sweet, quiet, and plain. Now, well…

Trying to temper the nervous anticipation about her date that night, Mary Bell polished off breakfast and joined her guests in the dining room.

"Hey, y'all," she began.

The room quieted. The guests peered up, smiling. Mary Bell loved to see the transformation in visitors during the course of a few languid days in Priory. Twists of concern faded, knotted brows softened, and worn faces regressed a decade. They were youthening like Merlin.

"How's breakfast going?" she asked.

"Wonderful food."

"What's in these grits?"

Mary Bell smiled and said, "I'm sworn to protect Lafitte's deepest culinary secrets." She switched her tone to something more formal before beginning her weekly history lesson. "I want to thank you all for coming and tell y'all a little something about our home. It was built in 1850 by Dr. Kent Deauville and his wife, Susanna Hafferty Deauville. The portraits on the wall above the fireplace are of the great doctor and his wife, and we're very proud to have them in our possession."

Mary Bell pointed to the black marble mantle. Dr. and Mrs. Deauville stared ahead, portraits of elegance in distressed oval frames.

"They spent only ten years in this house before moving downriver to New Orleans and selling the property to General Gerard Bateau, whose portrait is in the front parlor. He and his descendants, myself included, have been living here ever since."

A middle-aged woman with a face full of bright makeup asked, "Why is this inn called The Retreat?"

Mary Bell answered, "Well, one of General Bateau's sons became a priest. When Father Bateau came back to visit his family, he said this place gave him a sense of peace, like a retreat house." Admiring the details of the room, she added, "When his siblings turned their home into an inn, they named it The Retreat in his honor."

Heads nodded. Lafitte poured an unsteady cup of coffee for a balding gentleman.

Mary Bell concluded, "Again, thank y'all so much for coming to The Retreat. If you have any questions, Lafitte and I will both be around to answer them."

The guests rose and began to chat amongst themselves. After a few minutes of polite banter, Mary Bell disappeared beneath the staircase into the privacy of her quiet suite. She couldn't shake the morning's images of Henry Shane from her mind: his wavy chestnut hair, his white and easy smile, his ample biceps, his boyish eagerness to have dinner with her.

Opening her nightstand, she withdrew her journal and flipped to the back page. In various inks, scrawled over the past several years, were Mary Bell's *Rules for Dating*:

Don't be too aggressive.
Don't be too indifferent.
If he says all the right things, he's not trustworthy.
If he can't be found, he doesn't want to be found.
If he brags too much, it'll always be all about him.

And so on. Some days, Mary Bell found her own scribblings to be amusing. Other days, she remembered the failed relationships that led to each of the notes, and sadness chipped away at her optimistic spirit. Would she need such caution with Henry? She'd known him forever. Maybe rules didn't apply if you knew a guy since before his voice changed. Mary Bell hoped the list was complete. Surely, Henry Shane wouldn't be the man who prompted her to add another adage to the page.

No. She would not begin the evening by distrusting Henry. They were old friends. Maybe it was nothing more. Still, a spark ignited in Mary Bell. One that grew throughout the afternoon, rising into her eyes and her smile, despite her reluctance to believe in it. By the time she finished dressing for dinner, Mary Bell Bateau was incandescent, her inner glow bouncing off every glass doorknob in The Retreat.

CHAPTER FOUR

Not sure which direction to head, Tom decided against Mississippi. There were too many gambling temptations on the Gulf Coast for a young priest, even a fake one, so he steered his Jeep onto the I-10 West. He slid sunglasses over his cat-like green eyes.

He passed through marshes of arthritic cypress stumps that looked charred. Tall grasses rose from water as dark as root beer. Tom was surprised, as if he had never noticed it before, that the murky water was so close to the road. White roadside crosses were far too common. Crosses leaning sideways under the weight of plastic flower arrangements.

Tom knew how wrong his plan was. How sinful and depraved. Yet it also ignited him. Gave him some sort of twisted hope. He felt like a kid skipping school, except that his school years were long behind him.

He tried to envision what he would miss most about work while he was gone. His buddies were the obvious answer. They'd have to shoulder the burden of his unexpected departure and cover for him. A pang of guilt thumped his stomach.

His departure e-mail to his boss had been short and vague. They'd all be wondering where he went. Soon he'd be the object of so much speculative conversation. Tom shook his head to clear it and focus on the road. In order to disappear, he didn't need to wander far from home. Most of his family and friends were in New Orleans. He'd been born, raised, educated, and employed within a twenty-mile radius.

PRIORY, LOUISIANA

A buzz filled Tom's car: a combination of the purring motor and droning tires on pavement. Rain began to drop wistfully onto his windshield, shrouding him from the world. The car's wipers marked time like an upside-down pendulum, and he became mesmerized...so mesmerized he didn't notice the glassy-wet exit signs for Houmas House, Laura Plantation, and Oak Alley. The brown sign for Tezcuco finally caught his attention. The next exit, San Francisco Plantation, got him to thinking about the River Road, but he kept driving. The further he drove, the harder the rain fell.

Before reaching Baton Rouge, signs appeared for the northern plantations at Priory, in West Feliciana Parish, and Tom followed them. Priory, Louisiana. A small speck of a town that tugged at his soul.

Shortly after college, he'd driven his girlfriend there for a weekend jaunt. Charlotte was headstrong, energetic, and beautiful. She had an Oxford, Mississippi, accent that was a world away from his New Orleans cadence. His mix of y'alls, truncated words, and fires that sounded like "fie-uhs" were not nearly as dramatic as her exaggerated inflections and her sing-songy speech.

One morning she asked, "Tom, would you take me on a little spring trip to Priory this weekend?" "Spring trip" sounded like "spreeng tree-ip." How could he refuse?

That weekend, with azaleas blushing and water trickling through streams of seemingly wild plantation gardens, Tom fell hopelessly in love. Maybe the air was unusually dry, or the flowers excessively vibrant, or her eyes too luminous. Maybe it was the way her long, dark hair stood out against the crisp white pillowcase, or the way every kiss of hers brought with it the need for more.

The one night they spent in Priory was the best night and the worst night of his life. It couldn't have been more perfect, but then other nights had to be measured up against it. Nothing had come close. Tom couldn't believe she had chosen *him*.

When Charlotte left him a month later to go back to her high school sweetheart, doors closed inside Tom. He had known he wasn't worthy of her, but he was stunned nonetheless. She seemed so sincere, so taken with him, so amused by his ridiculous jokes. He had ingested her lure only to be yanked, gasping with desperation, to die slowly on dry land.

More than ten years had passed. Tom sometimes felt like it had been a dream. Wasn't sure it ever really happened. Maybe he should try to find their bed & breakfast. He didn't remember exactly where it was or what it was called.

He pulled into a fast food drive-thru near the interstate. A greasy burger slid into his trembling stomach while he sat in the car. He hated that his first stop was in such a nondescript place.

By the time the gently rolling hills of Priory appeared, his stomach felt like it was loaded with frogs. Thunder rolled. The sky darkened. He passed through the historic district, with wooden cottages lining its path, then turned onto a side street to find the Roman collar and put it on. Tom ran around to the back of his Jeep, reached in to unzip his duffle, and grabbed the white piece.

He couldn't believe he was going to impersonate a priest. How had he sunk this low? There was such an overwhelming force within him that wanted to try it, he couldn't refuse. He tried to talk himself out of it so many times, but finally gave in to the dark desire.

Tom needed to shake up his life. That was undeniable. And he wanted to be a better person. Seemed like every time he tried to better himself, the result was disastrous.

Maybe pretending to be a holier person would help. He was going to be an inspirational priest, not one like Father McMann. Besides, this ruse would only last a couple days.

The only way to get through this charade would be to not take it too seriously. Have some fun with it. Learn some lessons. Go home.

Soft raindrops clung to his slick hair. He was standing in front of a peach-colored home. A sign hovering over the front porch read "The Retreat." Tom looked at the inn, up at the menacing clouds, blinked hard when a raindrop caught his eye, and stuck one end of the collar into his breast pocket. As he walked toward the front door, the white collar flapped conspicuously.

 CHAPTER FIVE

The clinking of the round bell on the front desk summoned Mary Bell to the parlor. "Hey. Can I help you?" she asked.

Tom shook off raindrops. "I…I'm lookin' for a room. Do y'all have anything?"

"I do," Mary Bell said. "How many nights will you be staying with us?"

Tom took a deep breath and inhaled a subtle lavender scent. "I'm not sure how long I'll be here. It's sort of an open-ended trip."

"Wonderful. It's so special to have a priest visiting."

The priest-statement pricked Tom's skin like a burr. "Thanks."

Mary Bell stood behind a pulpit-looking desk and surveyed her reservation book. "I have a nice room with a double bed in it. Would you like to see it?"

"Oh, that's not necessary. I'm sure it's fine." Her eyes were as blue as a 2-ball, and the dark curls of her hair sat like springs upon her shoulders.

"The bathroom's in the hallway, Father. I hope it won't be too much trouble."

Hearing the word *Father* made him blink. It turned his voice into something soft and formal. "No. That'll be fine."

"Wonderful. Your name?"

"Uh…Tom. Father Tom."

"Last name?"

Tom hesitated. "I'd rather not say, if that's okay with you."

Mary Bell wrinkled her brow.

"What's your name?" Tom asked.

"Oh, I'm sorry. I'm Mary Bell Bateau."

"Mary Bell. That's pretty. Anyway, Mary Bell, I've been in need of a little retreat. Then I got lost and wound up at a place *called* The Retreat. What are the chances?"

She smiled at him.

Tom lowered his voice. "I'd like to hide out here for a few days, if that's okay with you."

"Sure, Father."

Tom wanted to wrap his arms around her and tell her he wasn't a priest. Maybe she could save him from his swirling demons. After a quick glance at her bare ring finger, Tom straightened his posture. Now, if he could miraculously be transformed into someone she would want…

"Priory's the perfect place to relax," Mary Bell said. She leaned toward him and whispered, "And I'm very good at keeping secrets."

Tom drank her sweet, breathy words, but he recognized the familiar aftertaste of impossibility. A woman like Mary Bell would never be interested in a guy who would fake his own priesthood.

She continued, "You're in Suite 2B, at the top of the stairs. Do you need help with your bags?"

The fingers of Tom's left hand twitched, instinctively typing out the word b-a-g-s into the humid air, a bad habit rooted in too many years of keyboarding. "No, thank you, ma'am. I'm travelin' light."

Tom took the iron key from Mary Bell and hiked up the stairs. When he turned to sneak another peek at her, Mary Bell was watching him with upturned eyes.

He closed the door to his room and threw his bag under the highboy in the corner. In front of a full-length mirror, Tom pondered his attire.

He fastened his top button. After removing the white tab from his pocket, he slid its ends into his collar. His eyebrows took turns rising and falling. The impact of that white rectangle was startling.

Tom cocked his head and pulled at the stiff neckline of his shirt. The Australian-shaped birthmark on his neck was partially covered. It bore a closer resemblance now to the Smoky Mountains than it did an island continent. Tom didn't remember having only half of Australia when he wore this costume during college. Had Australia moved over the years or was he too tanked to notice it last time?

Back downstairs, Mary Bell fidgeted with paperwork. The front door opened again, amplifying the patter of raindrops. Through the open door, she admired Henry Shane's chiseled profile. He clutched a bottle of wine under one arm, closed his umbrella, and left it in the brass stand.

"Hey, Mary Bell." Henry closed the door, pecked her cheek, and handed her the bottle. "I hope you like it."

"Thanks, Henry." The kiss melted through her skin. "I'm sure I will."

Henry tried to remind himself to take things slowly, but he'd been daydreaming about Mary Bell all afternoon. He wondered if it showed.

"We're going to eat on the back porch, if that's okay with you."

"Sure, of course. I'll follow you."

Mary Bell led him through the dining room and into the kitchen. A tempting mix of rosemary and browned butter greeted him. Henry felt droplets of good fortune falling upon him. What were the chances he would come back to town and find Mary Bell Bateau unattached?

In the kitchen, they encountered Lafitte making a pot of coffee. A stainless steel scoop crunched into coffee grounds.

"Lafitte, you remember Henry Shane…" Mary Bell said.

Lafitte offered a firm hand to Henry, who accepted it with confidence. "I do," Lafitte replied. "Henry, good to see you again. Say, you're quite a bit taller than you were in high school."

Henry smiled. "Good to see you, too, Lafitte."

Out of the corner of his good eye, Lafitte saw Mary Bell's gaze bounce off various parts of Henry's physique like a fly trying to get through a pane of glass. "I guess I'll leave you two kids alone. I hope y'all enjoy your dinner."

Lafitte turned to leave the room, and Mary Bell said, "Oh, I almost forgot to tell you. A priest just checked into 2B. I gave him a key, and he went upstairs a couple minutes ago."

"Good. I'll check in on him and give him the lowdown on breakfast and what-not."

Lafitte exited through the swinging doors but wished he could stay to spy. Mary Bell was a grown woman now, and he had known Henry's family for decades, but Lafitte was hesitant. Mary Bell hadn't been lucky in love, and it had been hard to witness.

PRIORY, LOUISIANA

Mary Bell led Henry onto the back porch. The wide painted floorboards moaned. Henry couldn't believe his eyes. The scene was alive with flickering candles, swaying plants, and raindrops beyond the screens.

Henry never remembered feeling this special. He'd dated plenty of women, even some who had pursued him, but this was different. If he had ever dared to think of it as a young man, he would have lusted after Mary Bell. Everyone in high school lusted after Mary Bell.

Henry was speechless, and his silence filled Mary Bell's ears. Was he thinking she was foolish? While he stood spellbound by the flames, she wondered if she'd been wrong about his intentions. Maybe he had just come as a friend…a friend who wanted to catch up on missing years.

"Henry, I thought it might be fun to listen to some old music," she said, hurrying over to the stereo. She fumbled with a newly burned CD and managed to get it started, but was afraid to turn around.

Henry, without uttering a syllable, walked up behind her, moved her spiral curls to one side, kissed the nape of her neck, then reached down to cradle her hands in front of her petite waistline. He saw no reason to dawdle and couldn't convince himself to hold back.

Thank you, God, Mary Bell sighed, closing her long lashes. *Thank you.*

Neither one of them moved. Hootie & the Blowfish crooned "Only Wanna Be With You" and they smiled nervously. Henry held Mary Bell. Her heart beat through her back and onto his chest.

She turned around and put her hands behind her, bracing herself on the baker's rack. Henry stayed close in front of her, covering her hands with his and kissing her full-on. Mary Bell was trapped between the baker's rack, Henry's body, and Hootie. He kissed her passionately and with a sense of urgency. Then the kisses became gentler and more relaxed.

Henry pulled back, but he smiled a triumphant grin. "How about some wine?" His vision was blurry.

"I'd love some." Mary Bell grinned, too. She felt the victory was entirely hers. Staring at his lovely teeth, she re-noticed his one slightly crooked incisor. It made his smile all the more contagious and endearing.

Henry removed the cork and filled crystal goblets. Rain veiled them in secrecy. They clinked glasses and took a sip.

"Hungry?" Mary Bell asked, trying to focus on the meal Lafitte had prepared.

"You bet." Henry teased her, "What did you make me?"

Mary Bell laughed. "You might not already know this, but Lafitte's the only cook in this household."

She disappeared into the kitchen and returned carrying two warm plates with tea towels. She placed them on the table, and Henry pulled out a chair for her. He pushed her chair in and sat next to her but already felt too far away.

The distance between them was less than a foot of porch air, but it felt like the length of a football field. Grasping the leg of Mary Bell's chair with one strong hand, Henry pulled her toward him. They were closer now, knees touching. He moved her plate closer, too.

When he rested his hand on her thigh, she gasped inaudibly. Was he going to move it up further? If so, how would she have the strength to stop him? His hand lingered there. Then Henry leaned over and kissed her cheek. His breath brushed across her cheekbone and tickled the inside of her ear. Shivers wiggled down her back.

Mary Bell imagined clearing the table and throwing herself on it.

While Henry and Mary Bell nuzzled, Tom went into the kitchen in search of a drink. He looked out the window. *Shit.* The kitchen door creaked, and Lafitte caught Peeping Tom.

Tom turned his back to the window. "Oh, hey." An explanation for his presence was stuck to the roof of his mouth like peanut butter. Finally, he freed his tongue. "Do you mind if I get a glass of water?"

Lafitte eyed him, retrieved a clear plastic bottle from the fridge, and stuck around long enough to make sure Tom left the kitchen.

Scaling the steep staircase, Tom noted two of his least favorite things about his fake priesthood: a half-covered Australian birthmark and the expectation of obedient chastity.

Outside, enveloped by August's heat and a prophetic rainfall, Mary Bell and Henry talked for hours: laughing, flirting, and remembering youthful dreams. They kissed until Mary Bell thought her lips might chap. Holding her in his arms, Henry whispered, "I've been thinking about you all day…"

Mary Bell nodded to a glowing candle, "I guess it's pretty obvious I've been doing the same."

PRIORY, LOUISIANA

Running his hands up and down her slim back, he imagined going outside the invisible boundaries, moving his hands to her butt or her breasts or underneath her shirt.

Mary Bell couldn't get enough of him, couldn't ask him to leave, didn't want to break the spell.

When they did finally separate and Mary Bell walked Henry to the front door, it was with a heavy, throbbing reluctance. It took every ounce of respectability and social propriety not to rip each other's clothes off.

PRIORY, LOUISIANA

CHAPTER SIX

After Lena spent the morning in her joyful spot on the levee, she walked home, showered, and put her nightgown on. It was broad daylight, but she was exhausted. If someone came over, maybe she'd say she was sick. The day passed while she lay tossing in bed, awake and asleep, awake and asleep. Sunbeams leaked through her plantation shutters, casting rods of harsh light across pine floorboards. As the day dimmed and waned, shadows crawled up the walls.

Lena had grown to hate Sundays, and worried about the sinfulness of such feelings. Although it was her only day off from her job at The Retreat, she had nothing to do. She went to church on Saturday night because, again, she had no plans. It was hard to explain to Mary Bell that she didn't want a day of rest. Who could understand such a thing?

She didn't think Mary Bell could comprehend such an empty social calendar. Mary Bell had led a privileged existence, was pretty, and she'd had a string of enviable boyfriends. Everyone liked her, including Lena. Could a person like Mary Bell have any real regrets?

Lena imagined the heart to be a locked box full of secrets, hidden behind velvet curtains. If Mary Bell had any secrets in her locker, they were well kept. Lena's box had been dragged out from behind the curtains and smashed into splinters. Her mistakes littered the Priory streets.

The public knowledge of Lena's shame was a price to be paid for the simplicity of small-town life. Lena's drinking problem, her accidents, her recklessness... People knew. Most folks were nice enough not to say anything, considering all she'd endured, but she felt their eyes upon her when she walked through town. Once she overheard someone whisper, from the pew behind her in church, that Lena's spirit had been broken. It seemed as true an assessment as Lena had heard.

One Sunday—*was it last week or the week before?*—Lena lay in bed and imagined herself sitting at a desk, deep within a cypress grove. Each person in Priory stood in line before her, a queue of neighbors stretching toward the horizon, weaving through the trees. Lena wrote words for them onto small pieces of paper, phrases like *Car Accident #2* or *Truancy Day #9*, before folding the papers in four. She handed the notes to her first grade teacher, then the lady that ran the dress shop, then Lafitte, and so on. She fell asleep that Sunday, trying to run out of mistakes before she ran out of people.

Lena knew her future didn't have to be lived in the shadows. She'd already been down for too long. Life is cyclical. An unknown, vast future spread out before her. It was time to put down her old pen, step away from the desk, and follow her knowing neighbors out of the cypress grove.

# CHAPTER SEVEN

From her veranda in Pass Christian, Mississippi, Ria Legrange watched the sun rise over the Gulf's gentle waves. Anyone could admire the setting sun, she thought. It was spectacular and bold. She preferred dawn, with its subtle, diffused light and understated elegance. On Ria's best days, from a scrolled iron bench on her front lawn, she could pretend life was perfect. Anyone driving down the road might presume as much.

Ria barely heard Victor approaching, but his hair tonic mixed with the salty breeze, so she knew he was near. He laid an impeccably groomed hand upon her shoulder. She covered it with her own. The warmth of Victor's flesh still sent gentle aches throughout her body, but after all their flawed years together, she now only gave him a piece of her heart, not the whole throbbing thing.

She turned her eyes away from the soft glow of morning, looked past Victor, and reflected upon her family home. Ria remembered playing croquet on the front lawn as a child, remembered barefoot games of kick-the-can with neighbors on breezy summer nights.

Her childhood home had been masterfully crafted many years earlier and had undergone countless renovations. Under the direction of Ria's mother, it had been painted white on the outside and shades of pastel inside. The dining room was seafoam, the sunroom was crème brûlée, the kitchen was the color of beach sand.

PRIORY, LOUISIANA

Ria could still picture her father passed out in a rocking chair on the front porch, damp with morning dew, key in hand, one too many martinis on his breath. He'd been a sweet and pleasant drunk. Full of hilarious stories, dark sunglasses, and apologetic mornings-after.

Victor's meanderings were not quite so easy to endure. Not quite so endearing. Ria smiled weakly at her husband and turned back to the Gulf.

The bobbing water was calm that morning: so tender, so forgiving. The Legranges didn't know a storm was approaching. It was still far away, above a distant sea. Ria was ready, though. She was always ready. She'd been weathering storms on the Gulf her entire life.

CHAPTER EIGHT

Tamika lay atop her lumpy bed in New Orleans' Ninth Ward, her ears filling with teardrops. Her body was limp and achy. When she'd left for church that morning, she'd had a brother. A big brother named Tyrell. She laid her hands upon her chest and talked to the cracked ceiling.

"Dear Jesus," she whispered, "help me."

Her mother, Nichelle, wailed in the other room.

"Please help Mama, too. I'm only nine years old…I can't do this by myself."

When the policemen had arrived after church, Tamika was sent to her room. She hadn't been told her brother had been shot, but she knew he was dead. Her mama had never cried like that before. How strange it was to become an only child so abruptly, with no warning. No time to prepare for the emptiness of it.

"We need a miracle," she whispered. "You're our only hope."

Tamika wiped her eyes, stood up, and pulled back her worn, fitted sheet. Rusty springs poked through the surface again, their barbed tips all too familiar. She rearranged the old towels on top of them, and stretched her sheet back over the uneven mound.

After Tamika lay down again, she wanted to weep—felt the urge for it rise from her belly—but the tears refused to leave her open eyes. They thickened on top of her eyeballs like a salve.

She interlocked her fingers upon her breastbone. Looking back up to the crack in her ceiling, she added,

"Mama says you can move mountains." Tamika had never seen a mountain before. The highest thing she'd ever seen was Monkey Hill at the zoo. She fell asleep trying to imagine God moving Monkey Hill.

Monday morning, Nichelle's sisters and neighbors flooded into her house to mourn the tragic loss of her son. Nichelle cried and rocked on the edge of her sofa, while her sister Demetra kept saying, "He's with the Good Lord now, honey. He's in a better place."

Nichelle didn't want him to be with the Good Lord. She wanted him to be in his bedroom, blaring his music or calling to say he'd be late.

Too often in the past few weeks, he'd been late. Nichelle hadn't known what to do. He was practically a grown man, so it was hard to enforce his curfew or give him advice. When she lectured him about his choice of friends, about the strange scents he brought in on his clothing at night, about his increasing truancy, Tyrell kissed her on the forehead.

Now that he was gone, a familiar scene played in Nichelle's head.

"It's okay, Mama," Tyrell said. "Ain't nothin' gonna happen to me. Everything's gonna be okay."

"Go to school, Tyrell," his mom insisted.

"I go to school, Ma."

"Go to school *every day*, Tyrell."

Tyrell flashed his charming grin and walked away. "Ma, you worry too much. Maybe you're watching too much TV."

She had felt him slipping away. "It's my fault," she cried into Demetra's shoulder.

Demetra held her tighter.

"It's all my fault he's gone," she said again.

"Now, hush, Nichelle," her sister insisted. "You know that ain't true."

The sisters both knew what temptations were on the streets for their boys. Demetra's own son was fifteen now, and she wished she could somehow fast-forward his life.

Tamika pretended to be asleep whenever someone opened the door to her bedroom. Her eyes were crusty and sore, and she kept thinking about Lazarus. Jesus made Lazarus rise from the dead. Maybe He would do the same for her brother. She wondered whether or not it would be scary if Tyrell walked back through the door today. She wondered if such things really were possible.

PRIORY, LOUISIANA

 CHAPTER NINE

Tom returned to his suite, dislodged the white plastic from around his throat and tossed it onto the bed where it flailed about. After undressing, he let his clothing lay in a brooding puddle on the wooden floor, slipped into a t-shirt and boxers, and crawled under the cotton sheets.

He looked up at the ceiling. The medallion around the chandelier was an intricately carved montage of leaves, berries, and acorns. It was beautiful. Rolling onto his side, he studied the antique nightstand. Then he slid the drawer open to find what he expected he would find: a Bible.

With apprehension, Tom lifted the Bible from its resting place, leaned up on one elbow, and placed the Book on the bed. He flipped through worn pages, skipping past the Old Testament. The Old Testament was a mystery to him, and he didn't have the mental energy to tackle it.

Tom stopped flipping and read a passage in Luke, Chapter 21: "Take care not to be led astray. For many will come in my name, say, 'I am He,' and, 'The time is at hand.' Do not, therefore, go after them."

He turned more pages, and his eyes found John, Chapter 10: "Amen, amen, I say to you, he who enters not by the door into the sheepfold, but climbs up another way, is a thief and a robber. But he who enters by the door is shepherd of the sheep."

A draft circled the room and rested its cool hand upon Tom's neck. He glanced around. *Is this place haunted?* So many plantations were. That would be just his luck.

He rested the Book upon his chest and closed his eyes. His thoughts turned to his least favorite priest, Father McMann, whose love of drinks and po-boys was well known. Father McMann seemed so unhappy, as if he hated his job. As if it was a chore, not a calling.

Tom's all-time favorite priest was Father Fenn, who was briefly assigned to Tom's grammar school. Father Fenn was young and startlingly handsome; the girls had instant crushes on him.

Once a month, he gathered up Tom's sixth grade class, huddled them around the altar, turned off the lights, and prayed by candlelight. Tom and his classmates stood throughout the service, pre-teen bodies nearly touching.

Father Fenn was not on a pedestal, and the altar was not on an island. The breaking bread snapped in Tom's young ears. The wine's tannin was addictive and pungent. Tom was an arm's length from the action, like an apostle. Looking back, he wished he'd been Baptist or some other demonstrative religion. Catholics were taught to be silent and reverential in Church. Not emotional. When tears had stung his eyes during Mass with his classmates, he'd refused to let them go.

I wonder where Father Fenn is. How did I wind up with a priest like Father McMann? Why did they give him his own parish?

Over the years, the more Tom believed that Jesus lived in the same world he did, the more his schism with the Church had solidified. He disliked his parish priest, and he felt the Church was wandering too far from Jesus' teachings. When Father McMann gave a homily about excommunication, Tom was outraged.

Excommunication? Who has the right to separate us from God? Let he who is without sin cast the first stone. Tom wondered what would happen in the afterlife to those who built walls. Jesus loved sinners. Why couldn't the Church? Although Father McMann had made it clear that some excommunications were necessary, Tom couldn't envision Jesus giving the same sermon.

Why couldn't God's presence be more obvious in this world? Tom wanted God to tell him what to do. Not give him some sign that he might mistake as an ordinary chirping bird. He loved it when God was palpable, like when it poured down rain on Good Friday. Or when Tom's cousin was born the same day his grandfather died.

As Tom got drowsier, his soul floated outside of his body, bouncing gently off the walls. It was restless, that soul. When it settled back within Tom, he fell asleep with the Bible open on his chest. Its wisdom seeped into him, pierced his hardened arteries, invaded his insipid mind, and turned his whole being inside out.

PRIORY, LOUISIANA

Mornin', Y'all

Monday, August 22, 2005

"*Mornin', Y'all.* This is Melody Melançon and you're listening to WPRY 90.5, bringing you and your mama up-to-date on the latest in Priory.

I have got to tell y'all what my delicious husband, Randy, did for me this morning. You will not believe it. While I was showering and putting on this mask full of makeup, my hubby was toiling away in the kitchen making me grillades and grits. I kid you not. I am still daydreaming about it. There's no better way on God's green earth to prepare veal.

I said to him, 'Darling, what are you doing? I'm on a diet. I already lost five pounds.'

He did not miss a beat, y'all.

'Five pounds?' he said. 'Nobody's gonna notice that, hon. That's like throwing a doubloon off an Endymion float. Eat the grits. You look good no matter what.'

That man has a way with words. And he can cook like John Folse himself.

What a perfect lead-in to my next bit of news. Dr. David Westerfeldt is in town tomorrow night to sign his book, *Lean or Mean: 20th Century Hurricanes by the Decade,* at the Little Red School House. He says that some decades, like the 1980s, were lean, having only a few hurricanes. Other decades, like the 1960s, were mean like your Aunt Lula after she's had a few too many Sidecars.

Oh, now isn't this nice? Says here that iced tea and cheese straws will be provided by Miss Angela's

Sweets & Eats. I might go see this author myself if he's got cheese straws on the side. Everyone in town knows that Miss Angela's are to die for. Just the right amount of crunch and cayenne.

That's it for now. But remember, if you're not listening to *Mornin', Y'all*, you might as well be living in Oregon."

 CHAPTER TEN

The sun rose and spread pale apricot light upon Priory, making the morning fog glow from within. Tom walked over to the long window, pulling aside its lace curtain. Heat seeped through wavy panes of glass. The thick lawn glistened with dew.

He turned around to face his room and its simple bed: a maple pencil-post with clean lines and worn edges. It was a world away from the bed he shared with Charlotte in Priory: a carved half-tester draped in opulent fabrics. He couldn't picture their lovemaking in this earnest bed. In this bed, he was a man pretending to be a priest. This, too, was an unwelcome image.

A debate seeped inside Tom's head over whether he should leave town and discontinue this charade, or stay and stick it out for a while. He didn't have the strength to think clearly with his stomach growling so loudly.

After getting dressed, Tom went down the staircase and straight out the front door so he wouldn't have to deal with Mary Bell or Lafitte. He knew the general layout of town and figured he could at least find Main Street.

The blacktop road in front of The Retreat had no sidewalks. It wasn't much of a road, really, more like a wide asphalt path. No curbs, no painted lines. The rough tar surface didn't end abruptly at the edges. It thinned, crumbling into irregular black nuggets in the grass. Tom crunched upon the nuggets because he liked the way they felt under his high tops.

A white Eldorado approached.

"Hey, Father! You need a ride?" A loud, gravelly female voice called out. Grace leaned out her window, dangling a cigarette from her stained hand. Her fingernails were as yellow as rice pilaf.

He moved toward the car. "No, but thanks for askin'."

"Where you headed, Padre?"

"Just out for a walk…no place in particular."

"Oh, fine, then, fine." Grace coughed. Smoke floated around her car's interior, searching for something before it billowed out the window. "Where you from, Father? I haven't seen you around here before."

Tom didn't want to answer. "Umm…I'm visitin' The Retreat so I can take a little break. I've never been here before." The lie pressed upon his temples.

"Oh, the Bateau's place. Mary Bell is such a sweet girl." Ashes floated from her cigarette to the ground in waves.

"Yes, she seems to be."

"Well, Father," Grace said, noticing a dead dragonfly on her windshield. "I guess I'll go if you don't need me. You sure you don't need a ride?"

"I'm sure, thanks." Tom smiled.

"Alright then. Enjoy your walk. Wha'd you say your name was?"

"Father Tom."

"Nice to meet you, Father Tom. I'm Grace Swannee. Double 'n', double 'e'. Where you from again, Padre?"

Tom talked over his shoulder as he walked away. "Gotta go, Grace. Thanks for offerin' me a ride. Maybe I'll see you around town…"

PRIORY, LOUISIANA

He was relieved to hear the car roll away behind him.

"See you, Padre!" Grace shouted.

The asphalt path ended, and he turned onto a shelled street that lasted only a hundred yards or so before reaching the cobbled bricks of Main. These streets were not produced by anyone's master plan.

Tom stood at the corner of Main and Ibis, put his hands on his hips, and marveled at Priory's smallness. Nothing was taller than one story. The façades along Main were varied: glass windows, worn bricks, painted clapboard. The rooftops weren't uniform either: flat roofs, slate slopes, asphalt gables. The shops were utilitarian: a hardware, a grocery, the Post Office.

He wondered how he would pass a whole day here until, like an oasis, Bob's Bar appeared. The large picture window said "Air Conditioning" and "Tables for Ladies." Wide blinds hid the pub interior from street traffic. A hot summer breeze whisked Tom inside. He blinked hard and adjusted to the dim lighting.

The front room was speckled with a few wooden tables and a couple of leather booths. A bowling game, the size of a pinball machine, glowed in the corner. Its fist-sized pins were chipped, suspended by ancient ropes, and resting on an alley marked with shallow scratches and sawdust. The world went silent for Tom as he approached it.

Inside Tom lived so many fond memories of Grandpa Dirk. Saturday morning haircuts followed by lunch at The Final Turn near the racetrack. Shrimp po-boys, fried pickles, and mini-bowling. Life lessons learned over root beer. "A man's handshake is his word." "If you're not having any fun, you're doing something wrong." "No one can fault you for being too kind."

Tom knew, standing in an unknown barroom in front of this truth-evoking bowling alley, that he had failed his grandfather. He hadn't become the man Dirk had trained him to be.

When sound rushed back into his ears, Tom turned around to face the room. Beyond the restaurant stretched a slim, musty bar, accentuated by neon beer signs and gleaming liquor bottles. There were already, at this late morning hour, patrons on stools, frosty mugs in hand.

"Have a seat, Father. What can I get you?" the bartender asked.

Tom sat on a padded wooden stool, folded his hands in front of him, and said, "I'd love a draft."

"You got it."

By now, the other bar flies stirred, interested in the newcomer. Tom was closest to the front door, so everyone cranked around to cast a curious eye on him. One by one, they made welcoming gestures. He smiled and tugged at his collar. *No one can fault you for being too kind.*

Tom gulped his beer. The cold stabbed his chest. Thin sections of ice slid from the handle. His lips melted a half circle onto the glass. *Ahh.* He took another swig.

"Father, I'm Gus Leddy," the man next to him sputtered, extending a fat hand.

Tom shook it. "Father Tom."

"What brings you to these parts, Father Tom?"

The men leaned toward him.

"I'm sort of on vacation. Just passin' through."

The bartender wiped his hands on his apron. "I'm Bob Parsons, owner of this joint. Glad to meet you."

"Thanks, Bob. You've got a great place."

"Yeah, she's a beauty." Bob nodded then turned to restock liquor.

Gus continued, "Where you from, Father?"

"Oh, all over, I guess."

"You gonna be saving any souls while you're here in Priory?"

Tom remembered a line the cool Father Fenn had used. "On a good day, I'm hopin' to be saved myself," Tom replied. To take the edge off, he added, "I'm just gonna relax here for a while."

"This is a good place to relax, Father. In fact, if you're not careful, you'll relax yourself to sleep here. Pretty damn boring in Priory." Gus's round face wobbled when he spoke. His wild eyebrows were two halves of a handlebar moustache that had been separated by a patch of skin and moved skyward.

Tom smiled. "I just got here last night, so I wouldn't know."

"Where you staying?" Gus asked.

"At The Retreat, down the way."

"Oh," a skinny old man said, from three stools away. "The Bateau's place. That Mary Bell's a hottie, huh, Father? I bet you wouldn't mind getting a piece of that!"

Gus slapped Slim on the back. "You idiot. This guy's a priest, for God's sake."

"Yeah," Slim said, "like *that* makes a difference." The men snickered. "He's still a man, ain't you, Father?"

Tom looked over his shoulder at the front door.

Bob intervened. "Never mind them. You know they're just screwing with you."

Tom shrugged it off. He didn't have any respectable comebacks. The real Tom Vaughn might have had a clever, curse-laden comeback, but Father Tom was weighing his words. His stomach was growling, so he read a laminated menu then ordered a shrimp po-boy with some cheese fries. When his food came out, he moved to a nearby table.

Slim pulled his tattered ball cap low on his face, laid money on the bar, and started to leave. He stopped by Tom's table on the way out.

"Father Tom," Slim said, tugging down the bill of his cap as if tipping it reverentially. Tom shook Slim's thin hand and smiled at the gray-eyed gent.

"I didn't get your name," Tom remarked.

"Stan. Stan Ball. But everybody calls me Slim."

"Nice to meet you, Slim. You're a real character."

"Oh, yeah, well, Father, I say what I mean," Slim Stan explained. "And if some girl's a hottie, she's a hottie. It dudn't matter what shirt you got on. See you 'round." With that bit of wisdom imparted, Slim Stan left Bob's Bar.

Tom grinned, shook his head, and took a huge bite of his po-boy. Ah, the crunch of French bread. He wiped his mouth with a linen napkin and took a healthy gulp of beer. Gus was next to appear at Tom's table.

"Mind if I join you, Father?" Gus asked.

Tom shook his head and kept eating.

"Father Tom," Gus said quietly, scrutinizing the smoky room like a spy. "Can I talk at you?"

"Sure."

"What kind of a priest are you?"

Tom hesitated then answered, "Roman Catholic."

"Oh, good. Me, too. Listen, Father, I have a question for you about confession."

Aw, shit. I hope I know the answer.

"Go on." Tom hadn't been to confession in eons.

Gus looked over to the bar to see if anyone was eavesdropping, but everyone seemed preoccupied. "Father, sometimes I'm embarrassed to tell my priest my real sins, you know? I can say the simple ones: I cussed, I lied. But there are times when I don't wanna tell my priest my really bad sins. Know what I mean?"

Tom nodded.

"I've known our priest for years. He knows my wife, my mama, my kids, my whole family. Now, I know he's not supposed to remember all my asinine mistakes, right? I mean, a priest can't hold no sins against me, can he?"

Tom paused. He knew what he'd been taught in Catholic school. "No, he can't, Gus. After he's absolved you, the sins are forgotten."

Gus squinted.

Tom continued, "Besides, whatever your sins are, your priest has probably heard worse." Tom hated to see Gus squirm. He seemed to be a pretty decent guy. "Everyone's a sinner, Gus. We all just have different sins."

Tom knew his own vices all too well.

"I haven't been to no confession in a long time," Gus said. "Not even sure I believe in it, to tell you the truth."

Tom wished Bob would refill his mug. He looked behind the bar, but Bob was on the phone.

"No offense," Gus continued, "but I don't see why I hafta say it to a priest. Why can't I confess it to God in the privacy of my own bedroom?"

"You *can*."

"I can? Are you sure?"

"I don't know. Maybe the Church would frown upon it, but I don't. I mean: Gus, if you're really sorry, and you tell God you're sorry, and you promise never to do that sin again, I think God would be okay with that."

A dozen years of Catholic education and hundreds of Sunday Masses seeped through every pore in Tom's body. He felt a rush of nervous excitement. "God *is* forgiving," Tom added. He hoped it was true.

"You're okay, Father Tom. You're an okay guy."

Tom's mischief and curiosity joined forces. His eyes twinkled. "That bein' said, Gus, I *am* here for you. Is there something you want to confess? Lay it on me."

Gus laughed. "No, thanks. I'll do it tonight before I go to sleep." Gus stood up, shook Tom's hand, and exited into the unbearable summer heat.

His work and his meal at the table being finished, Tom returned to the bar to settle up. "Bob, that po-boy was great."

"Thanks, Father."

"What do I owe you?"

"Nothing, man. This round's on me."

Cool. A perk. "Thanks." Repeating the words of Gus, Tom said, "You're an okay guy."

An elderly man was at the far end of the bar, head bobbing like a buoy on Lake Pontchartrain. He crooned in Tom's direction, in a Dean Martinesque voice, the slurred words to "Memories Are Made of This."

Bob pointed at the guy, "That's Dino."

Dino winked a golf ball-sized eye and struggled to keep his bloated belly centered over the barstool while he sang.

Tom liked it here and was glad a Catholic priest could have a few beers. There might not be any place on earth as comforting as a cool barroom on a hot summer day.

PRIORY, LOUISIANA

CHAPTER ELEVEN

A burly wind swirled around The Retreat Monday night, fluttering cypress leaves, toppling flowerpots, and stirring people within their beds.

Mary Bell didn't pay any attention to it. After an amazing first date, she had enthusiastically accepted a second one with Henry for the next evening. He hadn't waited until the weekend, hadn't wanted to miss a single day with her.

On Monday night, Mary Bell and Henry wandered the streets of Priory. It was dark and windy. The leaves overhead were noisy and congratulatory. The two held hands and recalled stories of their childhood: what happened under the Dueling Tree or on the City Park playground. He rubbed her hand with his thumb then pulled her behind the smooth cinnamon-colored bark of a crape myrtle tree to kiss her. They flirted unashamedly.

Mary Bell couldn't stop feeling that somehow the universe had been rearranged to make this reunion possible. Henry walked her back to The Retreat, and she invited him to her suite for a drink. When she returned from the fridge with a beer for him, Henry glanced out the window with what seemed to Mary Bell like the smallest wedge of hesitation. The moment passed quickly so she dismissed her initial insecurity as nervous imagination.

After his moment of pensive distance, Henry set his beer down on the table and moved toward her, pushing her gently against the wall. Gentleness was replaced by fierce desire. Clothing was stripped off and thrown to the ground like penalty flags.

Their lovemaking was deep and hungry. They danced all around her suite before landing, exhausted, in her waiting bed. Spent energy pulsed through their bodies.

Lying amidst a pile of down pillows, trying to steady his breathing, Henry smelled Mary Bell's hair. He kissed her fingertips and ran his warm palms over her naked curves. A tear of joy slipped from the corner of Mary Bell's eye. That tear had been hiding for a very long time. She buried her head in her pillow so he wouldn't see it. It was too soon. She would look pathetic.

In his attic bedroom, Lafitte was lying in bed, too. He was listening to the cacophony of whistling wind bleeding through the roof. He'd been awakened by its ferocity but blessed by its timing. Before waking, he'd been in the throes of another relentless nightmare. Same thing, over and over. Fires. Bloody fields. Dirty people begging for mercy. Body parts. His calloused trigger finger.

It had been so many years since the war. Why wouldn't God make the nightmares stop? Lafitte had not bothered even asking anymore. His prayers weren't being answered. Dawn was hours away, so he flipped on his lamp and made a scratchy list of jobs that needed tending around The Retreat.

In room 2B, Tom Vaughn heard the call of the wild wind, and he woke into a mystical half-awake state. He opened his eyes but couldn't move his head. Searching the room, he wondered if God had come to lecture him.

PRIORY, LOUISIANA

After a few moments, his body regained its strength. Tom sat on the edge of his bed, surveyed the dark images in his room, and felt certain they were all inanimate. He stretched, then walked over to the window, flipped the lock, and hoisted the huge pane. The nighttime chirpings were amplified, and blustery evening air exploded into his space.

Lace curtains passed him on their flight into the darkness. They fluttered on either side of him. Tom closed his eyes and took the biggest breath his body could bear. Then he closed the window, grabbed the soft quilt and headed down the steps, careful not to make too much noise.

On the front porch, Tom witnessed a godly experiment that mixed the forces of frantic wind, leeching moisture, and a blueberry sky. The moon-silhouetted trees, the pulsing bushes, and the blonde rope hammock on the front porch came to life. This house seemed to be the only thing on earth.

He sat down on a wooden rocking chair. The wind ran her fingers through his hair.

Tom closed his eyes and pictured how he must look to God: a speck of a man, sitting on a borrowed front porch, watching the earth sway. In his mind, the camera zoomed out, putting the intimate porch in the context of the neighborhood, the city of Priory, and then the whole world. Tom loved feeling small.

Across town, auburn-haired Lena Melendez lay in her bed and twirled a loose pillowcase thread. She was grateful to have her housekeeping job at The Retreat. It had been an exhausting and productive day. She hoped to fall asleep easily.

But as she lay there, and the wind outside increased in speed, it began to sound mournful. It ran menacingly around her cottage, taunting her. Life had come to this juncture by her own hand, and she couldn't forgive herself for one horrible decision. The drinks, the swerving, the tree…

Lena steered her thoughts back to The Retreat. Mary Bell said a priest was staying with them, but Lena hadn't seen him yet. Maybe she would seek him out and ask for advice.

The wind slowed down to whisper something to Lena, but she had no idea what it meant.

PRIORY, LOUISIANA

Mornin', Y'all

Tuesday, August 23, 2005

"*Mornin', Y'all.* This is Melody Melançon and you're listening to WPRY 90.5, bringing you and your mama up-to-date on the latest in Priory.

Hold on tight, y'all. We got us something brewing in the tropics. Hard to say what it's gonna be, but with the low pressure hanging over the Bahamas, it's shaping up to be real interesting. Mmm-hmm.

Now don't y'all go making any plans for a late summer Florida fling neither. They're saying this girl might be real fast—just like your cousin SuSu on your mama's side—and that's never good, if you know what I mean. She could be upon us before you know it.

Now onto something more personal. I want to give a shout-out to my beautiful friend, Darla, who is battling breast cancer: *Darla, you look good even with no hair.*

I swear to God. Prettiest cancer patient in town. The most curvaceous eyebrows you ever saw, even when they're drawn on. Looks like a festival queen. You hang in there, honey. Me and Randy are praying for you.

Hey, y'all. Even if you don't know Darla, say a quick prayer for her. Prayers that rise up from Priory have a special power. My mama always told me that and she never lied. Bless her heart.

That's it for now. But remember, if you're not listening to *Mornin', Y'all*, you might as well be living in Nebraska."

CHAPTER TWELVE

On Tuesday in Pass Christian, Mississippi, rain pittered upon the sand. Thunder rolled in like a trolling motor. A switch of self-preservation flipped within the locals. Uncertainty descended upon them.

"Charles," Ria Legrange said into the phone, "have you been watching the news?"

"Yeah, Mom, I'm watching it right now." Charles lay on his leather sofa just a few minutes from his parents' Gulf-front home. He scratched his thin stomach and readjusted his boxer shorts.

"Well, honey, I thought it might be nice if you came over to help your father board up the house."

Charles yawned and clicked to a skin station. "The storm's not even in the Gulf yet, Ma. And it's still only a tropical depression."

"I know, honey, but your father doesn't like to wait until the last minute. Can't you help him?"

No response.

Ria counted silently: *One Mississippi, two Mississippi, three ...*

She usually granted him up to seven seconds before repeating herself.

"What, Ma? What did you say?" Charles tried to concentrate on his mother's words while a half-naked nurse was preparing to examine some longhaired, bare-chested plumber.

Ria turned her volume up a notch. "I said I thought it would be nice if you'd help your father board up the house before the storm. It won't take y'all very long if you do it together."

Charles blinked hard and turned the TV off. His head was pounding, and his mouth was pasty. He was sick of boarding up the house. His parents were probably just using it as an excuse to go to Priory again. No one would be boarding up houses this soon. For all they knew, the storm would dissipate or head toward the Yucatan Peninsula.

"Sure, Mom, I can help." His voice was not enthusiastic.

"He's going to the hardware today and plans on boarding up tomorrow. Will tomorrow work for you?"

Charles strained to remember his plans. "If we wake up tomorrow, Ma, and the storm's in the Gulf, I'll come over."

Ria was relieved but apprehensive. Just because he said he'd show up didn't mean he would. She'd make sure the gardener came, too, as insurance.

"Do you want to go to Priory with us?" Ria asked.

Charles contemplated their last evacuation to Priory. He'd made a pass at Mary Bell and had been dismissed. He hoped one day she'd regret her decision. After all, he was going to be a famous Mississippi author in the tradition of Tennessee Williams or William Faulkner. Some day, from behind a book-signing table, Charles hoped to look up and see Mary Bell. He, of course, would be unavailable. He'd be juggling a bevy of supermodels, and there'd be no time for a sweet, small-town girl from Priory. He shook his head to clear it.

Why did his parents have to go to Priory every time a storm entered Gulf waters? He knew his mother's attachment to Mary Bell's mom. They were practically sisters. But why did his parents have to be so set in their ways, so ingrained within their routines? What would be wrong with a little spontaneity? Maybe his parents should go wild and fly off to Paris before the storm. They could afford it.

Charles wasn't disrespectful enough to suggest this. They had paid for his English degree and his bungalow and had even given him a generous allowance while he contemplated his novel, so he wouldn't weigh them down with suggestions of a better life.

"No, Ma, I think I'll pass on Priory this time."

Ria wondered where he would go and how much it would cost her to send him there.

"I'm going to take off and drive north until I'm sick of driving," he said. "Maybe I'll end up someplace interesting, you know? Maybe I'll even end up with new material for my book."

Ria wished he'd show her some sample pages. "Sure, hon. That's fine."

"Maybe I'll see you tomorrow then."

Ria's grin was loving but weary. "Thanks, Charles. I'll make those peach muffins you like so much…"

Charles started scratching his arms. "You know I love 'em…"

When they hung up the phone, Ria walked over to a window. The waves shimmered just beyond the Gulf road.

She thought back to when she had given birth to Charles. Both Ria and Victor had thought the name Charles Dalton Legrange sounded dignified. They wanted their son to start life with every possible advantage, so the first gift they gave him was a distinguished name, a name his future in-laws would be proud to print on expensive parchment.

PRIORY, LOUISIANA

But when Charles was in third grade, Victor had decided to give him a buzz cut. Ria objected because she didn't want him to look like a military brat.

Victor held his ground. "Every boy needs a buzz cut once in his life, Ria. It's a rite of passage."

There was no point in arguing with Victor. He did as he pleased.

After the shearing, curious hands ran across the top of Charles' new hair, and his friends began calling him Buzz. Buzz Legrange. Victor and Ria cringed each time they heard it, but the nickname stuck around for years.

Ria watched the waves, her eyes fixed upon the horizon. *Why does Victor have to always be so bull-headed? So wrong?*

Her thoughts flipped back a few weeks to a dinner party.

"That's right," her friend Sally Ann had declared. "Each of us has one hundred twenty soul mates on this earth. Not one, like some naïve romantics would have us believe."

Sally Ann's husband was working late that night, so he was not there to defend himself. She continued, "I've already told Daniel that he is not one of my soul mates, but he just laughs at me."

Everyone enjoyed a good chuckle. Ria forced a smile. Bubbles of anxiety rose within her but were dispelled by the gentle eyes of her friends. She wanted to know more about this elusive set of mates.

"How did y'all come up with the number one hundred twenty?" Ria asked.

"Oh, I didn't come up with it. Some big lah-dee-dah psychologist did. And I believe her." Sally Ann peered around the dining room table. "And I've told Daniel in no uncertain terms that if I should ever be so fortunate as to meet one of mine, I will not pass up the opportunity."

One of the men challenged her, "What if Daniel finds one of his true soul mates before you find one of yours?"

Sally Ann turned her eyes upward and studied a crystal hanging from the chandelier. She paused. Her smile relaxed for a moment. Then her grin reappeared, her shoulders settled, and her eyebrows ascended.

"I will be thrilled for him," she continued, straightening her back and raising her glass. "To each of us—every last one of us—finding one of our glorious soul mates."

Ria looked across the table at Victor and raised her goblet. She knew he wasn't her soul mate. If he were, he wouldn't have held her heart in his hand and squeezed it the way he had. A mate would feel the pain he was inflicting. If he'd made a mistake once, he wouldn't find himself justifying similar mistakes over and over again.

Because of his indiscretions, Ria had withdrawn into a circle of loving but cautious women who'd also suffered similar journeys of quiet pain. They could go out to lunch, garden together or go antiquing, knowing none of them might bring up an uncomfortable subject or cast a judgmental glance. She trusted her friends, the beautiful women seated at this table. They knew what Ria knew: A soul mate wouldn't peel the

PRIORY, LOUISIANA

dignity away from you, leaving you exposed to society's stinging pity.

 CHAPTER THIRTEEN

Tuesday morning, Mimi sat in her favorite wing chair, flipping between The Weather Channel and the local news. The door opened behind her, and Cora walked in. Tuesday was Cora's day. Mimi looked forward to it.

"Morning, Mimi," Cora greeted, pacing across the room.

"Mornin'," Mimi said, flipping back to The Weather Channel. "There's another storm in the Atlantic, darlin', and it looks like it's headed for the Gulf. You been watchin' it?"

"No. I don't mind those storms until they get closer. They make me nervous." Cora started emptying the dishwasher.

"Yeah, you're probably right. You know I couldn't care less, anyway. Storms don't scare me. But Thomas is out on a road trip, and I'm wonderin' if he's payin' any attention."

Cora appeared in the kitchen door. "Thomas? On a road trip?" Cora's voice ascended an octave. "Thomas doesn't usually go *nowhere*."

Mimi looked up from the TV and laughed. "Yeah, and that grandson of mine had a priest's shirt on when he left," Mimi said, flashing her winning-hand smile.

Cora's face dropped. "Oh, my Lord, what in the world is that all about?"

"I don't know, hon, but I think it's a good sign. That boy's been a mess lately."

Cora went back to the kitchen but kept talking. "I dunno, Mimi. It doesn't sound like a good sign to me.

Sounds like something that could get him struck by lightning. I'm gonna be praying for that boy all day long. Yes, indeed. I'm gonna say me some prayers."

Mimi worried that she'd blabbed too much. "Now, Cora, when you go over to my daughter's house tomorrow, don't you say anything about the priest's shirt, you hear?"

"I know, Mimi, I know."

"I don't need Sylvia lecturing me about keeping a closer eye on Thomas. He's a grown man. He can do as he pleases." Mimi thought about it for a minute. "If Sylvia asks, you can tell them he's gone for awhile, but don't say anything about the shirt."

Cora wasn't listening. She was already in the back bedroom, folding clothes and watching her stories on the TV.

CHAPTER FOURTEEN

Tom woke up with bear hair and a recharged spirit. After sitting on the small-world porch last night, he felt younger, like he was back in college. He slipped into a polo shirt and jeans and bounded down the staircase.

Lafitte saw Tom leave The Retreat with his civilian clothing on and grew increasingly curious about their guest.

Tom got into his Jeep and headed to Baton Rouge, speeding along the state highway. He rolled down his windows and cranked the music. Exhaust fumes and gravel dust filled his car. He'd been weighing every move, every uttered word since he'd gotten to Priory, and it was stifling. Tom joined The Meters in a rousing rendition of "Hey Pocky A-Way."

When he arrived in Baton Rouge, his first drive-by was fraternity row. Some of his friends had pledged here, and Tom had spent many drunken nights at their parties. Ghosts of his former life danced on the front lawns, and he wished he could join them.

After cruising frat row, he went to lunch at a tavern near campus. Tom wondered if he would recognize anyone, but he didn't. In plain clothes, ten years post-college, no one paid much attention to him.

To his dismay, Tom noticed how young everyone was. Guys' chests were inflated, and weathered ball caps were perched upon their heads. The girls had sleek ponytails, miniscule shorts, and clinging t-shirts. Tom looked down. His chest had fallen into his stomach.

PRIORY, LOUISIANA

Tom still frequented college bars in New Orleans, but rarely during the day. A nighttime barroom smelled like cigarettes, hair spray, and cheese fries. This place reeked of stale beer, bleach, and used grease. He felt surprisingly out of place.

After lunch, he went to his favorite snowball stand. Sitting on a picnic table out front, he devoured a nectar cream snowball with a dollop of soft-serve vanilla ice cream on top. Maybe sugar would pep him up.

A brain freeze was setting in when he spied the camera shop next door. His thoughts strayed to his own camera, packed safely within his duffle. Maybe it was time to add some new equipment to his collection.

Tom finished his snowball and walked in.

"Hey, can I help you?" a man asked.

"Yeah, sure, I'm lookin' for a digital camera."

"Anything in particular?"

"I hate to say it, but I learned to take pictures a long time ago and I don't know much about the new ones. I have a film camera and a couple lenses."

For the next hour, Tom was riveted by his conversation with a knowledgeable man whose wiry, straw-colored hair and tortoise-shell bifocals made him look like an intelligent scarecrow. While the summer sun headed westward, printer options were discussed and picture clarity was considered. Pistons fired within Tom's body, and it wasn't long before he plopped down his credit card.

Tom Vaughn could have bought half the shop with the money he'd saved over the years. No wife, no children, free housing, and a fairly decent salary had padded Tom's accounts with a comfortable stash. He bought what he wanted and left.

He sped back to Priory, grinning ear-to-ear as if he were standing on a balcony in the Quarter above a well-endowed woman begging for Mardi Gras beads. It was a grin that held with it the promise of something spectacular.

Although years had passed since Tom had taken a photo, he was, at one time, quite passionate about it. When he squatted next to the girls' soccer field in high school and focused the lens between his nimble fingers, popular girls swooned. With practice, his framing skills became more astute, and he became amazed at the intimacy of photography. Muscled flesh was delineated; wild, sweaty, ponytailed hair was caught in mid-flight; a fleeting moment of athletic grace was immortalized on film.

It wasn't long before he began to call it his Secret Agent camera. He could hide behind the lens and become someone entirely different.

One day, Tom's photography class took a field trip to the Garden District to sample architectural features. His favorites were the tall columns that stood like sentries: plumed Corinthians, scrolled Dorics, and simple Ionics. While studying columns, Tom spied a set of harlequin leaded-glass windows within his camera's eyehole. The light from inside the house shone through the glass, bending at each beveled edge. The windows sparkled like vertical chandeliers. He struggled with the settings on his camera until he thought he might do the image some justice.

He had printed it in sepia, which gave it a beautiful patina of caramel and chocolate. It was crisp and dreamy. Mimi put it in an antique frame and hung it in her bedroom. He was proud when she made a fuss over it.

Tom looked at his new camera and wondered how long it had been since he'd done anything to be proud of. When he couldn't remember that far back, he turned the camera on.

CHAPTER FIFTEEN

On the rocky banks of the Mississippi River, behind Audubon Park, Nichelle and Tamika stood by the wide, swift current. Tyrell's ashen remains rested inside a small wooden box. Nichelle held it in her hands like a Biblical offering. It was a hot, bleak, drizzly day. The sagging sky and Tyrell's powdery remains were nearly the same shade of pewter.

Nichelle's son had loved coming to the river. When he was younger, he thought it was the most mystical, dream-laden place on earth. She still pictured him flying his kite on the levee or playing tag with Tamika, who was now standing next to her in stunned silence.

Maybe Tyrell loved the riverfront because it was the one place where he felt free to revel in green grass, frolic under blue sky, and hunt for marbled rocks. Their neighborhood was gray. Its tone was omnipresent, seeping into Tyrell's veins, overtaking his judgment and his senses. Life had been washed in watery ink. No pure right or wrong, only justified means.

"Tamika, honey," Nichelle said.

Tamika looked up at her mother with swollen eyes.

"It's time to say goodbye."

Tamika placed her small brown hand on top of the wooden treasure chest, a chest she had given Tyrell for Christmas one year, a chest she had gained in a trade. He loved it. She remembered how his face lit up when he removed the newspaper wrapping.

Tamika felt odd about Tyrell's remains being inside, couldn't figure out how it was possible, couldn't mentally reduce Tyrell's large-framed body to a size that would fit inside the box.

Nichelle placed her shaking, sweaty hand on top of Tamika's, and they both closed their eyes.

"Dear Jesus," Nichelle said, tears racing toward her chin. "Take him to your loving breast, forgive him his sins, help him find rest."

"Amen," Tamika whispered.

"Amen."

Together, they heaved Tyrell's treasure chest into the Mississippi River, whose current carried it downstream toward the heated waters in the Gulf.

PRIORY, LOUISIANA

☀ *Mornin', Y'all* *Wednesday, August 24, 2005*

"*Mornin', Y'all.* This is Melody Melançon and you're listening to WPRY 90.5, bringing you and your mama up-to-date on the latest in Priory.

Whoa, y'all. This tropical depression is looking like a doozy. She might even get upgraded to a tropical storm. They're gonna name her Katrina, just like that snotty girl I sat next to in Sister Mary Joseph's art class.

She was a witch, even at the tender age of twelve. One day, I was passing a note to the love of my life, the very same Randy that I married (only we were in the seventh grade at the time) and Katrina raised her hand so high she rose up out of her chair.

'Sister! Sister! Melody is passing a note.'

It was so embarrassing, y'all. Sister Mary Joseph saw all the hearts I'd doodled on that tiny piece of paper. Sister folded it into a wad and then stuck it up her black sleeve, where she usually kept her Kleenex.

But don't you worry, y'all. God cursed that poor Katrina with the worst case of zits you ever saw. All because she ratted me out to Sister Mary Joseph. And then God really got her good. He transferred her father to some far away place like Seattle or Tacoma or some place like that.

Anyway, hold on to your grass skirts if you're in the Bahamas. Katrina's almost outta there. But fill the tub with ice if you're in Southern Florida. She's probably coming your way. And if she doesn't come your way, you can put some beer in the ice and have yourselves a real nice party.

That's it for now. But remember, if you're not listening to *Mornin', Y'all*, you might as well be living in Utah."

PRIORY, LOUISIANA

CHAPTER SIXTEEN

Wednesday morning, before Lena went to work at The Retreat, she decided to do something new with her hair. It was a superficial gesture, but a change nonetheless. After her car accident, she'd begun wearing her hair in a low ponytail behind her neck. This hairstyle hid most the scars on her scalp, but it made her feel like an old-fashioned school marm.

She tried pulling the auburn hair from her temples up and fastening it atop her head in a clip, but under the hair was a glare of scalp and more scars. Lena remembered her friends saying that they'd visited her old car in Priory's car graveyard. How chunks of her hair were dangling from the crackled windshield.

Maybe she'd wear braids. She nimbly intertwined her hair. Each braid stopped just below her shoulder. She finished them with clear rubber bands and smiled.

When she sashayed into the kitchen at The Retreat, Lafitte took notice and grinned. "Hey, Lena. What's up?"

"Not much."

She knelt down to retrieve some supplies from underneath the cabinet. Lafitte sliced an orange and placed it into the juicer. He snuck a peek at the part in the back of her head. He'd never seen her in braids, and he wasn't sure whether he should laugh or cry, but a strong emotion rose within him.

She left the kitchen to go clean Lafitte's room. Tom was coming down for breakfast. They met at the foot of the stairs.

"Morning, Father."

Tom would have walked right by, but she had that I'm-looking-for-a-conversation air about her, so he stopped. "Hey."

"I'm Lena Melendez."

"Tom. Father Tom."

At first, Lena was reluctant but then she said, as directly as possible, "Father, I want to talk to you about something." She looked down at her cleaning supplies. "I could use some advice."

Tom liked that people suddenly wanted his advice. "I'm goin' out to shoot some pictures today. Wanna come? We can talk while we're out."

"Pictures? Of what?"

"I don't know. I'm open to suggestions. I bought a new camera yesterday, and I want to give it a workout."

Tom noticed freckles on her face. She was attractive, in a quirky way, what with all that auburn hair and the dangling braids. "Are you a photographer, by any chance?"

"Oh, no," Lena replied, rubbing the back of her neck. "I'm not a photographer at all."

"Doesn't matter. Come anyway." He paused, "I've got two cameras and I could use some company. While we're there, you can tell me what's on your mind."

Tragedy and melancholy intrigued Tom. The scars on her face and the pain in her voice were magnetic.

"Well, it's going to take me a few hours to finish my work here, but then I can help, if you want."

They made plans to wander about that afternoon, but Lena worried she wouldn't be brave enough to bare her soul to a total stranger, even if he was a priest.

She was drawn to his eyes, though. They were kind and familiar.

Within the sanctuary of the owner's impeccable suite, Henry Shane propped himself up on one elbow and admired Mary Bell. She opened her eyes and caught a glimpse of him over her shoulder.

"What are you still doing here?" she chided through half-open eyes. "Don't either one of us have to work today?" she asked the wall.

Henry kissed the back of her head. "I do, but Doc Gainard can cover for me until I get there," he said. "*If* I get there..."

He slipped an eager hand around her supple body and pulled her in, kissing her exposed neck and shoulder. Her whole body flushed under his touch. He cupped one of her breasts in his hand and marveled at its velvety perfection.

"Let's go for a drive this afternoon," he suggested, nibbling at her. "We'll pack up a picnic lunch, leave late this afternoon, and go fool around on some deserted stretch of grass." The vanilla candles burning in her bedroom last night made the sheets smell like a decadent dessert. "We'll eat dinner and wait for the stars to come out." From behind her, Henry watched half of her gorgeous face grow pensive.

"What's wrong?" he asked.

Mary Bell didn't know how to say that she was worried they were moving too fast. Lust had gotten the better of both of them, and she wanted this relationship to last.

"Mary Bell," Henry said, holding her hand in his, speaking into the back of her tousled mane, "you must know I'm crazy about you. I've always been crazy about you."

Mary Bell had made so many bad decisions where men were concerned. Maybe she should have made him chase her longer.

"Please come with me," Henry said.

She rolled over to face him. He kissed her cheeks, pushing her dark curls aside.

"Okay."

Henry pulled her up against him. Being with him was incredible. He was selfless and passionate. She lost herself in him. All she wanted to do now was barricade the door of her suite and stay there forever. If only such moments could last.

CHAPTER SEVENTEEN

Victor slid leather work gloves over his blotchy hands and prepared to board up their waterfront home. The calfskin was cool and smooth. His younger self tried to resurface.

He lifted a huge piece of plywood, carried it across his back lawn, and rested it against the picket fence. The humid Gulf air steamed wet patches onto his cotton t-shirt. When he stood erect, his back creaked. Victor arched it to readjust and then returned to the storage room in the carriage house to get more plywood.

Manual labor made Victor's skin tingle. Maybe not in the same way a vigorous day in the courtroom would, but in an altogether different, salt-of-the-earth way. He hoped Ria was watching him from a window, appreciating his still-fit body. After stacking plywood sheets, he walked onto the wrap-around veranda and made his way to the front of the house.

Ria was carrying out a pitcher of lemonade and some clear acrylic glassware on a mosaic tray.

She is stunning, he thought. She had a straight, upper-crust nose that flared out a bit at the nostrils. In the victorious moments of his life, he felt like he absolutely deserved her.

He pulled off his gloves and laid them on the table. While sipping lemonade, Victor saw Ria turn her eyes to the water. He'd never known anyone so hypnotized by the sea.

Interrupting the Gulf view was their son's approaching car. Their eyes followed it up the long driveway. Ria touched Victor's arm, smiled at him, and went inside to get the peach muffins.

"Hey, Dad," Charles said, ascending the front steps.

Victor shook his hand and patted him on the shoulder. "Glad you could make it, son."

Charles' dark sunglasses sheltered his burning eyes. He grabbed a glass of lemonade and sprawled out on a padded chaise.

"Resting already?" Victor complained.

Charles smiled and sipped his drink. Ice slid up to rest against his lip.

"Hey, honey," Ria crooned. She placed another tray on the table.

Charles stood when she neared him, and he kissed her cheek. "Hey, Mom."

She handed him a muffin, and he gratefully plopped back down onto the padding.

"It's so wonderful to have my men together," Ria said. Her voice softened Victor's mood, and he sat down.

"This storm looks like a doozy, huh?" Charles said.

"Sure does," Victor replied. "I think we need to board up and leave soon."

France crept into Charles' imagination again. *If they'd go to Paris, I'd go with 'em.*

"I might stay here," Charles said. "You know, get a first-hand account. I could write about it."

Victor and Ria locked eyes. Charles tried to ease their concern. "That storm might not even come here, you know. We've all been through this dozens of times."

"Yeah, but honey, even if it comes close, it'll be a mess," Ria said. "Why don't you come to Priory with us? I'm sure Mary Bell would love to see you again."

Charles shook his head. Some sea gulls pecked at nothingness along their expanse of beach. The sand was pretty far from their porch: beyond their sprawling lawn and the beach road. It made the birds appear tiny and insignificant. "Nah, not this time, Ma."

"But remember…" Ria started.

Charles finished her sentence. "I know, I know: remember Camille."

Everyone talked about the disaster Hurricane Camille had wrought upon the coast in August of '69. Many people died trying to ride out the storm.

"Don't poke fun, Charles. If this storm is another Camille, you'll be glad you left."

Victor stared at his son until Charles agreed.

"Fine, I'll go somewhere. I promise I won't stay."

"But you won't come with us?" his mother asked.

Charles shook his hung-over head slowly so he wouldn't disturb the vodka that might still be sleeping in it.

Ria was proud of his independence, even if it was at her expense.

The men went to work, and she caught herself eyeing her husband. In casual clothing, Victor was handsome. Much better than when he was all buttoned up.

A cloudy sky supplied some thunder, and the Legrange men spent the rest of the afternoon working side-by-side. Ria moved her family jewelry to the attic. Even in the worst-case scenario, if the storm surge flooded their home, her jewelry would be high and dry. It certainly wouldn't reach their third floor safe.

CHAPTER EIGHTEEN

Lena knocked at Tom's door. He answered it with digital camera instructions in hand. "Hey, thanks for comin'."

"You're welcome."

Tom looked down at the brown paper bag Lena was carrying.

"Lafitte and I made us some sandwiches," she said softly.

"Cool."

Tom handed her the silver camera, and she put the thin strap over her wrist. The woven band of his old camera bag slung like a guitar strap over his shoulder.

"Where do you want to go, Father?"

The word "Father" hit him in the chest like a basketball. He took a step backward.

"Last time I was in Priory," he said, "I went to an abandoned plantation. I dunno where it is anymore. Do you?"

"Sure," Lena said. "Coeur de Vie. It's a short walk from here."

"Well, what do you think?"

Lena's eyes brightened. "It's amazing."

"Then we're off to Coeur de Vie. I'll follow you." Tom's stomach jumped at the thought of seeing the ruins again, but he was drawn to them.

The air was clammy as they walked the quiet streets. Their path was lined with live oak trees, pink azalea blossoms, and multi-colored wildflowers. A white egret took flight from the swampy woods beside them and soared low to the ground, brushing against long grasses.

With Tom away from The Retreat, Lafitte went out to Tom's Jeep and peered inside. A pile of CD's were strewn upon the passenger seat, and they weren't religious music. The New Orleans slant was easy to follow: the Neville Brothers, Dr. John, Marcia Ball, Allen Toussaint. Around back, Lafitte's good eye saw something even more mysterious and alarming: software manuals. He clenched his jaw.

Tom and Lena approached a set of tall, stony pillars and a wrought-iron gate. The ruins of the plantation spread out in the distance, among wise trees dripping with Spanish moss. Sunlight streamed through holes in the intertwined branches, and Tom instantly recognized the scenery. His heart hid behind his breastbone.

"Isn't this place gorgeous, Father?"

"Yeah," he said. His brain was jiggling around, trying to retrace his steps here with Charlotte. Through his peripheral vision, he saw Lena unpack their lunch on an iron bench, but his eyes searched for familiar terrain, picturing Charlotte everywhere. She had been so beautiful, so elusive. So temporary.

She had never given herself entirely to him. He had been only a pleasant diversion. Tom's eventual admission of this point did nothing to lesson its sting.

While Tom and Lena ate lunch, he checked out the lighting. The sun played games with wispy, scattered clouds. The hues of the earth changed under the sun's whims.

Lena squinted and watched a young couple walking across a wooden footbridge in the distance, hand-in-hand. *They look happy*, she thought, chewing her lunch in slow motion.

After they cleared away their mess, Lena had still not broached whatever subject was on her mind, so Tom began unpacking his camera gear. He affixed a lens to his Secret Agent camera and handed it to her.

Her eyes widened. Tom removed the lens cap. "Wanna get started?"

"Sure."

"Okay, then, I guess we'll start with something that won't move. Hmmm… Look at that window frame in the building over there."

Lena raised the camera up to her eye.

"Line up the cross-hairs in the middle so it's in focus, you see?"

She held the camera steady with her left hand. Tom leaned over her and showed her how to move the lens, clockwise and counterclockwise, back and forth. Her fingers were long and delicate.

"What're you lookin' at?" Tom wondered.

"I see the stones around the window frame…" She rotated the lens. "The wildflowers inside the house…" More tuning and fine-tuning. "I can see the back wall, well, what's left of it anyway. Wow, it's so clear."

She took her time and snapped one shot. Hovering over her, Tom showed his new student how to advance the film. Her aroma—a mix of succulent oranges and baby shampoo—wafted upward. He couldn't stop staring at her as if he was trying to find hidden orange peel in her hair.

Lena was deliberate while focusing, this time concentrating on a ledge of chalky stone. She snapped again and stood.

"Why don't you hang on to that camera," Tom began, "and I'll try to figure out this guy."

"Okay."

He gave her his other lens but instantly longed for it. "If you run outta film, let me know and I'll show you how to change it."

"Okay."

Lena's economy of words challenged Tom. He wanted to wait her out. Make her say something substantial. But her patience was greater than his, so he continued, "There are a couple things I learned in high school photography class…"

Lena cocked her head. It was funny to hear a priest mentioning high school.

"My teacher had a lot of tips, but only a few I can remember. Let's see. Number one: Don't center your picture. An off-center picture is more compelling, and you can showcase the background. Hmmm… Number two: If you're takin' a picture of a person, try to catch him not lookin' at the camera. Be sneaky."

Tom peered at the heavens and squinted. "Number three: Don't worry about wastin' film. You're one click away from the next one bein' great."

Lena smiled, and Tom was surprised he remembered that. It had been years since he'd thought of photography class. He encouraged Lena to venture off, and she agreed, but Tom kept her within eyesight.

The digital camera soon showed its limitations to Tom. Focusing with the "tighter" and "wider" buttons was constricting. Using the LCD screen to frame a picture was like listening to the radio and watching the TV at the same time. Too much background noise. He wanted to close his left eye tightly, peer through a tiny hole with his right eye, and become totally immersed in another world.

After deleting a few pictures, he wished he could switch cameras with Lena, but she was focusing on a crumbling tombstone nearby, and he didn't have the heart to do it.

Tom wandered through summer flowers, dodged industrious bees, and followed a meandering creek. Every few steps, he looked for her. They did a slow-motion dance around the property, careful not to bump into each other.

On the surface, this plantation seemed to be abandoned, but Tom realized it was bursting with life, in a constant state of evolution. Stones secretly became worn, changed hues, and shifted. Wild flowers burst forth and waved about arrogantly.

People left imprints on the ground and invisible fingerprints on the bridge railings. Everyone who'd ever visited this land had become part of it. The collective history of it wrapped itself around Tom's soul. He would never be able to capture the essence of it on a memory card.

Lena walked triumphantly toward him. "Father Tom?" Her voice was light. In her approaching hazel eyes, he saw something special. "I finished my first roll."

Tom gave her instructions for changing film and then let her try. While she fumbled with the plastic cartridge, he snuck a few discrete photos of her. It was easy with a camera that could be focused at arm's length.

By the end of Lena's second roll of film, the sun had sunk below the top of the tree line, so they packed up their equipment and began to leave. They passed through the gate. Tom paused by the weathered stone columns. "Coeur de Vie" was chiseled into the stone. He pushed his index finger into the worn "V".

He turned away from the column. Lena was a few feet ahead of him, talking to someone. Before Tom neared, he sized the guy up: sixtyish, salt-and-pepper, gaunt, reserved. He was wearing a tunic, khakis, and running shoes.

"Father Tom," Lena said, hand outstretched. "Come meet Father Abelli."

Shit.

Tom's throat closed as if he was suddenly allergic to Spanish moss. Against his better judgment, he approached Lena. Father Abelli gave half a smile and shook Tom's hand.

"I didn't know there was a visiting priest in town," Father Abelli started.

"I just got here a couple days ago." Tom's face was expressionless.

"I'm Francis Abelli, the pastor at Our Lady of Good Hope. What parish are you from?"

A single car rolled down the street, pausing while its passengers gawked at the ruins. Tom's mind whispered, *Get out of the car. You can't see Coeur de Vie through your window.* Tom refocused and answered Father Abelli, "I'm not assigned to a parish right now. I'm on sabbatical." *Do priests use the term "sabbatical"?* Maybe there was a more religious term for it. Tom rested his sweaty hands on his hips.

Lena spoke up, "Father Tom is staying at The Retreat for a few days. We're out here taking pictures together."

Father Abelli smiled paternally at Lena. His clear blue eyes turned to Tom. "Are you a photographer, Tom?"

The sun was falling, but the heat was still insufferable. Tom wiped his brow. "I was, once, a long time ago. It seems like another lifetime."

Francis Abelli looked contemplative. "Why don't you come by the rectory? I'd love to visit."

"Sure, Francis, I'll do that." Tom didn't know if calling another priest by his first name was standard operating procedure, but he went along with it. He wondered whether Father Abelli could see through his disguise.

They said their goodbyes, and then Lena and Tom watched Father Abelli walk through the gates onto the hallowed ground. His hands were clutched behind his back.

"He's such a wonderful priest," Lena said, "so giving and understanding." Looking into Tom's eyes, she said, "You'd love him."

Tom wondered if he himself—given the right set of circumstances—could have become a priest. If so, would he have fallen into a narrow path like Father McMann or followed the wider path of Jesus? He hadn't been much of a model-citizen, so maybe he wouldn't have been a model-priest either.

They walked away from the ruins. The searing sunlight had given way to a soft summer sky. The sounds of nature followed them.

"Father Tom, what brought you to Priory?"

"I dunno, Lena. I kind of wound up here by accident. I was tryin' to get out of my rut. Answer some questions."

"Any luck?"

Tom laughed weakly. "Unfortunately, the longer I'm here, the more confused I am."

"Confused about what?"

"I don't even know. My place in the world maybe?"

Tom's heart pounded. He wondered if she could hear it. While they ambled down a hill, he tried to find the right words, wishing he could pick them up like pebbles in the path.

"I read the Bible, but it doesn't give me answers, ya' know? Lots of parables. We're supposed to figure it out for ourselves 'cause it's personal, right? But sometimes, I just wish He'd come right out and tell me what to do. I don't wanna wonder if every move I make is wrong."

He sighed and then turned his attention to her. "What about you? You said you had somethin' to talk about…"

Lena stopped in the road and turned to face him. Tom steadied his camera case and did the same. With nothing but humidity between them, it was easy to see small veins through her thin skin.

Lena felt like she was on the diving board of a frigid pool, imagining what it would be like if she jumped in. Pre-feeling the pain and immersion. Counting down from five to summon the courage. It was time to jump. "I had a bad car accident in high school. And it was my fault."

"I'm sure it wasn't *totally* your fault."

Lena strained to look at him. "Father, I was drunk. And I was driving. There was a tree. Anyway, even before that, I caused a lot of trouble. It wasn't a one-time thing. That was just sort of the end of it."

A weight pressed upon Tom's chest. "We all make mistakes…"

"Yeah, I know, but…"

Tom knew there was more, but he couldn't listen to it. He turned and began walking again. What was he supposed to say? What was he supposed to do? He couldn't tell her that he'd driven drunk so many times he couldn't count them all. Didn't want to confess that some mornings he'd woken up unaware of how he'd gotten home. How would that make things better?

He wanted to hold her, brush the wispy hair away from her face and say that everything would be okay. But he had a feeling things hadn't been okay in her world for a long time.

He was trying to be an inspirational priest, but nothing was coming to him. Tom's mind was a tangled mess. He didn't have any words of wisdom for her. Even though he longed to know more, he found himself unable to continue the conversation. Being a confidante was not his strength.

Lena walked in confused silence. She imagined that Father Tom was condemning her. Is that why he'd abruptly stopped their conversation?

When they reached The Retreat, Lena handed Tom the camera. He wanted to ask her more about the crash, but didn't know how. All he knew was that he had to have more time with her.

"Hey, wanna develop this film?" he asked.

"Ourselves?"

"Sure. Why not? Hmm, only problem is: no darkroom. Maybe Mary Bell would let me convert one of the bathrooms for a day."

PRIORY, LOUISIANA

Tom knew he was being impulsive. Setting up a darkroom would be expensive and time-consuming. Plus, he'd be leaving Priory soon, so he'd have to pack it all up before then.

"You can use one of my bathrooms if you want. My house is so empty…" Lena's hazel eyes were enchanting.

He was fighting a strong desire to kiss her. "How 'bout tomorrow?" Demons circled him.

"Sure. I'll be finished at The Retreat around two."

He wondered what would happen if he leaned forward and pressed his lips to hers. A scandal would immediately swirl around them and consume the town. "Two o'clock. I'll meet you here on the front porch."

Lena walked away from The Retreat, thinking about Father Tom. Maybe he wasn't condemning her, after all.

Tom watched her from the front steps. Birds chirped in the surrounding trees. She was walking home, not driving. Unable to maintain a straight path, she hobbled a bit and seemed to be favoring one leg. He turned away and hung his head, wondering how he would ever do right by her.

PRIORY, LOUISIANA

Mornin', Y'all   *Thursday, August 25, 2005*

"Mornin', Y'all. This is Melody Melançon and you're listening to WPRY 90.5, bringing you and your mama up-to-date on the latest in Priory.

Hold the phone, y'all. I told you this Hurricane Katrina was going to be a curse. She slammed into Florida, tore across the Southern tip, and left again. She seems to be in a real big hurry. Katrina was only a Cat 1 when she hit, but she left some major damage, y'all. I'm starting to hear reports that say some people died. That just breaks my heart. Water and wind can be powerful enemies.

Anyway, Katrina's huge now—like my uncle who hid Moon Pies in his pockets—so take her serious. If y'all got relatives on the Gulf coast, tell them to come and visit for a spell. Priory's real nice right now. Hot, humid, overcast paradise.

Hang tight, y'all. Make some homemade ice cream (I like the Creole Cream Cheese flavor myself) and brace yourself for some visitors, 'cause Katrina is a witch.

Oh, and one more thing. I want to sincerely thank the Priory Knitting Circle. After I gave the shout-out to my beautiful, bald friend Darla, they planned a chemo cap knit-a-thon. It's tomorrow morning at nine in the church hall at Our Lady of Good Hope. That warms my soul like a spicy, hot Bloody Mary. You ladies are the best. I am gonna be there to hang around and cheer you on. I can't knit to save my soul.

PRIORY, LOUISIANA

That's it for now. But remember, if you're not listening to *Mornin', Y'all*, you might as well be living in Kansas. Does anybody really live in Kansas?"

CHAPTER NINETEEN

The world spun on its axis in a predictable way Thursday morning even as Tom's life and Hurricane Katrina were becoming increasingly unpredictable.

Lafitte was at the front desk fielding an endless array of calls from potential evacuees. With one room already occupied by Tom, the three other rooms were booked in no time. The rest of the day was spent putting people on a waiting list that Lafitte knew they'd never need.

Tom was in Baton Rouge, watching his black clothes spinning inside a coin-operated dryer. Visions of Lena crowded his thoughts. Pieces of her flashed in his brain: her fragile eyes, her freckled and scarred skin, her quivering voice. He imagined trying to tell her the truth about his priesthood. There was no way to make it sound noble or sane.

Although his future was unclear, Tom decided to leave Priory on Friday morning. He didn't know where he'd go, but he didn't want to disappoint Lena or drag her into a scurrilous affair. He knew he'd been a disappointment to his parents, and he couldn't keep hurting people. Didn't want to maintain the worn pattern of regret.

Tom put his clean priest-shirt on and drove back to the camera shop. The wise scarecrow greeted him again but with a more surprised tone this time.

"Hey, Father. Why didn't you tell me you're a priest?"

Tom smiled and shrugged. He'd forgotten that his last visit was in plain clothes.

"I wish you would've told me. I could've given you a discount when you bought that camera last time."

"Not necessary," Tom replied.

"How'd you like the digital camera?"

"It's not as much fun as my film camera. Too much instant gratification."

He handed his silver camera across the counter. The man pressed the browse buttons back and forth. While the clerk was flipping through his photos, Tom noticed the guy's nametag: "Paul."

"These are pretty good shots, Father. Have you printed any of 'em yet?"

"Not yet." Pointing at the nametag, Tom said, "Paul. Like the apostle, right?"

"Yeah, Father, that's right. What's your first name? I can't remember."

"Tom."

"Also an apostle. The doubting one, right?"

Tom hesitated. "Yeah, the doubting one."

"Do you want me to develop these?"

"Please."

"You got it. Anything else I can do for you?"

"Maybe so. I need to set up a darkroom to develop the black and white rolls we shot yesterday. Can you help?"

"Sure, do you need instructions with the supplies?"

"Probably not a bad idea."

"Okey-doke. I'll stick this card in the printer and round up your other stuff."

The straw-haired apostle went to work, leaving Tom to wander around, gawking at an endless display of camera supplies and gadgets he suddenly wanted to own. While making a lengthy mental wish list, Tom wondered whether or not he should buy a camera for Lena.

Do priests buy people presents? Especially expensive ones?

He honestly didn't know. Some of them took vows of poverty, so maybe a priest wouldn't have been able to afford big gifts. Paul handed Tom his photos.

"You can look these over, Father. I'm almost finished getting your stuff together." Paul placed chemicals, clips, plastic containers, and a timer on the glass countertop and walked away.

A grin overtook Tom as he relived the day's adventure on 4x6 glossy paper. He flipped through a close-up of a ladybug on a piece of grass, an overview of the ruins that had no focal point (he needed to work on that), a squirrel perched atop the wooden bridge railing, and various other shots of flora and fauna, some hitting their mark, some lying blandly upon the paper. Tom's grin disappeared, though, and he stopped flipping through photos, when his first shot of Lena appeared.

She was slightly off-center, as planned, and was looking down into her camera, loading the film. Determination lit her face. Her braids hung down playfully like ends of an auburn jump rope, sunlight glimmering on their edges. Wisps of hair decorated her delicate features. In the background was a blurry smear of grass, flowers and shells. Tom gently touched the picture of her face with his fingertips.

"That's it," Paul declared, interrupting Tom's trance.

Tom left the picture of Lena on top of the stack and placed the photos back into their yellow envelope. Paul rang up expenses, gave a generous discount, and filled two large bags with supplies. Standing in a camera shop in Baton Rouge, Tom's future became increasingly uncertain.

He drove back to Priory, talking aloud. "God, seriously, what am I supposed to do?"

A patch of sky pressed against his windshield. "I don't get it. Where am I supposed to be goin' with this?"

Lena was sitting on the front stoop waiting for him when he pulled up to The Retreat at 2:10. She cocked her head. She'd noticed the green Jeep in front of The Retreat the past few days, but she hadn't once thought it might be his. So many things about Father Tom were peculiar.

"I thought you'd forgotten me," she said when he approached. Her eyebrows formed an upside-down V like a roof gable.

"I didn't forget you. I just had to get some stuff for our darkroom, and I lost track of time. Sorry."

Hearing the apology cemented her already warm impression of him, and her eyebrows relaxed. "That's okay."

"Lena, do you mind if we *drive* to your house? I know you like to walk, but I'm worried about how little time we have."

Would she get into a car with him? Had she been in a car since the crash? He searched her eyes for answers.

"I guess it's okay," Lena replied. She stood and stretched, as if she'd just woken up from a long nap.

He opened the car door for her, threw his CD's into the backseat, and held her hand while she got in. It was the first time they'd touched, and they both felt oddly charged by it. Behind Tom, the screen door creaked.

"Father Tom," Lafitte said.

Lafitte's face was red and his chest was pumped up. Tom was almost afraid to go near him, but he closed Lena's door and walked toward the front porch. Lafitte seemed to grow exponentially as the distance between the two men shrank.

When Lafitte was within whispering distance of Tom, he said in a voice as low as a bullfrog, "If you do anything to that girl, I will kill you myself."

Tom stood still and tried to maintain his priestly dignity. "Lafitte, I'm a little confused. I don't know why you think I'd do somethin' to hurt her, but I never would."

Lafitte gave him one intense eye and said, "Tom whatever-your-last-name-is, are you going to be heading out of town any time soon? People are trying to evacuate the storm, and you're taking up space."

Tom realized Lafitte had not called him "Father" and his underarms started to sweat. The storm? He'd overheard people talking about it, but hadn't given it any attention. And although Tom had planned on leaving the next day, he wanted it to be his idea and his alone. If Lafitte was going to be such a jerk, maybe he wouldn't leave. Maybe he would stay awhile longer. He'd noticed Lafitte giving him the suspicious eye, and it was starting to get on Tom's nerves.

Could Lafitte know his true identity? His instincts said Lafitte was fishing. Tom wasn't going to be idiotic enough to jump into the net.

"Don't know, Lafitte," Tom whispered. "I think God might be callin' me to stay here a while longer."

Tom challenged Lafitte's stare. His new bravado spewed forth like a spring.

"We'll see about that, *Tom*," Lafitte said in such a calculated manner that the hairs on Tom's arms stood up. "If you don't leave soon," Lafitte continued with intensity, "you and I will have some serious shit to discuss."

Lafitte turned around and headed back into the house. Tom felt a headache forming. He climbed into his Jeep.

"Is everything okay?" Lena asked.

"Oh, sure. Lafitte was just givin' me a message."

Tom was unsettled when they started their drive. His palms were sweaty and his throat was parched. In need of an attitude adjustment, he donned his wrap-around sunglasses and turned on the CD player. Lena grinned in recognition of the funky, cool Dr. John.

Glad to be back in his own domain, priestly attire aside, Tom returned the smile. He rolled down the windows and searched forward to "Traveling Mood." Tom drowned out the hot wind, singing with Dr. John, while a lone whistler and an enthusiastic horn section underscored the lyrics about searching the countryside for a lost love.

Tom and Lena might have looked like two young lovers on their way to a drive-in movie, bouncing their heads to the music. He rapped his clammy hands against the steering wheel. She whistled to the tune. Except for his stiff white collar, her pink scars, and premature lifelines on both their faces, they were teenagers again.

They pulled up to Lena's house, a purplish-blue clapboard shotgun, the vibrant violet of a Louisiana swamp iris. It was finished with neat white trim and charcoal shutters. A wicker swing hung sideways from the beadboard ceiling of the front porch, in front of a solitary window.

Lena led Tom through the feminine, cozy living room and sparse but immaculate dining room into the kitchen. It smelled of cypress wood, turnip greens, and hot tea.

"My father was a carpenter," Lena explained, showing him the cypress cabinets her father had made. Tom rubbed his hand against the surface of one of the doors. Its gray-green luster impressed him. "He did all the woodwork in the house himself."

When Tom inhaled the wood's depth, he remembered the chest-of-drawers Mimi had given him. Every time he opened a drawer its scent came alive, as if it was freshly hewn once again. He thought of the chest presiding proudly over the corner of his bedroom in New Orleans.

"The woodwork is awesome," Tom said. "Where's your father now?"

"Oh, he passed a couple years ago."

"Sorry."

"Me, too, but it was quick, which was a blessing. My father and I both watched my mother die of cancer. *That* was agonizing."

"Wow. I'm really sorry." Tom knew it must have sounded feeble. He tried to think of what a priest would say without making it cold or distant. "At least they're in a more peaceful place now, right?"

"Yeah. They sure went through hell here on earth." Lena looked out the kitchen window. "I guess I should say I *put* them through hell."

Tom took her two hands in his and turned her toward him, looking into her hazel eyes. His wild blood was uncertain which direction to flow, as if it was a stream traversing the Continental Divide.

"Lena, everyone makes mistakes. You would've never made your parents suffer on purpose."

She pulled back and turned away. After pausing, she said, "My parents spent a lot of money and time helping me get better. They looked ancient when they died, even though they were still pretty young. *I* did that to them, Father. Maybe not on purpose, but it was my fault all the same."

Lena pointed to a picture in the hallway. "This is them."

Inside a black frame, Tom saw a picture of a sturdy Latino man and a petite auburn-haired woman. They were smiling politely, but not beaming. They looked genuine, like people you could trust. Lena's face so resembled her mother's.

"Do you have any other family?" Tom asked.

Lena thought about it for a minute and then said, "Yes. Mary Bell and Lafitte." Tom started to understand Lafitte's threats.

"Lena, you need to forgive yourself before you can move on, and I don't think you've done that."

She lowered her eyes.

Tom continued. "Did you ever tell your parents you were sorry?"

She sighed. "Sure. Many times."

"Did they forgive you?"

"Of course, but…"

"Then who are you to deny them that privilege? You owe them that, Lena."

She had never thought of that before, had never considered she was withholding something from them they would've wanted. The pain in her eyes melted. It was so simple.

Tom wished he would've apologized to his parents, but with all the mistakes he'd made, where would he start?

Lena changed the tone of the conversation, grinned softly and said, "Hey, I want to show you something."

She led him through a sitting room and then her bedroom. "Sorry about this, but it's the only way through the house."

"Yeah, I know," Tom said matter-of-factly, having been through many shotguns in New Orleans. On his quick trip through the room, he spotted a sleigh bed, an armoire, and a simple wooden vanity with a glimmering Venetian mirror perched over it.

Passing through the heavy back door, they came upon an intimate brick courtyard shrouded by tall walnut trees on two sides and what appeared to be a large shed in the back.

"My father used this shed for his woodworking," Lena said. "But I think it would be perfect as a darkroom. It doesn't have any windows."

They walked into a nearly empty room, and Lena flipped on the lights. A sink and countertop traversed one entire wall.

"Where's your father's equipment?"

"Oh, I sold it. I didn't want to keep looking at it, and I didn't know how to use it. Besides, before I got my job at The Retreat, I needed the money. My parents left me the house and a little cash, but not a lot."

PRIORY, LOUISIANA

Tom was proud of Lena. She didn't need his pity. She'd been strong and self-sufficient. He surveyed the room. Not a cobweb in sight. It smelled faintly of sawdust and oil.

"Did you just clean this?"

"I swept it out, that's all. It didn't take me very long. We don't want our pictures to be dusty, do we?"

Lena looked happy. Molten lava poured into Tom's chest. He scanned the room. In an upper corner, a fan was mounted to the wall. "Does that work?"

"I think so, but I haven't tried it lately."

Lena walked over to the switch and flipped it. The blades turned. Warm air slid across their skin.

"This is perfect," Tom said, pushing aside a rising tide of unwelcome feelings for someone he shouldn't be considering. "Let's get to work."

They brought in bags from the car, unpacked chemicals, and made various soups and baths. Tom instructed Lena through every step, pleased with how easily it came back to him. They ran a clothes line across the room and hung clips on it, ready for their dripping pieces of Coeur de Vie.

For the rest of the afternoon, Tom and Lena slipped in and out of darkness. He bumped into her once or twice, reaching for supplies. And it was hard not to accidentally touch her hand when trying to maneuver without light. She felt his steady presence in the room—trustworthy and full of knowledge.

Tom loved the anonymity of darkness. No visuals. No collared shirt. No blinding sunshine to betray him. He wondered if he could now be anyone he wanted to be.

As photos evolved, Lena beamed and Tom praised her. Her work was elegant and mesmerizing, especially the tombstones.

When the day was spent, they ate dinner on the front porch. Crickets sang. Tom and Lena talked effortlessly, swinging back and forth on the wicker swing. She fed him leftover gumbo and crusty French bread. They rested their bottled beers on the wooden porch floor.

Tom told some of his silly Boudreaux jokes and she laughed softly, cupping her hands over her eyes when they were particularly awful. Whenever she hid her eyes, he stole secret glances of her. Her neck was long and graceful. The nighttime glow made her skin look peach.

He stopped talking but kept staring. Lena had no other choice than to look at him. She nervously studied his intense green eyes.

"Lena, when you were younger, what did you want to be when you grew up?"

She looked down at her bare feet and wiggled her toes. "I don't know. I didn't really have any big dreams. I was just happy hanging out with my friends. Hoping to go to college, I guess."

Tom looked away from her into the sweet olive bush beyond the rail. His whole body ached for her. He knew it was a mistake to keep wanting her, but he couldn't stop. *Why not think about it? What would be so wrong about falling for a girl in Priory?* Tom tried to project forward a potential relationship with Lena. Sylvia Vaughn would suffer multiple asthma attacks upon hearing that her son was falling for a housekeeper.

"What about you?" she asked. "Did you always want to be a priest?"

Tom laughed and gave her an honest answer. "No. I didn't always wanna be a priest. In fact, before I became a priest, I was a techie. You know, a computer guy."

Lena made the gabled-eyebrow expression again. "What made you do that?"

Tom had never put it into words before, had never tried to figure it out, but now it became clear. His whole face opened up. "I think I was tryin' to make my parents proud of me, and I did what I thought I needed to do," he said. "One day my dad was reading the paper, commenting on how the computer industry was the next great horizon, and the next thing I knew, I had chosen it as a major in college."

"Did it work?" she asked.

"Did what work?"

"Did you make your parents proud?"

"No, I didn't, I guess. I was never passionate about it, never did anything more than the bare minimum at work," he admitted. "My dad wanted me to own a computer company, invent a new chip, blaze some new micro path by now, but I never got outta the small box I put myself in."

s-m-a-l-l b-o-x was typed onto his legs, including the thumb tap marking the space bar.

"So, did you become a priest to please them, too?"

"No," Tom answered with hesitation. "I think I did that for myself."

Lena was intrigued.

"But it's a mistake," Tom added, locking eyes with her. "It was a mistake to go down a path that wasn't meant for me."

She quickly rose from the bench, picking up their dirty dishes and fumbling into the house. Tom helped Lena clean up the mess in silence. She wouldn't look at him, feared how deeply she felt for him, and he knew he'd pushed too far. Every part of his body wanted to be with her.

When they returned to the warmth of the front porch, Lena sat back down again, uncertain what to do next. Tom came outside, carrying his Secret Agent camera. He placed it into her cupped hands and wondered if he would ever see her again. Regret and desire consumed him.

"Lena, I want you to have this. You're a natural."

If Lena had not been so afraid of herself, so afraid of her feelings for him, she would have asked him to stay for a while longer. But one monumental mistake in a lifetime seemed like plenty. Her stomach fluttered.

"When are you leaving town, Father Tom?" she asked, staring at the gift.

"I dunno. Soon."

"You'll let me know before you leave, won't you?" Her pleading eyes rose to meet his.

Tom wished she wouldn't look so irreplaceable. "Sure," he said with uncertainty. "I'll let you know."

CHAPTER TWENTY

Full from a picnic of cheese, alligator sausage, and wine, Henry turned the lantern on low and set it next to the blanket. Blades of grass reflected amber light.

A blood orange horizon was stuck between the treetops and a darkening sky. Henry wanted to pause it so it would always look that way, but the orange narrowed and slid into the earth.

Mary Bell lay on her back, her curly hair spread out below her as dark as oil. They looked up to the heavens, snuggled together in the open field, and held hands. Stars ducked behind clouds and then reappeared. The night air smelled of their mosquito spray, mud, and moss. Mary Bell was light-headed from the alcohol.

"There's Orion," Henry commented, pointing to the hunter.

"Where?"

"Right over there. You see those three stars together? That's his belt."

Mary Bell liked the profile of his hand against the twinkling summer sky. His hands were muscular and square.

"The two stars above it are his shoulders."

She remembered his hands exploring her. Her breasts and legs tingled with longing. Was he thinking of her or was he charting constellations? Why couldn't she control herself around him?

He kept talking about two of the stars pointing in a straight line to something else, but she couldn't concentrate with his body nearby. The sky seemed farther away than usual. An early owl hooted.

She loved listening to Henry. When they were growing up, he was one of the brainy boys. He'd grown even more impressive with time. How had she overlooked him? She marveled at his earnest profile. He turned his head, and they looked at each other in silence. Inhibitions were stripped by wine.

He rolled over on top of her, the natural weight of him grounding her, hiding her, making her feel safe. In this position, her breathing shallowed and shortened. Even that small change heightened her desire. Henry played with a ringlet of hair at the edge of her face. His heart was thumping wildly. His whole body pressed upon her.

He was looking all around her face. For what, Mary Bell did not know. She wondered what he was thinking.

Henry wondered how to keep sand from slipping through his hands.

He kissed her gently but passionately. Then, as if he had just remembered a dying relative, he rolled over, sat up and ran his fingers through his hair. Even in the warm humidity, Mary Bell felt a chill. He turned to look at her. His furrowed brow made her heart sink.

"What's wrong?" Mary Bell asked. As soon as she said it, she felt desperate. There was a painful silence.

"I've got a long day ahead of me tomorrow," he said.

Mary Bell propped herself up on one elbow, confused. She wanted to ask him more but felt herself shutting down.

"I think we should head back, hon," he continued, reaching over and touching her fingertip.

She hoped he was kidding, but she already knew that wasn't his style. Henry rose, helped her up, and grabbed the blanket and lantern. They crushed blades of grass on their trek through the field.

In the car, Mary Bell put her hands in her lap and concentrated on the front windshield. Henry grabbed her hand and wove his fingers through hers, holding onto her for the duration of the ride.

He was distant, though. Distant and quiet. They drove home in total silence. He wouldn't look at her. Outside the car, under a starlit sky, the leading winds of a storm whipped into a frenzy.

Mornin', Y'all

Friday, August 26, 2005

"*Mornin', Y'all.* This is Melody Melançon and you're listening to WPRY 90.5, bringing you and your mama up-to-date on the latest in Priory.

I wanna welcome all you people who are coming to our quaint little town to get away from that whopper of a storm. I swear you will find no more hospitable people in this entire world than you will here in Priory.

I especially want to welcome Miss Annie from Pensacola. I met Annie yesterday at The Corner Grocery. Lovely lady. Gray hair, blazing blue eyes.

Hey, Annie! I hope you like those Camellia red beans you bought yesterday. You tell your sister Fanny she needs to let them soak overnight. Never mind what it says on the package. And don't forget to add the green Tabasco if you're wanting to try something new. I know most people swear by the red Tabasco, but I like the green one on almost everything.

So, people of Priory, if you have someone staying with you while they're riding out this hurricane, you make sure you feed them real good. If there's one thing we know here in Loo-siana, it's red beans. I love 'em. Especially with some smoked sausage on the side. Of course, you can't go wrong with a pork chop on the side neither.

That's it for now. But remember, if you're not listening to *Mornin', Y'all*, you might as well be living in Iowa."

PRIORY, LOUISIANA

CHAPTER TWENTY-ONE

Friday morning, Katrina's path pointed to the Florida panhandle. Her counter-clockwise swirl covered nearly the entire Gulf. Coastal people prayed not to get hit, but it was too much like praying someone else *would* get hit.

Batteries, flashlights, and plywood flew off store shelves. People stocked up on bottled water, canned goods, liquor, and gas.

New Orleanians discussed Betsy's wrath in '65 as they helped each other board windows. The storm would be a Category 4 or 5. If she came anywhere close to their city, the very least they could expect would be loss of electricity for several days. Hundred-degree summer days.

Offices were as empty as churches on Fat Tuesday. Sustained winds, a strengthening eye wall, and higher than average sea temperatures were daunting.

Mimi was having a highball and watching TV when her phone rang. "Hello?"

"Mama, have you been following the storm?" Sylvia asked.

"Of course I have, darlin'."

"Well, we're packing up, so throw a few things in a bag. Richard and I will be picking you up early tomorrow morning."

Mimi thought of the last time she'd left town with those two and their miniature poodle, Bitsy. Bitsy had circled Mimi's lap over and over again with nervous energy, scratching up Mimi's terrycloth lounge pants, pulling the loops until the pants looked like an old throw rug. Mimi had been miserable: the sunlit backseat made her stomach heave, and the incessant barking and circling gave her a splitting headache. They'd sat in bumper-to-bumper traffic on the I-10, turning a five-hour jaunt to Houston into a ten-hour nightmare. Nowhere to stop for gas or bathrooms or food.

Completely uncivilized, as Mimi remembered it.

Tom had refused to go with them, smirking and waving goodbye to the miserable threesome while he perched atop his Jeep, drinking an icy cold hurricane from a souvenir Pat O'Brien's glass.

When the real hurricane had taken a turn and hit Florida, Tom teased Mimi about her miserable, unnecessary trip. This all resurfaced in Mimi's mind as she contemplated her potential evacuation.

"Where y'all goin', darlin'?" Mimi asked her doting daughter.

"I know what you're thinking, Mama. We are *not* going to Houston."

"Oh, thank the Good Lord."

"We're going to Natchez."

"Mississippi? What for?"

"It's closer. I-55 should be less crowded than the I-10, and I know you adore Natchez."

"Have you heard from Thomas?" Mimi baited.

"No, I haven't. What's up?"

Mimi thought about it and then said, "He went out of town for a couple days, but he called today and said he's comin' by to get me."

"Out of town? Where is he?"

"Didn't say, sugar, just said he'd be here soon. Cora didn't tell you he was gone?"

"No, she didn't."

"Oh, well. He said to tell you not to worry. He's gonna come back and scoop me up."

Sylvia was proud of him. Finally, a display of responsibility. "That's great, Mama. You two will have fun together. Where y'all going?"

Mimi paused momentarily. "Didn't say. I'm sure he's got a plan, my darlin' Thomas."

Sylvia didn't know why she felt uneasy. Tom was a grown man, and he could certainly take care of his grandmother as well as anyone else, but the logistics of it were hard to believe. Tom was out of town? That alone was very odd.

"Mama, the I-10's only going to be one-way by tomorrow morning. All lanes will be heading out. How's he going to get here?"

"Well, sweetie," Mimi assured her, "he must be comin' in tonight. Or maybe he doesn't need the I-10. Like I said, I don't exactly know where he's been."

Sylvia might have wanted to prod her mother further, but Sylvia's own best interests wrestled all doubt from her mind. Being in the car with Richard and Bitsy was stressful enough without adding her flask-carrying, bladder-challenged mother to the mix.

"Okay, Mama. If for some reason that falls through, call us before nine tomorrow morning. We want to get on the road early so we can get to Natchez by lunch."

"Sure will, Sylvie. Y'all have a great little trip. Say, Cora's leavin' town, isn't she?"

"Yes, thank goodness, she's going to her cousin's in Shreveport."

"Good then. See y'all in a couple of days."

Richard and Sylvia packed enough clothing and dog food to last three to four days, tops.

Mimi took Tom's spare house key out of her kitchen drawer and went out her front door. It was hard to believe a storm was coming. There was no rain in sight, and it was only partly cloudy. Heat bore down. Sweat crept into her cleavage.

She turned the key and let herself into Tom's place. In his kitchen, Mimi opened several upper cabinet doors until she spotted it. Pulling a wooden chair over to the counter, she carefully climbed up and reached for the top shelf, pushing aside various and sundry fraternity favors until she found her prize: the Pat O'Brien's hurricane glass.

It shone like an hourglass with the top third sliced off. The recipe for a hurricane was imprinted in kelly green ink upon smooth, glassy curves. Mimi's eyes sparkled. She knew Tom would love her plan. She could hardly wait to have her own Hurricane Party and wondered if he really would surprise her. She believed he might.

PRIORY, LOUISIANA

CHAPTER TWENTY-TWO

Tamika sat next to her mom on the tattered sofa, watching the local news. The weather forecaster was telling everyone to leave New Orleans. The anchor woman wondered aloud whether or not this was the end of New Orleans as they knew it. It was hard to concentrate on their messages with Tyrell's dead voice still bouncing off their walls.

The storm was drifting further west than the Hurricane Center had predicted. Katrina, too, had a message: *Life is unpredictable.*

The projected path now had the eye crossing onto land along the Mississippi-Alabama border. The western edge of the cone of probability was swallowing up half Louisiana.

"We leavin', Mama?" Tamika asked, turning her brown eyes up to her mother's face.

"Don't know, baby," Nichelle answered, "we really got nowhere to go."

She snuggled Tamika in closer to her and worried. Their raggedy old car might not make an extended road trip, particularly one in which they might roast for hours on the interstate: car overheating, fluids leaking, belts popping, expensive gas being sucked up.

"Maybe it's not really comin'," Nichelle said. "They keep tellin' us the big one's comin', and it ain't never showed up."

Nichelle decided they would go to her sister's apartment instead. Demetra was safely ensconced on the third floor and, even if she lost power, would at least stay dry. Nichelle and Tamika's first-floor apartment took on a couple inches of water during any given cloudburst, stinking like mildew for weeks afterwards.

Nichelle already knew the rain-soaked routine. After the water seeped in under the sliding doors and saturated the dining room shag, she'd leave the windows open. Humidity would smear a damp film upon everything she owned. Once, in a moment of atypical generosity, her landlord had given her a brown bag full of solid blue deodorant sticks that she distributed around her sopping apartment. If there were available funds in her paltry bank account, she might rent a wet-vac from the grocery to help speed the process. Often, she would have to call the meat market to tell them she'd be late for work until she found someone to keep Tamika. She didn't want her daughter to catch any waterborne diseases. Just the thought of all that inconvenient hassle wore Nichelle out.

"Maybe we'll go over to your auntie's house 'til it passes, okay?" Nichelle said.

"Okay."

Nonstop hurricane coverage lit up their sparse apartment. The glowing screen dominated the room. When it showed waves heaving in the Gulf, Nichelle looked hard at them, wondering if they contained Tyrell's treasure chest.

PRIORY, LOUISIANA

CHAPTER TWENTY-THREE

Three days before Tom left New Orleans pretending to be a priest, he lay in bed, staring at a napkin on his nightstand. It was white, cheap, and fragile like tissue paper. With its crumpled shape—corners pointing to every nook of his bedroom—it resembled a Mexican flower like the one he'd made in third grade.

He considered throwing away the cocktail napkin, like so many others before it, but instead he sat up and smoothed the napkin between his warm palm and his bed sheet.

Callie. He vaguely remembered flirting with her at Grayson's party. Her handwriting was a mess, but he felt drawn to how illegible it was. How scratchy and desperate it seemed.

Callie answered after two rings. While Tom fumbled through the awkward call, he tried to paint a mental portrait of her. He was almost sure she was brunette. She sounded pleasant, but her voice felt thin and unfamiliar.

The next day, on his way to meet Callie for lunch, Tom's twitching fingers tapped the steering wheel. He cracked the windows and fidgeted in his leather seat. At a red light, humidity oozed in the windows. It spritzed beads of sweat upon his forehead and upper lip. Tom watched a priest walk down the sidewalk and turn onto Jackson Avenue. The image of the priest became blurred in striated layers of August heat.

A priest. Walking down the street. That was odd, even for New Orleans. A car honked behind Tom. He rolled forward but kept looking down Jackson. The priest's backside shrank with each step until his steamy silhouette smeared against a backdrop of fluffy, white camellias.

Tom continued toward his date at the oyster bar, but he couldn't shake the image of the misplaced cleric. *Since when does a priest just walk down the street?*

While Tom drove majestic Saint Charles Avenue, the sun flashed a series of leafy patterns through the massive oaks, transforming his car with a constantly changing camouflage. Its variations made Tom feel invisible.

How do I know that guy is a priest? What if he's not? Maybe he's just some nut-job looking for a free meal. Maybe he's on the Most Wanted List. Maybe he just wants to feel important.

New Orleans was a city in which you could find someone in costume on almost any given day. Tom himself had donned priestly attire at a "Dress As Your Favorite Sinner" fraternity party. Did he still have his black shirt? He was pretty sure he did. Being the only dark item in his whole faded wardrobe, it had caught his eye from time to time, hanging in the back of his closet, squashed behind an array of shrinking frat jerseys.

Tom had seen plenty of costumed, fake priests in the Quarter over the years. Wasn't it possible that this guy on Saint Charles was just a costumed crazy? Some guy masking even though it wasn't Mardi Gras?

At his destination, Tom stood in the crooked doorway of the oyster bar, upon the black and white pharmaceutical tile, and scanned the room. No single women. Maybe she wouldn't show. Part of him wished she wouldn't.

Tom bellied up to a wooden stool at the marble bar where Eddie was shucking oysters.

"Hey, man," Eddie said, glancing up.

"Hey, Eddie. How they lookin'?"

"Fat and salty, man. Perfect."

Eddie reached into the bed of crushed ice in front of him. With his thick rubber glove, he hunted for another shell and scooped out a knotted mound.

"You eat any today?" Tom asked.

"Always do. Ain't no better way to start the day."

While Eddie pried the oyster open, the door jingled open behind Tom. He turned around, and recognition clicked. It was her. She had a long, slender nose, glowing olive skin, and dark hair pulled into a neat bun. Brunette, not blonde. He'd been right.

She was kind of pretty. Not gorgeous, but attractive. Her nose was a little longer than Tom usually liked, but her figure was impressive and fit nicely into her pinstriped suit. Even though the pinstripes said "conservative," her plunging neckline and visible décolletage declared "open to suggestions."

After exchanging niceties, he ushered her to a pink linoleum table and pulled out her chair. He smiled as he snuck a look down into her cleavage. Tom thought to himself that since oysters were an aphrodisiac, and breasts were one of God's greatest creations, lunch could end well.

Tom wondered what she thought of him. Was he just as she remembered? Had she wondered about the color of his hair? Was he taller than she thought?

Conversation was a little awkward at first, but she was a talker, so that helped. They shared mutual acquaintances. Common barroom hangouts. If they'd left after their first round of oysters, he might have called her again. But the second dozen oysters arrived, and Tom squeezed a cut lemon over them. He was mixing a concoction of ketchup, horseradish, and Crystal hot sauce when things began to fall apart.

"Do you like foreign films?" she asked.

Tom plopped a dollop of creamy sauce onto the moist oyster and shook his head. "Nah." He stuck his fork into its goo, lifted the dripping mass from its shell, and placed it in his mouth. The horseradish cleared his nasal passages.

"Oh, too bad. There's a new French film I thought I might go see. It has English subtitles."

Tom took one bite and swallowed. The salty cold blob slid down his throat, aided by oyster water.

She continued. "What about the art museum? Maybe we could go see that exhibit…" blah, blah, blah.

Tom lifted his freezing longneck to his lips. Foaming hops chased the oyster down his throat. *What happened to the girl who wrote the scratchy number on the Mexican flower?*

Disengaged from their conversation, Tom's mind wandered back to Jackson Avenue. The image of the priest was stuck in his mind like a splinter. *I bet that guy wasn't a priest. A priest wouldn't be just walkin' around. He'd be drivin' a Marquis or a Town Car.*

Tom paid the tab and offered a noncommittal, "Well, it was fun."

"Yeah, thanks for the invitation." She saw his far-away look. Her throat hurt when he dug for the keys in his pocket. "Hey," she added, "do you want to go to Big Monty's and play hooky this afternoon?"

Tom gave up half a smile. Big Monty's: eternal night, cheese fries, more beer. Since it was Friday, and nothing productive was ever achieved on a Friday afternoon in New Orleans, the decision was amazingly simple.

Six hours later, uncertain he could spell his own name, let alone navigate a car, he got behind the wheel of his Jeep and drove home from a tony apartment in the Warehouse District. In his wake was a lovely woman, half-clothed and nearly asleep in her bed, unaware she would never hear from him again.

When Tom got home, he fumbled to the bathroom and grabbed the sink to stop the room from spinning. An invisible dagger pierced one of his temples and ran through to the other side. In the toothpaste-spotted mirror, he looked old. If he weren't drunk, and if he didn't look so disheveled, he would swear he was staring at his Grandpa Dirk. "Grandpa D," he said, looking up to his white bathroom ceiling, "I'm a mess."

He reinspected his reflection. It wouldn't stay still. His eyes glazed over. How long had it been since he'd promised himself this wouldn't happen again? Not that long.

He contemplated calling Callie and envisioned how pleased she'd be. Tom knew he wouldn't do it, though. Knew he didn't have it in him. She was too good for him. After she put her suit back on, it wouldn't take longer than one Southern afternoon for her to figure that out.

Tom reached up and grabbed two fistfuls of hair. He began to think of the priest again. The one who'd become smeared upon the camellias. That man, whoever he was, walked casually, as if he hadn't a care in the world.

An idea was pushing its way into Tom's brain, and it couldn't be halted. His head pivoted like a silent owl's towards his bathroom door. Beyond that door was his bedroom. And his closet.

He stumbled toward the closet door, turned the knob and opened it. Something unseen was pulling him forward. He felt disconnected and numb.

Hangers screeched when he pushed them around. In slow motion, Tom grabbed the black shirt, shuffled over to his bed, and passed out on top of it. Outside his window, wind howled through the towering pine trees.

Tom Vaughn had been struggling for years through the dull ache of an ordinary life. Suddenly, ordinary was over.

PRIORY, LOUISIANA

CHAPTER TWENTY-FOUR

Lena touched the flat package in her back pocket and ascended the stairs of The Retreat. Each stair creaked louder than she'd ever noticed before. She pressed on, all the while staring at the brass 2B, hovering in the air as it approached her.

Behind the door, in his new favorite chair, Tom was reading the Bible again, searching for answers. Flipping the soft, thin pages, Tom stuck his finger into the Book, opened it up and read from above his fingertip, "Commit to the Lord whatever you do, and you will succeed."

Outside his door, Lena stood, knuckles suspended in mid-air, afraid of what might lie ahead if she did this. She closed her eyes and knocked, unable to talk herself out of it.

Tom opened the door. His pulse raced. After an awkward silence, he started, "Hey, Lena."

"Morning."

The back of his head tingled. "Come in," he said, stepping aside.

She walked past Tom, and he closed the door. Lena's eyes jiggled around the room: to the hurricane lamp, the tall window, the landscape painting on the wall, then up to the medallioned ceiling. This room was so familiar to her, but with him in it, it seemed foreign. Undiscovered.

From the back pocket of her denim shorts, she withdrew a crumpled photo envelope. Lena held it in front of Tom, her hand shaking. She looked down upon its yellow rectangularness as if it contained the mysteries of the universe.

Tom wouldn't look at it. He couldn't take his eyes off her flowing waves of hair, the after-effects of a day's worth of braids, now flirting with her shoulder blades.

Lena carefully opened the flap of the envelope and pulled out an image of herself. It was a picture she didn't know existed until last night, after he'd left. She'd gone back to the shed to soak up a few final moments of joy, to wander among the laundry lines of beautiful paper.

While folding up bags from the camera shop, she felt a lopsided heaviness. Almost stuck to the bottom was an envelope containing photos. She retrieved them, lifted open the flap, and pulled the stack of 4x6s out. Lena couldn't believe her eyes when she saw the top picture. It was *her*.

She was awake half the night, wondering and praying in such a dizzying array that her doses of intermittent sleep were interlaced only with odd pieces of dreams about Father Tom kissing her. She worried about the repercussions of such a dream and prayed for forgiveness. Asleep again, the same forbidden dream recurred.

By the time dawn was breaking, Lena wasn't sure what to do. She just wanted to see him again. Standing in front of Tom, she trembled and almost dropped the photos. When he looked at the picture, he realized he had two choices. One: he could be flippant and nonchalant. Two: he could be honest.

He reached over and touched the photo again with his fingertip. His heartbeat rolled like the drum in a jazz funeral.

"Lena," he said, still gazing at the photo, contemplating his next line, "I think you're beautiful." Their eyes locked. A stillness overcame the space between them. Lena panicked, tossed the pictures on his bed, flung the door open, and left.

Lafitte and Mary Bell were greeting guests in the parlor when Lena came hobbling down the stairs and hastily exited The Retreat. They looked at each other with concern, but Mary Bell returned to her guests.

"Aunt Ria, Uncle Victor, I'm so glad to see y'all again." She kissed Ria and Victor each on the cheek. Ria and Mary Bell's mother were sorority sisters, like extended family members.

Ria Legrange had elegant, shoulder-length gray hair and wore linen pants. Victor had on white Bermuda shorts and a canary yellow polo shirt. They could have done a commercial for *Chic Senior Living*.

"We're glad to see you, too, honey," Ria said. "It's always a treat to be here."

"That's quite a storm coming," Victor said. "It's huge. They said it's the next Camille or Betsy."

"How's Charles?" Mary Bell asked.

Before Ria and Victor's response, Lafitte abandoned the conversation. He couldn't take the small talk. Lena had come bounding down from Father Tom's room, obviously upset, with no explanation. Lafitte climbed the steps two at a time, and knocked on 2B, trying not to guess ahead.

Tom opened the door, hoping it was Lena returning. When Lafitte's huge presence appeared in his doorway, Tom backed up. Lafitte entered and closed the door behind him. Pictures of Lena were strewn across the bed. *What the hell?*

Lafitte's brow furrowed. He looked at Tom and then down at the pictures again. He didn't know what it all meant, but The Retreat was going to be packed, a storm was approaching, and he did not have time for this shit.

Lafitte took one huge step toward Tom and threw a right hook to Tom's chin. Tom, having been in a couple of barroom brawls over the years, instinctively turned his head sideways to soften the blow. Lafitte's huge knuckles made contact but didn't do serious damage. He was an expert at hand-to-hand combat and could have put an end to Tom whatever-his-name-was right there and then if he wanted to, but he held back because Mary Bell would have been livid. Besides, there were guests in the house.

Tom spun around and fell against the wall next to the window with a pain that shot from his chin throughout his entire body.

"Shit!" Tom said, holding a hand up to his mouth, tasting the sharp, hot blood sliding out from between a couple of his lower teeth. "What's your problem, man?"

"Stay away from Lena," Lafitte said, punctuating each word with clear diction. Pointing a shaking index finger in Tom's direction, Lafitte reiterated, "Stay …away…from Lena." And with that, Lafitte left, creating a gaping hole in the room.

Tom wiggled his jaw around to make sure it wasn't broken. It was usable, but his mouth was pooling with blood, and he didn't want to swallow it. He hurried down the hallway to rinse his mouth out in the bathroom sink.

Hanging over the porcelain washbasin, Tom swizzled and spit until the water became more pink than red. He stood up and looked at his reflection in the mottled mirror above it. He was struck by how little his reflection had changed since his drunken luncheon date in New Orleans.

Wasn't he supposed to be transforming his life? Why was he still such a mess? Tom didn't want to leave Priory, but his options were dwindling.

Lafitte went back downstairs, breathing heavily and shaking his hand out.

Ria and Victor Legrange had already gone to 2A to settle in, so Mary Bell was alone. She wanted to call Henry so badly, but wouldn't do it. She was readying herself for the disappointment and wouldn't beg him for an explanation. She already missed him, though, and couldn't stop wondering what had gone wrong. It was so hard to wrench her face into a fake smile for her guests when all she wanted to do was weep.

Lafitte's reappearance downstairs startled her. When he reached for the registration book, she saw his red knuckles. Her eyes grew wide and accusatory.

"Lafitte, what happened?"

"Nothing." He closed the book and walked into the kitchen to avoid her, but she followed.

She grabbed his arm after they both passed through the swinging cypress door, "This has something to do with Lena, doesn't it?"

Lafitte was adjusting his eye patch, something he did when he was worried.

"Lafitte, did you hit Father Tom?"

No answer. Mary Bell's whole body tingled.

"Mary Bell, trust me. I know what I'm doing." He pulled a glass from the cabinet, filled it with tap water, and poured the water into his burning throat.

Mary Bell's eyes were as big as the gibbous moon. The deepened lines on his face worried her.

Lafitte sighed and said, "Look, Mary Bell, we're gonna have a lot going on this weekend with the storm and all, so I don't want you to worry about it. I'll handle it, okay?"

Mary Bell nodded but was weak. More change was coming. She felt like fuzzy caterpillars were crawling all over her.

PRIORY, LOUISIANA

CHAPTER TWENTY-FIVE

Charles sprawled out on the chaise on his parents' veranda. The waves were choppier today and creeping up the beach. It was time to leave Pass Christian, but he had a problem.

He closed his eyes and thought about his lack of funds. How could he explain his squandering of this month's allowance at a strip club in New Orleans?

He envisioned making a potential confession to his father. It went something like this:

"Dad, I'm broke."

"What happened to the money we gave you?"

"Gone."

"Gone? Where?"

In his daydream, Charles put on a manly grin, winked at his dad and said, "French Quarter. Strip club. Nice girl, dancing her way through nursing school… I was just trying to be helpful."

His dad might not think it was funny, but it was the truth, even if not a very elegant truth. Over the years, Charles had heard rumors about his father: ladies' man, quite the Romeo. Word on the street was that Victor Legrange was constantly taking up with some poor paralegal, a single mom, or an aging debutante divorcée.

Charles had found a way to live with that, had been extra kind to his mom when the rumors surfaced, so wouldn't it be a brotherhood-of-men confession to admit to his father that he'd done the same thing? Wouldn't that forge some sort of bond between them?

PRIORY, LOUISIANA

Not having a clear answer to that question, he sat on the porch, refilling his martini glass with chilled vodka until the day was almost done.

He had maxed out his credit cards, spent all his cash, and had no money in his account. And his mother was right. This storm looked wicked. He knew he shouldn't stay. He'd promised he wouldn't.

Charles walked into the house to take one last bathroom break. The grand staircase caught his attention. One hand lingered too long on the carved wood. He shook off the unwelcome feeling that he was getting ready to do something wrong.

When a wave of pre-sinning would darken his spirits, he usually concentrated on trying to talk himself out of such depravity, but his better self almost never won this argument. By the time an immoral deed became lodged within his psyche, the only way Charles found he could progress was into the deed itself, never around it.

It was as if he stood at the edge of a great forest, wide and shady. He knew he'd be looking for trouble in the forest, but trying to avoid the evil might mean edging along the patch of darkness for ages, thinking and re-thinking it. He'd become obsessed by the forbidden act and eventually surrender to it anyway. At least if he walked straight into the darkness, he'd pass through it in the shortest period of time, and maybe find the light again.

He went into the bathroom and peed into the basin, swirling unsteadily. When he re-emerged, his demons took over. The alcohol in his system made his head feel separated from his body in a way that suited him. Disconnected. He walked up the stairs, turned the corner and opened the attic door. Ascending a less decorative set of stairs, he found himself in the stylishly musty room. Except for the layer of dust, it was quite the grand little space.

Step by step took him closer to the safe until he stood eye-to-eye with it. It was a fairly recent addition to the home: waterproof, fireproof, built into the wall. The digital combination was seared into Charles on many different levels. It was his birthday: 12-08-80. Feast of the Immaculate Conception.

His chest was thumping erratically. He feared the vodka was trapped inside his heart, swelling it, preparing to explode. After his shaky index finger punched out the code, the heavy door popped open. Branches of imaginary trees shrouded him from the world.

PRIORY, LOUISIANA

CHAPTER TWENTY-SIX

Sitting upon her slipcovered sofa, Lena felt sick. She lay down on her side, slid a pillow under her head and looked sideways at the coffee table. Her father had carved it out of an oak tree, felled years ago by a lightning bolt. Lena rubbed the surface with her palm. It undulated beneath her touch. A tear snuck out the side of her lashes, dripped down her temple, and landed on the cotton pillow.

"Papa, Mama, where are you?"

The sideways room was disorienting, but that seemed fitting. Lena wondered whether her parents were angels, still hovering over Priory. Could they see her? Were they in this sideways room? Were they ashamed of her?

After everything I've been through, haven't I learned enough lessons? Do I really need to be falling for a priest?

Back at The Retreat, Tom had chosen to deal with his own crazy morning in another way. After Lafitte's blow, Tom initially considered leaving town, but he changed his mind. Jesus didn't run from his problems. He stayed there and let the crowd crucify him. If Tom truly wanted to be Christ-like, maybe he should stay in Priory. While thinking this through, it occurred to Tom that he probably shouldn't be comparing himself to Christ. There were very few similarities.

Drinking had always helped clear Tom's mind and strengthen the divide between black and white. With a little help from hops and barley, all choices would morph into their extremes and Tom could sort them out. In this too-sober state, things were confusing. On top of that, his chin was burning and a little medicinal alcohol would be comforting.

Still in his room, but preparing to head to Bob's Bar, Tom lifted his white collar up, preparing to slide it into place, drawing it near his chest. He stared it down but didn't insert it. Tom found that it wouldn't go any farther skyward than his chest. Its flaps stuck out like helicopter blades, threatening to whirl about and lift him off the ground. When he released it, the collar spun to the floorboards in an uneven pattern, as if shot down by a sniper. He left it there.

Confusion, shame, and desire all mixed violently inside Tom, creating a cocktail that blurred his vision. He snuck out of his room, slithered down the staircase, and crunched upon the asphalt gravel into town. By the time he reached the slatted blinds of Bob's, he was dying for a beer.

Once inside the door, it could have been any time of day. The blinds were closed enough to lend an aura of dark mystery to the space, and Tom was pleased to join the time warp. When he approached the bar, he noticed Dino was atop his horse at the far end, and Slim Stan was rubbing elbows with him. Gus was missing.

Bob bellowed, "Hey, Father. What'll you have?"

"A draft beer, please." Tom hoisted himself onto his regular stool, leaving Gus's stool empty in case he showed up.

"You got it." Bob withdrew a frosted mug from the cooler and tilted it under the tap. Tom's mouth tingled with anticipation.

A blaze of light flashed briefly behind them. Everyone turned toward the front door to see who it was. Gus appeared, newly shorn and practically bald.

Dino fell off his barstool, pressed his huge back against the wall, waved one hand grandly like a circus ringmaster and sang out in a low, wavy tone. The lyrics from a Dean Martin classic wafted across the bar. Dino kept singing but everyone spoke over him.

Bob started, "Hey, man, what the hell happened to your hair?"

"Yeah," Slim Stan prodded, "what's with the cue-ball?"

Gus smirked and spread his legs, frog hopping onto his padded stool. Dino silenced himself and spent considerable energy trying to remount his horse.

"It's too damn hot to have hair anymore."

They all nodded in agreement, downed some brew in solidarity, and turned their eyes toward Father Tom, their newest bar mate. It was then that Gus noticed the flaming chin.

"Father, what's up?" Gus asked, eyeing the bulge.

Stick to the truth, Tom reminded himself. "Lafitte slammed me good this mornin'."

Beer mugs suspended in mid-air. Eyes grew huge, and Tom felt like an instant ass. He deserved this trophy. Lafitte was trying to protect Lena, and Tom respected him.

"In all truth," Tom continued, "I was askin' for it."

Silence blanketed the crowd. The constant drone of hurricane coverage hovered over them. What could a priest do that would make Lafitte belt him? No one could imagine.

"What the hell didja do?" Slim Stan needed to know.

Tom turned his palms upward and refused to go explain any further. He put his hands down on the bar again and pecked against the bar rail. F-a-t-h-e-r.

In a frenzied hurry to alter reality, Tom chugged his first beer so quickly his throat went numb. Bob was surprised but filled it up again. Tom chugged the next one similarly and then ordered an oyster po-boy and fried pickles.

The barkeep refilled his glass yet again, and all attention came to rest upon the priest. Something scandalous had happened, and they wanted to know about it. They wanted to have their very own Jimmy Swaggart confession right now in Bob's Bar.

Tom slurped another beer before Bob even had time to put his order in at the kitchen.

"Hey, Father Tom," Bob said, "what's up?"

The carbonation rose into Tom's eyes.

"Yeah," Gus said, concerned. He put an oil-stained hand on Tom's upper arm. "What's up?"

"Sorry, guys. I just can't talk about it…"

Disappointment filled the room.

"Fine, that's fine," Gus said, elbowing Slim. "Right, guys? If Father here dudn't want to tell us what happened, we're not gonna pry."

Stan said, sloppily, "Okay by me."

Dino continued his song from the safety of his stool.

The rest of the men resorted to small talk to make their way through the awkwardness. An hour later, after dissecting the strengths and weaknesses of every position player the Saints had acquired over the last ten years, the men's speech was as incoherent as if they'd been shot with anesthetic. Tom said something garbled about it being time to go.

"Father," Dino said, his body making broad circles around an invisible pole, "whatever's wrong, it'll straighten itself out, don't you think?"

Tom, with half-open eyes, smiled weakly and said, "Yeah, man. I'm gonna straighten it out myself."

Dino put his hand out. Tom grasped it in a shaky hand sandwich, trying to keep his balance.

"Thanks," Tom added. He turned and wove his way toward the door.

Outside, the heat of August thawed him. He peered up at the sky. Stars twinkled brighter than ever. Even though his world blurred, it was obvious that to most sober folks, it was a clear night. Maybe the storm was heading to Florida. He hadn't been paying much attention to it, with his own drama swirling about. Worst they'd get in Priory, so far from the coast, was a torrential rain. Nothing they hadn't all seen before.

Still, the clear sky was menacing. It could be the proverbial calm before the storm. He tried hard to keep looking up but couldn't steady himself and was afraid of falling off the sidewalk.

Thank God I didn't drive.

A long car eased down the cobbles of Main Street and pulled up in front of him.

"Hey, Padre, what's up?" Grace Swannee asked. Her yellowing hand rested atop her sideview mirror.

"Oh, hey." Tom turned to look at her. "Grace, right?" His shadow swayed onto the façade of Bob's Bar.

"Why don't I give you a lift, Padre? You going back to The Retreat?" *Cough, cough...*

Her furry image jumped about in front of him.

"I am. And I'd love a ride."

Crossing in front of her Eldorado, he used one hand to steady himself upon her white car hood. He let himself in the passenger side and tried to slide across the red velour seat, but his jeans couldn't be persuaded. He lifted up his behind and moved toward the center of the car. Falling out would be embarrassing.

Grace's car reeked of cigarette smoke, but no more so than the barroom. At least the smoke inside her car was mixed with some sort of sticky, fruity candy scent, masking its lethal potency.

Tom couldn't feel the car moving. His own equilibrium was more crimped than the uneven surface beneath her tires. He nodded off but woke up when Grace pushed on his arm.

"Okay, Padre, we're here."

Tom's head popped up. Hadn't he just closed the door? He dreaded going back into The Retreat. Uncertainty lived inside that place. Tom settled in and tried to focus on his new driver, but it felt like there was a brick upon his head, and he was trying to keep it from falling off.

"What's your story, Grace?"

Grace was amused by the drunken priest. She and her husband used to relish cocktail hour on their front porch at night. "Don't have much of a story, Padre."

Tom tilted his swollen head back to the headrest and looked at the red ceiling. "Everybody has a story, Grace." His own recent story was quite unbelievable.

He wished this car would stay still. It felt like a whirlpool that kept forgetting its starting point. It was exhausting trying to control it.

Grace placed both hands on the steering wheel and peeked through the dusty windshield into the night. "Yeah, I suppose I do."

Tom closed his eyes but vowed not to fall asleep. "What is it? Lay it on me."

Grace thought about the answer for quite awhile. Finally, she turned her head away from him, talking to the crickets outside. "My life was grand. It really was. Then one day, my husband dropped dead, and my whole world fell apart."

She tried to remember what she had looked like in her youth. The only image she conjured up was her engagement photo. Neatly placed curls. Hopeful cheeks. Tom was still breathing, so she continued. "I don't have any hobbies. I've got nothing to do."

Even in his drunken stupor, Tom felt her sorrow.

"Good story, huh, Padre?"

He opened one eye just wide enough so that he could see her profile. She was still clenching the steering wheel, and her knuckles were white, making them look like toasted marshmallows. Grace glanced toward The Retreat's front porch, so he closed his eye again.

"Don't know why I'm still here," she said.

Don't know why I'm still here. He could have said those words himself.

"I know why you're still here, Grace."

She turned to look at him, but he appeared to be half-asleep.

"It's 'cause there are still people here who need you." He said it to the ceiling but felt her gaze upon him. When he opened his eyes to look at her, she reminded him so much of Mimi. "I need you," Tom said. "Who else is gonna drive my drunken ass home?"

Grace laughed, wiped her cheek, shook her head, and let herself out of the car. What Father Tom needed was some rest. She helped him stumble up the front staircase, making sure he was safely inside the door. Then she returned to her luxury liner and navigated it into a new fog.

The fog was confusing to Grace. Was it friend or foe? Some nights, it was her ally, glowing brightly to warn her about approaching headlights from another car. Other nights, it was her adversary like the billowing clouds of heaven, just beyond her grasp.

CHAPTER TWENTY-SEVEN

Mary Bell couldn't fall asleep. The whole day had passed without word from Henry. She'd checked her phone for messages several times. Nothing. Late in the day, against her better judgment, she even asked Lafitte if Henry had called. Lafitte shook his head. Mary Bell hated the way Lafitte turned away from her when he did it. In the course of one day, she felt as if she'd become a creature to pity.

Had Henry used her? She wouldn't believe it. It wasn't in keeping with anything she'd known about his decency. If he didn't call by tomorrow, she would call him, no matter how humiliating it might be.

All day long, Mary Bell had refused to open her nightstand and re-read the *Rules*. As if her personal turmoil wasn't enough, a storm was looming. It wouldn't be much of a threat to Priory, maybe just some heavy rain, but so many other people were in danger. This much uncertainty always made sleep elusive for Mary Bell.

She drifted off after midnight. In the midst of a dream, she was startled awake by the sound of sharp, cracking noises. She struggled to leave the dream and make sense of her surroundings.

Her room was awash in blues and purples, bathed in darkness but colored by moon glow. *Crack* again. The sound was coming from her window, and it scared her at first. She slid out from under her sheets to pull back her curtains.

Standing about ten feet below her window, in damp matted grass, was Henry. When he saw her, rocks fell from his hand as if an invisible gnome had squeezed his wrist.

For a moment, neither one of them moved. They were motionless figures in a glossy photograph. Mary Bell backed up, slipped into a flimsy robe and hurried out the front door. Her heart beat erratically. Henry was at the bottom of the porch steps with a wild look in his eyes.

Mary Bell slowed down, tightened the robe around her body, and descended the steps to meet him. She crossed her arms like she was stepping out into a cool Wisconsin night, not a balmy Louisiana one.

"Mary Bell, I'm sorry," Henry started.

She looked down at her bare feet. "I think you owe me an explanation, Henry."

"I do."

His tone worried her. It was full of guilt. Also, he hadn't approached her. That couldn't mean anything good.

Henry started walking down the side hill, waiting for her to walk side-by-side with him, so she did. They ducked under low branches on the live oak, went behind a row of thick brush, and down the creek slope, trying to stay on moss and out of mud, until they reached the water's edge. The creek water was clear and nonchalant, gurgling in the moonlight.

Mary Bell felt exposed in the thin robe and short nightgown, but Henry wasn't wearing much more. Just some shorts and a t-shirt. When he led her to a large stone and asked her to sit down, Mary Bell grew light-headed and fearful of the unknown.

Henry paced the pebble-strewn space in front of her. He seemed to be gathering his thoughts. After a few moments, he stopped pacing and sat next to her on the rock. They both watched the creek catch the light and then melt to black. Night insects harmonized.

"Mary Bell," Henry said to the creek, "there's no easy way to say this."

She steadied herself on the rock with her hands.

"Before I moved back from Baton Rouge," he continued, "there was another woman in my life. I went back to Baton Rouge today to see her."

Mary Bell turned to look at him. "That's where you were today?" She said it so softly he barely heard her.

"Yes." He paused then added, "I haven't been with her for a couple weeks. She's been in California visiting a girlfriend."

Mary Bell and Henry had been together for less than a week. She forced herself to ask, "How long have you been dating her?"

Henry didn't want to answer that, but could think of no way around the truth. "About a year or so."

Blood rushed to Mary Bell's head, throwing off her equilibrium. She felt like she might fall into the skipping creek. There was a sudden desire to know everything, even if she didn't like what she heard. She turned toward him.

Mary Bell wanted to ask Henry what she looked like. Was she prettier than Mary Bell? Taller? Thinner? What was her name? Mary Bell realized she was being superficial. There was really only one question that needed an answer.

"Do you…" she whispered, "Do you love her?" Mary Bell's stomach folded onto itself. She turned her head away. Ferns waved nearby. A ringing noise in her ears drowned out the tumbling water.

Henry ran a finger under Mary Bell's chin. Her neck felt thick with pain, but to Henry it looked regal. "I thought I did, but it's not the same thing I feel for you."

Mary Bell didn't know what to think. She had never contemplated this. He had deceived her.

"I loved her because I grew to love her. Maybe that doesn't sound right, but…it just wasn't the same. I never thought I'd be with her forever. Time just sort of slid by."

He studied Mary Bell's profile and tried to read her thoughts, but she was not giving anything away.

"Anyway, it was a pretty rough day today," he said.

"It wasn't much easier here."

"Mary Bell, I told her that I can never see her again. I know I was a total jerk for not telling you earlier, but I couldn't believe what was happening between us. I couldn't break up with her on the phone, hon. I hoped you would understand."

Mary Bell's thoughts turned to Henry's girlfriend, as she realized that her own good fortune was someone else's misfortune. That part hurt. Mary Bell had been dumped for another woman before, and she remembered how devastating it was. She remembered picturing her boyfriend in the arms of his new girlfriend. The humiliation rushed back to her.

"I should have told you, Mary Bell, but I was afraid."

He had been afraid? Ever since he'd returned to Priory, he had been the embodiment of male confidence.

Henry was intense. "I was afraid I'd lose you. Afraid I'd never have the chance to win you before I'd lose you."

Mary Bell's hands were trembling. The smooth stone was growing tepid under her skin. The raw smell of peeling bark surrounded them. "Is it over for good, Henry?"

"Yes, Mary Bell. Whether you decide to stay with me or not, it's over for good. How could I go back to a relationship like that after…"

He stopped talking and turned his face away. Then he regained his composure, stood up, and reached down to hold her hands. Her chin was down but her blue eyes turned upward to look at him. "Mary Bell Bateau, I am in love with you. Head over heels, crazy in love with you."

She hadn't expected it. It had only been a few days, but a very intense few days. It was startling and wonderful all at the same time, as if he were a magician showing his best trick.

"Oh, Henry." Tears filled her eyes. "You love me?"

Henry nodded.

She mouthed, *I love you, too*.

There it was. Plain and simple. Mary Bell had searched for years, endured one-sided relationships, cheating boyfriends, and broken promises. She hadn't expected the whole thing, when it finally arrived, to be so obvious.

Henry stood back and helped her to her feet. He couldn't help but admire the way her satin nightgown and robe draped over her full breasts. She was so beautiful it hurt. He drew her closer.

PRIORY, LOUISIANA

Damp moss and mud squished between her toes. She pulled him up against her, nibbled his earlobe and whispered, "I have something to show you."

Mary Bell took his hand and led him along the creek bank for a few yards until they came upon a huge weeping willow. She parted the drape of greenery that fountained to the earth. They ducked under the foliage and let the drape close behind them.

The room they entered was a sanctuary of mossy ground, a bold trunk, and an umbrella of cascading leaves. Even the moon had trouble piercing the veil, leaving only small shards of the sun's reflected light upon the ground.

Henry couldn't believe it. Mary Bell loved him. If there was any way to suspend this moment, to make it hover above life's timeline, they both would have done it.

"I will never leave you, Mary Bell."

Mornin', Y'all
Saturday, August 27, 2005

"*Mornin', Y'all.* This is Melody Melançon and you're listening to WPRY 90.5, bringing you and your mama up-to-date on the latest in Priory.

I know I am not the only Southerner fixated on her television these days. That storm is starting to freak me out. I'm glad they don't think it's going to the Panhandle anymore. I love the Panhandle. All that white sand squished between my fat little toes. I just adore it.

Of course, I don't want it heading to New Orleans neither. You can't find a better way to pass an afternoon than by sipping a Pimm's Cup at the Napoleon House. Sit right next to an open French door and you'll think that time does not exist. Lick your lips and eat your cucumber slice. Anyway, we got lots of New Orleanians flooding into Priory. Did I just say *flooding*? Good Lord, I do have some trouble picking the right word from time to time. *To all you Who Dat's: I am praying for you and yours.* I am doing a triple Sign of the Cross.

I also wanted to give y'all a social calendar update. Even though the outer bands might bring rain to our fair town, the Sorghum Distillery is inviting all out-of-towners (and locals, of course) to their moonshine tasting tomorrow afternoon. Some of you may be surprised to hear that people are still dripping and drinking moonshine, but I tell you, it is all the rage once again. Sorghum Distillery claims that it tastes way better this time than when your Uncle Gaston made it in the bathtub.

And if craft moonshine isn't enough to draw you in, they'll be serving homemade pork cracklin's on the side. Am I reading that right? Homemade pork cracklin's? I will be there, y'all. Nothing is better for the soul and the arteries than fried pork fat.

That's it for now. But remember, if you're not listening to *Mornin', Y'all*, you might as well be living in Rhode Island, a state that is smaller on the map than my baby toe."

CHAPTER TWENTY-EIGHT

Lena lay on her back in bed. The sun's early rays began to light her quiet room. Too much confusion swirled within her. She'd been awake for hours, waiting for the darkness to dispel. Exhaustion held her body against the sheets. She couldn't even contemplate taking simple steps like running a shower or making her bed. She picked up the phone on her nightstand and dialed.

"Mary Bell," Lena whispered into the phone.

"Yeah?" Mary Bell sounded half-asleep.

"This is Lena."

"Lena? What time is it?" Mary Bell unspooned herself from a sleeping Henry and consulted her bedside clock.

"I'm sorry for calling you so early. It's just that…well, I don't feel very good." As if to confirm that she wasn't lying, an acid-like burn crept up her esophagus.

"Oh, honey, I'm sorry. What's wrong?"

"Hard to say exactly." She hesitated. "I know you'll be busy with guests and all, but I…I don't know if I can make it in today."

It was unlike Lena to call in sick. Mary Bell worried, but was too tired to get her head around it. "You'd be here if you could."

"Yeah, if I could…"

Silence absorbed the rustling of Mary Bell's bed linens. "Is there anything I can do?"

"No, thanks. I wish there was." Lena felt an impossible situation encircling her. They exchanged polite parting words. Lena hung up, rolled over on her side, and pulled her knees into her chest. In some ways, it was an extremely uncomfortable pose considering her scars. In other ways, it felt like the only thing to do. To occupy as little space on earth as possible.

Mary Bell furrowed her brow then slid back into the crook of Henry's warm flesh. "I hate to do it," Mary Bell said groggily, "but I need to get up. I don't know what time guests will start checking in, and Lena's not coming today."

Henry kept his eyes closed, but rubbed her upper arm. He, too, would be busy today. His veterinary office was already becoming a hotel for displaced animals, and it was only going to get worse. He didn't want to leave Mary Bell, though. He wanted to be back under the moonlit willow or stay here in this vanilla-scented bedroom.

His passion for her had a hungry edge to it, like he was afraid this feast of body and soul might disappear. Like *she* might disappear. He hid this as best as he could, but he wondered how long it would take before his desire might mellow into something less ravenous.

Within the hour, Henry was walking back home. His legs were shaky and his mind was spinning.

By mid-morning, Mary Bell was busy. The first storm guests, a frazzled young husband and wife from New Orleans by the last name of Laurelle, had arrived. In tow were their binky-sucking baby, a toddler, their twin Yorkies, a porta-crib, collapsible swing, pumpkin seat, diaper bags, duffle bags, and luggage. When this group burst from their van, Mary Bell was on the front porch. Watching them was like watching one of those comedies where an endless stream of clowns and luggage exits a taxicab.

Mary Bell welcomed them to The Retreat then suggested they board the dogs at Henry's veterinary office. Just saying his name gave her a surge of pride. Henry was caring and capable. His veterinary office was the best place, besides home, that a dog could possibly be.

Olivia Laurelle held her baby close to her breast and followed their toddler around the front yard of The Retreat. Tad had both dogs on thin leashes.

"I understand why y'all wouldn't want dogs at your inn," he said. He looked over his shoulder as his son attempted to yank a full hydrangea blossom off a nearby bush. The boy was unsuccessful, but pink snowflake petals floated to the grass.

Trying to be discrete, Tad continued quietly, "My wife is still a little unstable. You know, postpartum depression or something like that. It would really help her to have the dogs around."

Mary Bell rubbed her forehead. "I'm so sorry, Mr. Laurelle. But we've had a No Pet policy for years. It's for the comfort of all the guests." Mary Bell didn't want to seem trite by adding that she also worried about her hundred-year-old floors.

Still, these Terriers were irresistible. They couldn't have weighed more than five pounds each, and they seemed to be gentle and friendly dogs. Their black eyes were adorable. It took every ounce of Mary Bell's willpower to stand by her own house rules. Eventually, Tad relented. He scooped up one Yorkie in each hand, tucked them under his arms, and headed for Henry's office, using Mary Bell's directions. The little dogs folded their radar-ears back and began to tremble.

Upstairs at The Retreat, Tom Vaughn had been sleeping off his hangover. He started to wake as the Laurelles settled in with their kids and equipment, raising the noise level in the upper chambers by a decibel or two. Tom heard the thumping of small shoes on wood, running back and forth, up and down the hallway past his door.

He didn't want to open his eyes, though. He didn't want to confront the Bible on the nightstand or the black priest's shirt. The false reality that he'd built around himself had gone on too long. It was no longer entertaining to be sweating in blue jeans and a black shirt on hundred-degree days. He was tired of having half an Australian birthmark. But deeper inside Tom's soul, what he felt most disgusted about was the lying. Lying to people who had welcomed him with open arms, free rides, and full mugs.

He didn't know how to wiggle out of this ugly situation, but he got out of bed, threw on a pair of khaki shorts and a faded t-shirt, rolled up his priestly frocks, and stuffed them back into his navy duffle.

Tom saw how being a priest might be an attractive vocation. People were instantly nice to him, and he felt like a better person when he was behaving like a priest should behave. But the fact that he was just pretending to be a priest made him feel dirty and despicable. In retrospect, it was a really stupid idea.

He put his hand up to his throbbing jaw, which had become prickly and raw. What next? The answer to this question was painfully obvious, but telling Lena the truth would be awful. He didn't want to imagine how hurt she'd be, but he also couldn't stay here and make her the target of small-town gossip.

Tom sat and rubbed his eyes. He opened the Bible that both comforted and challenged him. Perusing the index of Christian virtues, he found several passages for Truth. He turned to Ephesians, Chapter 6: "Stand firm then, with the belt of truth buckled around your waist, with the breastplate of righteousness in place, and with your feet fitted with the readiness that comes from the gospel of peace."

A "breastplate of righteousness"? Tom didn't know what that meant. It sounded like something he didn't have. If he did have a breastplate, he feared that his had been crafted of tin. He placed the Bible back into the nightstand and went over to the window. "The belt of truth," he mumbled.

A midday sun was beaming down upon the side yard, making one patch in the middle of the lawn completely invisible to him. It seemed to be a bottomless white-hot hole incinerating the unsuspecting grass. Tom's head was lopsided and his blood still contained traces of alcohol, so it was hard to focus on anything for long. Especially a hole that looked like it led to hell.

Summoning his courage, Tom went downstairs for True Confessions: Round One. On his way down the steps, he had to keep willing himself forward. He kicked each foot in front of him like a marionette, letting it drop onto the step below.

Mary Bell was sitting in a chair by the registration desk. She was exhausted from her evening with Henry, and joyful at the thought of him, but nervous about the uncertain days ahead. She was saying into the phone, "We are bursting this weekend. I'm so sorry. I don't have any rooms available."

A pause.

"Keep calling around, but if you can't find anything, call me back."

Another pause.

"Y'all take care, too."

Mary Bell hung up the phone and scribbled on a pad. Tom knew she must see him approaching, but she wouldn't look up.

"Hey, Mary Bell."

"Hey, Father Tom." Mary Bell made notes in her reservation book, refusing to make eye contact. Lafitte had good instincts, and he had uncharacteristically decked a priest. Now Lena wouldn't come to work.

Tom stood there in forced silence until she had no choice but to look up. When she did, she saw the red bulge on his chin and the worn glaze in his eyes. She didn't know what to do or say. He wasn't wearing his black shirt and collar. In this outfit, he didn't look like a priest at all. His hair was a wild mess.

"Mary Bell, do you have a few minutes?"

Standing in front of her, with his black disheveled hair, his plain clothes, and his crusty chin, he frightened her a bit.

"Oh, I don't know…"

"I need to talk to you and Lafitte, if he's around."

Lafitte?

"Sure, Father," Mary Bell said with wonderment. "I think he's in the kitchen."

Tom followed her. The approaching bacon and flour scent made his mouth water. He hadn't eaten yet, and it was already early afternoon. Lafitte was washing something in the sink when he heard the swinging door creak. The sound crashed inside Tom's head and made his temples ache.

"Lafitte," Tom said, forcing a boldness into his voice that his spirit wouldn't support.

Lafitte turned around, wiping his dirty hands on his apron. The squashed tomato on Tom's chin caught his attention and made him feel a sudden surge of pride.

"I need to talk to y'all for a couple minutes," Tom said.

Lafitte gave a quick, sharp nod, and pulled a chair out for Mary Bell. He sat down across from her, and Tom began to pace the expanse next to the table, collecting his thoughts, running his fingers through his hair, making it stand on end.

He stopped pacing and turned toward them, "Have either of y'all ever made a *huge* mistake before? A mistake so enormous you can't even believe you were the one who did it?"

"Of course," Mary Bell admitted.

Lafitte refused to respond.

"I've made a real doozy, and I need to ask y'all to forgive me," Tom continued.

Lafitte suspected the impending revelation, and he hated that Tom was trying to soften them up.

"What is it?" Mary Bell wondered.

Tom neared the table and squatted on his haunches, holding onto the tabletop with both hands so he wouldn't fall over. "Lafitte, Mary Bell…until about a week ago, I was a somewhat normal, slightly messed-up guy who lived next to his grandmother in New Orleans."

Mary Bell's brow furrowed. "You weren't living in a rectory?"

Lafitte suspected it but still felt surprised.

"No, Mary Bell," Tom continued, "I wasn't livin' in a rectory."

Mary Bell looked at Lafitte's good eye. Lafitte raised his brows, shrugging. She looked back at Tom, who was having trouble balancing in this position, especially with a killer hangover.

"Truth is, last Sunday, I put that priest's shirt on for the first time since a college party, years ago."

Mary Bell's eyes widened at the storm that was Tom Vaughn. "*No.* Father Tom, that *can't* be true." She felt certain she'd heard him wrong.

Tom stood up, but his trembling hands stayed on the table, making it seem like a minor earthquake was underfoot. "It's true, y'all, and I'm not one bit proud of it."

Mary Bell seemed stunned, and Lafitte kept his eyes on her.

Tom continued, trying to squeeze everything in before he lost them. "I was tryin' to shake my life up a bit. Tryin' to practice bein' a better person. Maybe I went a little overboard."

Mary Bell and Lafitte both turned toward him.

"Okay, a lot overboard."

"Wow. Are you kidding me?" Mary Bell said, rolling her eyes. So many little things made sense now…

"I wish I *was* kidding," Tom said. "This is the God's honest truth."

Mary Bell needed more. "Father. Wait. What's your real name?"

"Tom. Tom Vaughn."

Lafitte stood up, inches from Tom's face. "What about Lena?"

"I swear, Lafitte," Tom said, "I never touched her."

He looked sincere. For some reason, Lafitte believed him.

"I want to tell Lena about this myself," Tom said to both of them. "She needs to hear it from me. I've been sending her mixed signals, and I need to straighten things out."

Tom's eyes were pleading. "I know I'm in no position to ask either one of y'all for a favor, but can you please not tell her? I promise to do it myself."

They nodded, but Mary Bell was aching to know what had transpired between those two. She raised her hand to the back of her neck and rubbed it.

For his part, Lafitte recognized that Tom could have snuck out of Priory, never to be heard from again. He was standing here, sorry and needy, and Lafitte could swim around in that. Truth was, in Lafitte's troubled and haunted mind, pretending to be a priest for a few days didn't seem like much of a war crime. He had seen a lot worse.

Tom had expected compassion from Mary Bell because she was so overtly kind, but Lafitte's now-compassionate face was as unexpected as snow in New Orleans. No wonder Mary Bell and Lena were so devoted to him.

Lafitte extended a shaky hand, which Tom received.

"Tom Vaughn, huh?" Lafitte smiled. "Good to meet you."

"Wow," Mary Bell was still saying, searching the kitchen for answers as if they might be printed on the side of a box of grits. "Wowee wow."

Lafitte left the kitchen, half-smiling, because he had seen enough, and he had a lot of work to do. Mary Bell stood and touched Tom's upper arm.

"Father…I mean, Tom. Boy, I am really going to have to get used to that. Didn't you just say you're from New Orleans?"

Tom nodded, his chest still pounding from his admission, feeling like a burden had been lifted, but not sure whether or not anyone would forgive him. The kitchen was spinning, and he wished Mary Bell would offer him a seat. His mouth began watering again. "Yeah, why?"

"The storm that's in the Gulf is supposed to be heading to New Orleans."

Tom thought for a minute. Shards of weather forecasts hung over his head in Bob's Bar. "I don't think so, Mary Bell," he said hesitantly, squinting his eyes. "Last night the news said it was headed to Alabama. New Orleans is gonna be on the weak side of the storm."

"What time last night?"

The night had folded over upon itself and swirled together in a psychedelic fashion that had no real beginning or end, so Tom couldn't pinpoint anything. "Not sure."

"It couldn't have been too late because the last forecast I saw, around midnight, showed it headed to New Orleans."

Tom tried to be calm about it, but he remembered that the hurricane's redness was massive.

"You said your grandma lives there?"

"Yeah," he said blankly. "All my family's there …my parents, my Grandma Mimi, some cousins…" He saw the concern on her face. "But they always leave for storms. They'll be fine."

"You should check on them."

Tom felt disconnected from the storm. "Mary Bell, do you think you could…do you think you'll ever …forgive me?" His tired eyes searched hers.

Mary Bell put her arms out and gave him a huge hug. It was accepting and non-accusatory. His shoulders rose and fell. Half his misery melted away, leaving through the soles of his feet, carrying itself out the back door into the steamy summer day. The other half was still co-mingling with dry mouth and a mounting hunger.

"You're a little crazy, Tom," Mary Bell said, "but I like you."

"Yeah, I'm a little crazy, and it's been a totally life-altering week for me here in Priory. Y'all have been great."

"Well, thanks. That's what we do. Want me to make you something to eat?"

Tom's stomach was begging him to say yes. *Always the hostess*, he thought. "No, thanks. I appreciate the offer, but I'm gonna go see Lena, make some apologies, then hit the road."

"Hit the road? Why leave now? You can't go home. The storm's headed that way. What'll you do?" *And what about Lena?*

"I dunno. Maybe head farther north. Start over? I don't know if I'll ever go back to my old life. There were reasons why I left."

"Just stay 'til the storm passes. Then you'll have more options."

Tom's ears were starting to ring, and his stomach was growling, but he was in a hurry to head across town. "Nah, I can't take up space here. I heard you on the phone a little while ago, and I feel like a total jerk not bein' able to help. Y'all need the empty room."

"Are you sure?"

"Yep, I'm headin' out. Already packed." He glanced at the kitchen door.

Mary Bell's eyes became blue crescents.

Tom cracked a smile. "You, Mary Bell, are one sweet girl." He held her hand and kissed its slender bones.

CHAPTER TWENTY-NINE

On the way to Lena's, Tom turned his cell phone on for the first time all week. Turning it off had helped him feel disconnected from his real life. Now that it was back on, he was confronted with fifteen new messages. The most recent message played first. It was his mother.

"Tom, honey, I'm so proud of you for taking Mimi this weekend. Call me and let me know where y'all are going. Maybe we can hook-up. Dad and I are heading to Natchez. Hope you've had a relaxing trip. I didn't know you were going out of town. Call me."

Shit. Delete. *Mimi's goin' somewhere with me? What's up with that?*

Next one was from his friend, Doug, "Tom, dude, we're not having our hurricane bash this weekend 'cause everyone is pretty freaked out, and I guess we're leaving town. I don't have to work 'cause they're even closing the bar. Serious shit, huh? Catch you next week."

Delete.

Next was his sister Rachel in D.C. "Tom, where are you? Do you have Mimi? Call me. I feel helpless being so far away."

Delete.

Tom felt like he was going to be sick. He was now sitting in front of Lena's violet cottage. The rest of his messages would have to wait.

Each time he pressed his speed-dial for Mimi, he got an annoying message telling him all circuits were busy. He tried his parents' cell. Fast busy. Redial. Fast busy. Redial. Fast busy.

I'm taking care of Mimi?

As he left his car and headed for Lena's front door, the birds shrilled in his ears. He raised both hands to his head to stop it from splitting open. Lena answered the door to find Father Tom, haggard and sullen, in plain clothes.

"Lena," Tom said in a soft voice, "I have a lot to explain to you…"

She opened the door wider. He passed her and went straight for the kitchen. What was that red abrasion on his chin? She closed the door and followed him.

The sweet smell of caramelized onions and greasy pastry filled the air. He opened up a worn cabinet door as if this kitchen were his own. After withdrawing a tall glass, holding it underneath the kitchen faucet, and filling it to the brim, Tom gulped it down in its entirety. The cool blandness of it made him feel marginally better. He wondered what she had cooked last night.

"Sorry, I was dyin' of thirst."

She stood there, staring at him, unable to speak.

"I went to Bob's Bar last night," he started confessing, "and I think I had too many…" He sat in the nearest kitchen chair, resting his elbows on the table and his forehead against his palms.

Lena backed up and leaned against the countertop, bracing herself with her hands. He looked strange.

A sparrow flew onto a branch outside her kitchen window. Its head twitched as it tried to eavesdrop through the panes.

"First thing I want to say, Lena," Tom said to the kitchen table, "is that I'm not a serial murderer or a total nut-job." He couldn't look at her, but he felt the warmth of her body from across the kitchen. He closed his eyes briefly and prayed for guidance.

"Well, okay, I'm a bit of a nut-job." Dropping his hands to the table, he looked at her with tired, twinkling eyes. "Remember those Boudreaux jokes?"

Lena was silent.

"I love those jokes," he said.

Outside the window, the eavesdropping bird was twitching like Tom.

"I'm sort of a Boudreaux myself, you know? Idiotic sometimes. But I'm not a bad guy, Lena. Not really. I'm a pretty decent guy…" Saying those words tied a knot in his throat. "I like cold beer, raw oysters, takin' pictures, hangin' with my friends, and playin' gin with my grandma."

"Oh, yeah," Tom added, trying to be charming, "I also love your gumbo. And your hair. And your scars."

What is happening here? Lena pressed her weakening body against the countertop. Something big was coming, but she had no idea what it was.

"There's something else you should know about me, too, Lena. Before I tell you the biggie, I just wanna say that I *am* Christian, and I *do* believe in God and sinners and salvation, the whole package." He paused and then added, "Even though I admit to falling squarely into the sinners' category."

Lena looked confused, so he went a different way. "I believe there's a reason for everything that happens in this crazy world," he said. "Don't you?"

Shaking his head and looking at the sparrow, he mused, "I don't always know what the reason is, but the details of life seem to fit together in some powerful and mysterious ways."

This was a truth Lena understood. She'd seen odd puzzle pieces fit together in ways that seemed hard to believe. Why had she chosen her own reckless path? Was it part of God's plan?

Lena had often thought that maybe in heaven the reasons behind life's trials would be revealed. Or maybe, the beauty of heaven lay in the possibility she'd no longer care what the reasons were.

From the sparrow's perch, the scene played out like this: the man sat in his chair and spoke; the woman raised her hand to her mouth and covered it; the man rushed to her side and helped her sit down; he pulled a chair up next to hers, flipping it around and straddling it; he reached up and pulled her hand down, resting it in her lap; the woman sank into the chair, shaking her head; the woman closed her eyes hard, opened them, and touched the tip of her finger to his, following one of his bones from his knuckle to his wrist; the man took her hand and kissed her palm.

Thank you, he mouthed. He kissed her other sweaty palm likewise then held both her hands in his.

Lena smiled weakly at Tom and wondered if she had ever been kissed in the valley of her hand. The answer came to her immediately. No, she hadn't. Even though some of her pre-accident life was blurry to her, if she had been kissed like that, she would have remembered. Besides, before her accident, she'd been so young…

Tom wiped his eyes and stood, backing away from Lena. "I have a few more confessions to go, then I'm headin' out."

"You're leaving?" Her voice broke.

Tom touched her auburn hair, which was hanging loose, wavy and shiny. "Lena, more than anything, I'd love to stay. I'd love to try to make this up to you."

His whole being longed for her, but he felt grim and defeated. "But seriously. What will people in town think if you take up with me? I'm gettin' ready to tell everybody that I've been a fake priest for the past week."

Lena's eyes were as broken as his, even with no alcohol in them. "Please stay," she whispered. *I'm so alone...*

Tom didn't know what to do. He had to finish his confessions before he went any farther. "I'm gonna try to fix all this," he said, heading for the door.

Lena heard the soft roar of Tom's stomach. "Wait a minute," she said. She went to the fridge, withdrew a plate, unwrapped its plastic, and grabbed a leftover meat pie. She folded the pie into a napkin, handed it to him, and added a cool bottle of water to the offering.

"You sound pretty hungry," she said.

He grabbed the pie in one hand, the water in another, and kissed Lena on her pink cheek. The citrus-y smell of her hair filled his senses. He took a bite. "You're the best."

Tom went out to the front porch and then turned back to her, realizing he had already checked out of The Retreat.

"What's wrong?" she wondered.

"If I do get this straight…" he started, "If it is possible for me to stay in Priory…I checked out of The Retreat a little while ago. Mary Bell was swamped with phone calls, with the storm headin' to the coast and all, so I gave up my room."

Lena's mind jumped to images of contraflow traffic out of New Orleans, all lanes redirected away from the city. She leaned her head against the front door. "Then I guess you'll have to stay here." It was hard for her to pinpoint why she trusted a stranger who'd been pretending to be a priest. But she knew, somewhere within herself, that he'd fight to become worthy of her trust. Within his eyes, the need to be decent welled up.

Tom knew he didn't deserve her. It was hard to look away from her glowing face long enough to get into his car, but the only way back to her was through Bob's Bar. Reluctantly, he slid into his Jeep and headed to Bob's for True Confessions: Round Three.

Lena watched him drive away, and her heart chased his car down the street like a dog.

 CHAPTER THIRTY

Tom's hasty departure from The Retreat left an empty guest room at a time when no beds should be so vacant. In Lena's absence, Lafitte helped Mary Bell change the bed linens and sweep and dust Tom's former room. Then they went down to the kitchen to have an iced tea and contemplate their next move. They sat across from each other at the kitchen table and weighed the situation. One bed. A waiting list almost a full page long.

"I don't know what to do, Lafitte," Mary Bell admitted. "Should I call the next person based on when they called us? There were some pretty desperate people who are further down the list. Maybe I should try one of the desperate-sounding ones."

Mary Bell put her hands underneath her thighs and sat on them. Lafitte knew that this was how she stopped herself from shaking when she was nervous or scared. He looked out to the screened porch because Mary Bell's gaze into his one good eye was too intense.

"I'll figure it out," he said, without a trace of exhaustion or frustration in his steady voice. "Don't you fret."

Lafitte rose from the table and went out to the registration desk to look over their book. He remembered clearly the ones he had written down in his scribble-scratch, but didn't know any of the stories behind the names written in Mary Bell's smooth, curvaceous script. Beneath his calm façade, Lafitte worried about making this decision. He didn't want the burden, but he wouldn't hang this weight on Mary Bell either. He imagined the ramifications of getting it wrong. What if he beckoned a troublemaker or a thief? What if he overlooked someone in his darkest hour of need?

Lafitte decided to proceed in the only order that made any sense to him. Whoever was at the top of the list would get the first chance. It was a simple decision that removed Lafitte from the equation. Lafitte referenced one of his favorite mottos: *In times of trial, let fate decide.* He had learned in Vietnam that fate had a way of defeating highly choreographed campaigns. He rested one hand on the phone's receiver to make the call.

On the solitary interstate out of New Orleans, thousands of vehicles were gridlocked. Nichelle and Tamika were in that pack. Nichelle, although initially hesitant to leave her city in their rundown car, had changed her mind. She didn't want the loss of one child to make her forget that she still had one precious child to raise.

She thought back to her unlikely decision to evacuate. Hurricane Katrina looked huge on TV. What if something happened to Tamika? Tyrell's death was already squeezing her soul. She was his mother, and she should have been able to stop his wanderings. Even if her pastor said it wasn't her fault, even as her sister Demetra insisted that Tyrell was making his own decisions, Nichelle assigned her own guilt in the matter. *If I'd been a stronger mother, I could have kept him from all that trouble.* It didn't help to tell her anything different.

PRIORY, LOUISIANA

Their old car crawled west in light rain on the I-10. Her crumbling wiper blades smeared the muck on her windshield into streaky arcs. The traffic was moving so slowly, though, that it didn't much matter. Just outside Priory, their motor started to sputter and jump. Nichelle felt the familiar clawing within her chest. Why? Why does it always have to be like this?

The car spewed rancid steam and lurched along until Nichelle veered off the I-10, and her car surrendered its soul in front of The Retreat.

Nichelle made a very simple sign of the cross and closed her large brown lids. Tamika did the same. Nichelle grabbed her cell phone from the bench seat between them. No charge. She sighed heavily and her shoulders slumped toward the steering wheel. So typical. She replayed her hasty packing job in her mind. No charger either. She tossed the useless phone back onto the bench seat between them and they both got out. Mother and daughter held hands and walked up the wooden steps.

They timidly approached the desk and saw Lafitte, who was about to make a phone call. Tamika was frightened by the black strap around his head, which seemed to be on crooked. She squeezed her mama's hand. Lafitte gave them half a triangular smile.

"Sir," Nichelle started, "we are desperate. Our car just died outside." She looked down to his calloused hands but couldn't bear to expose her eyes.

"Name's Lafitte, not sir. Where are y'all coming from?"

"New Orleans."

Lafitte nodded.

"We need some place to stay, but I don't have much money. If I pay you for a room, I won't have anything left for food." Nichelle wished she could cover Tamika's ears. She had always hoped to be a better provider for her kids, but it had never been easy. She refused to work two jobs because she didn't want to leave her kids at night. Her job at the meat market was respectable, but meager. She was living paycheck to paycheck, and her next paycheck was supposed to be in two more days. The last days of a pay cycle were painfully long.

Tyrell's cremation had cost so much more than Nichelle could afford. Folks at her church had taken up a collection, and Nichelle felt the grace of God flowing toward her through their good will, but she still had to come up with a few dollars. Those few dollars could have paid for a room during this evacuation. She might have even been able to get two rooms, if Tyrell had still been alive, and if he'd evacuated with them.

"Mr. Lafitte," Nichelle said, "I can't promise to pay you nothin', but we have nowhere else to go."

Lafitte's face softened around the edges. "Well, then. Nothing will just have to do."

Nichelle wrapped one arm around Tamika. "We can sleep anywhere you put us. Any small space you have."

Lafitte slid an iron key across the registration desk and said, "We can do better than that. Why don't y'all try Room 2B, at the top of the stairs? Someone just checked out."

PRIORY, LOUISIANA

At first, Nichelle feared he was teasing her. Her dark eyes darted up the staircase. How could a room be available? That couldn't be possible.

She didn't say anything while she studied Lafitte's face for signs of cruelty. Did he possess a hidden, evil smirk? Even though she had not encountered many people with eye patches before, the one eye that was visible was looking at her in a way that did not seem trivial or hurtful.

When she realized Lafitte's offer was genuine, a tear paraded down her cheek, even if she was too numb to feel its presence.

"I know I didn't do nothin' to deserve this," she said quietly. Nichelle looked down to her feet, pulling Tamika close to her. "Thank the Good Lord."

Tamika remembered how heartbroken she'd been when she realized God would not be raising Tyrell from the dead like Lazarus. She'd even begun to wonder whether or not miracles really happened. Until this moment. Until this unexplainable, miraculous moment. Tamika was experiencing her very own miracle, and she knew it. Her hair bristled with the quiet excitement of it.

Lafitte pulled a tissue from a gilded box and handed it to Nichelle, who then led her daughter up the staircase by the hand. Later, she would go out to her car and get their shopping bag full of belongings.

Upon opening the door to 2B, Nichelle sniffled. She wanted to say something profound, but nothing came out. The room was bright, airy, and pristine. Raindrops fell just beyond wavy panes of glass. The rain had a calming effect upon Nichelle now that she was no longer in her car. Now that she and Tamika were safe within The Retreat. Tamika hugged her mama, and Nichelle kissed the top of her daughter's braided head.

They were more wiped out than two people could ever imagine. Kicking off their rubber sandals, they slid under the cool sheets of the bed and marveled at the unimaginably plush mattress. *I wish Tyrell could be here*, Nichelle thought. She gently rubbed Tamika's forehead until Tamika closed her eyes. Then mother and daughter fell into a heavy slumber for the first time in nearly a week.

PRIORY, LOUISIANA

CHAPTER THIRTY-ONE

Early Saturday evening, Suite 2D had the good fortune of becoming occupied by a couple of college girls who had fled New Orleans just a few days after unpacking for their junior year. At The Retreat, it didn't take them long to drop their belongings and ask Mary Bell if she knew of someplace they might grab some dinner and a cold drink.

"Well, the best cheese fries in town are at Bob's Bar," Mary Bell said. "Y'all will love them. And I don't know whether or not you're beer drinkers, but Bob serves draft in frosty mugs."

Lucy and Becca grinned at one another.

Mary Bell wasn't much older than the girls. If she hadn't been so consumed in the goings-on at The Retreat, she might have gone with them.

The rain let up, so Lucy and Becca strolled over to Bob's Bar in the thick air of a summer's eve, as if they were on vacation, not running away from a storm. Their smooth shoulders slickened with sweat and humidity. Cotton tank tops clung to their graceful bodies.

Their appearance at Bob's Bar that night was as incendiary and mesmerizing as a sparkler on the Fourth of July. Dino spotted them first and belted out, nearly falling off his barstool in an effort to please them, the mostly-correct words to "That's Amore."

All heads turned because Dino saved this song for special occasions, those few elite moments when hot young women came through the front door.

PRIORY, LOUISIANA

The collegians brought a welcome levity to the room, which just a few minutes prior to their arrival had been spinning with Tom's post-confession buzz. As scandalous as Tom's revelation had been, after about an hour, it had played itself out. Sides had been taken. Good and evil had been loudly discussed. After some of the initial "sick bastard" slurs had been thrown, raucous laughter ensued. Then, with the room still spinning, Tom had quietly walked out into the night.

Into that supercharged environment strolled Becca and Lucy. Becca was a petite thing with tan skin and long brown hair, glossy from swimming all summer. She was darling and friendly and accessible. Men and women both wanted to befriend her, to take in her easy conversation and gregarious personality.

And then there was Lucy, a woman whose very presence could hush a pool hall. She was curvaceous and sultry and knew how to strike a pose when she felt men watching her. She had a thin physique, blue doe-eyes, and blonde hair twisted into a clip in the back of her head. Golden tendrils curled around her high cheekbones. Lucy's voice was breathy and almost hushed, just above a whisper. Men leaned in to hear her and feel her voice upon their ears.

Lucy and Becca became surrounded by an adoring group of bar mates. Gus, Slim Stan, Dino, Bob, and other men—some from Priory, others who were hurricane evacuees staying in Priory's numerous inns—treated the ladies to an endless supply of cheese fries and frosty draft beer. The girls introduced their new friends to an array of potent shots, including numerous things containing grain alcohol or medicinal herbs.

The regular crew told stories about how some guy named Tom had been in their midst all week, posing as a priest. Becca and Lucy wished they could meet him. He sounded like a lot of fun. When it was discovered that the former Father Tom was also a guest at The Retreat, the women could hardly wait to go back and meet him.

The girls laughed and flirted and basked in the glow of so much attention. Were there other women in the bar that night? Later, Lucy wouldn't be able to recall.

While they tipped back shot glasses, a drone of muted hurricane updates played out on the TV over Bob's head. The cash register drawer popped open so frequently that Bob felt as if it was a Spring Pilgrimage weekend, and everyone within Louisiana and its neighboring states had come to see the magnificent burst of azaleas.

Although the evening at Bob's crackled with energy and brilliance, it eventually fizzled out. When they were ready, Lucy and Becca pretended to go to the restroom, then snuck out the front door. They laughed and gossiped all the way back to the inn.

PRIORY, LOUISIANA

CHAPTER THIRTY-TWO

"Well, Dirk," Mimi said, sipping her red drink through a straw, "looks like it's just you and me, baby." Mimi winked at the gray and white photo of her late husband in the silver frame. His shoulders were broad and his hair was black, the same jet black as Tom's.

Saturday brought the outer bands of Katrina to town, sprinkling the city with the first drops of many to come. When thoughtful neighbors rapped on her door before they headed for the interstate, Mimi stayed in the kitchen. The phone didn't ring often but, when it did, Mimi waved it off.

The afternoon waned, her neighbors evacuated, and Lakeview began to grow quiet. Mimi gazed at Dirk's picture, had a refreshing cocktail, and talked to him again.

"Did you see Thomas leavin' here, Dirk?" Mimi laughed, her jowls shaking like hot water bottles. "That's your grandson, alright, full of spunk, just like you." Mimi took another sip. The hurricane flowed up the straw, met her lips, and recessed down its plastic tube again.

"He's a funny one, that Thomas." Into Dirk's eyes, she said, "You keep your eye on him, honey. I got a feeling he might need you."

Mimi settled into her big fluffy chair, thinking this storm was going to be nothing more than a nuisance, like the rest of them. She was glad to be riding it out in the comfort of her own home, surrounded by her memories, her few precious belongings, and a sense of strength. She was a tough old broad and wouldn't be chased out like a ninny.

A couple of days without electricity would be nothing. Back in her youth, they hadn't even imagined having an air conditioner, and she felt positively adolescent again. Open windows. Fluttering heat. She had enough canned goods and bottled water to last for weeks, so she was not the least bit concerned.

Hurricane what? Katrina? What a ridiculous name for a storm.

PRIORY, LOUISIANA

CHAPTER THIRTY-THREE

With the barometric pressure falling steadily, squirrels collected food. They led their wiry-haired young into the hollows of massive trees, hoping to choose a form that could withstand imminent disaster.

Dolphins in the Gulf sensed it, too. They left the panhandle of Florida and flirted with the coastline. As the eye of the hurricane tracked north, they tracked south until the pressure was more bearable.

Butterflies folded crepe wings and wedged their sensitive abdomens between lichen-covered rocks. Birds delayed migration through the unstable environment.

Numerous deer were felled by hunters in the hours leading up to Katrina's landfall because outdoorsmen know well that God's creatures feed feverishly before a storm.

It seemed that every animal—each stealthy alligator in tune with decreasing oxygen in the water, every coarse-furred nutria in tune with the vibrations of the earth beneath its webbed feet—knew enough to prepare for the storm.

Only humans took chances and stared it down.

CHAPTER THIRTY-FOUR

By the time Tom returned to Lena's on Saturday night, he was exhausted. He was still struggling with his hangover, weary of confessions, and drowning in a sea of absolutions, condemnations, and astonishment.

Lena had a cotton sheet, a hand-knit blanket, and a down pillow waiting for him on the sofa. They barely spoke before he crashed into a deep sleep in her living room. She sat on the floor next to the sofa and watched him for a while. He had laugh lines near the edges of his eyes. His lips were full plums. Lustrous, straight, black hair topped his head.

Tom's pulse was thumping against the side of his neck, making his Australia-shaped birthmark look like a volcano about to erupt. Lena loved its haphazard edges. One of Tom's hands came to hang off the edge of the sofa, and she felt his fingertips. They were soft and apparently had not done much manual labor in their lifetime.

His red chin was beginning to take on more muted shades of yellow and mauve. Even though she didn't dare touch it, and didn't want to wake him, the wound intrigued her. She looked up to the heavens, then leaned her head against the arm of the sofa and mouthed, *Thank you.*

When she woke up in her bed on Sunday morning, Tom was already making breakfast in the kitchen, and she smelled sausages frying. Lena couldn't remember the last time she felt this hopeful.

"Morning," she murmured, gliding into the kitchen with her terry cloth robe wrapped around her.

"Morning, sweetheart," he answered playfully. He placed a plateful of eggs and sausages proudly in front of her.

Tom had on gym shorts and a t-shirt. Lena snuck a peek at his hairy legs as he walked effortlessly across her wooden floors. It occurred to her that maybe she should throw a load of laundry in for him.

"Thanks," she said, looking up.

In this light, Tom thought her eyes looked like the color of a buttery, tawny roux. More of her scars were exposed because her hair was a mess. Seeing the pink jagged edges lying atop her creamy skin made his chest ache. "You're welcome."

He sat down. Lena crossed herself. Tom smiled and did the same.

"Will you say grace?" she asked. He nodded.

"Bless us, O Lord, and these thy..." He started over. "Dear God, bless everyone who I stunned this week with my temporary insanity. Bless my family and everyone in the path of the hurricane. Bless our food and help us to be thankful."

Lena thought he was finished, but his eyes were closed. "Oh, and bless Lena. Help me to not screw this up. Amen."

"Amen."

Her stomach was turning, but she tried to eat a bit of egg. Tom picked up a sausage link with his soft fingers and took a bite.

"How did everything go last night?" she asked.

"It was interesting," he answered, trying to be entertaining. "Stan Ball told me to go F myself."

"Oh, dear..."

"Gus was pretty understanding, though. He laughed and said he was glad he hadn't given me a full confession."

Lena pushed the food around on her plate.

"Dino wasn't sure what to say so he broke into song, singing 'Volaré' at the top of his lungs until he nearly choked. Then he slapped me on the back and ordered a beer." Tom took a swig of orange juice. "It was okay, I guess. I mean, how well could something like that go, anyway?"

After a moment of silence, he added, "The person I worry about most is Grace Swannee. Do you know her?"

"Sort of."

Most the town knew about Grace. Every day, she cruised the streets in her long Eldorado. It had been her husband's final purchase. Grace told one of Lena's neighbors that she wanted to be buried in it.

"Grace and I have bonded a bit while I've been here, so after I left the bar, I went over to Grace's to tell her the truth. She was ticked off," he said, sighing. "It took her about a half a pack of cigarettes before she could look at me. Another mark against me, I guess. Half a pack of cigarettes were my fault."

"Tom, Grace has probably been smoking since she was about ten."

"Yeah, I know, but that doesn't stop the guilt… Anyway, after the initial shock and anger, she laughed so hard she started coughing."

Lena's lips scrunched to one side.

Tom's eyebrows inched closer together, making a divot between them. "I've got more trouble than just this priest thing, Lena. I'm havin' trouble reaching my parents and my grandma."

"What do you mean?"

"They always evacuate during hurricanes, so I shouldn't worry, I guess." He pushed the food around on his plate. "But I can't reach my parents on their cell phone, and they left some cryptic message about my Grandma Mimi bein' with me. Why would they think *I* was takin' Mimi this weekend? They've got to be confused. Maybe she was leavin' with a friend or a neighbor or something…I don't know. It's just odd that I can't reach 'em. I tried callin' Mimi at home but no answer."

Tom looked out the window, staring past the panes into the puzzling world. "She wouldn't stay there. She never stays for storms."

Lena looked up to the iron chandelier. "Tom, why don't you and I go to church today? Might do us some good."

He wondered whether or not lightning would strike him if he tried to go to church. Father Abelli's face floated in front of him. "Oh, I don't know about that, Lena… Father Abelli will be there, huh?"

"Of course. He's the only priest we have."

Tom rose from his chair and paced the kitchen. He ran his fingers through his bear hair. He tapped F-a-t-h-e-r onto his boxer shorts.

"Tom, I really think we should. You've already told everyone else. You should tell Father Abelli, too."

He stopped pacing. Nothing could have appealed to him less.

"It's a beautiful little church," she said.

PRIORY, LOUISIANA

Reflecting on the cavernous, mausoleum-like building he had frequented for the last few years, inhabited by the likes of a finger-pointing, spit-strewing Father McMann, Tom had trouble envisioning a beautiful little church and an understanding pastor. Lena held out her hand, and Tom walked over and took it. It was impossible to refuse a request from her.

After cleaning up and taking showers, they were on their way. Tom tried his parents' cell again. Still a fast busy. Again and again: fast busy.

A heavy silence accompanied them in the car, drowning out the din of the motor. They were dizzy and tired. Lena was giving directions to Tom, and he was trying to concentrate. He glanced out his side window with a seemingly simple turn of his head, but he would wonder for many years whether this action had been mere coincidence or the magnetic force of history. Tom's foot let up on the gas. The car slowed to a crawl on its way uphill before stopping on the inclined blacktop.

He found himself in front of a stately red brick manse with gleaming white pillars, coal black shutters, and impeccably landscaped gardens. A weathered brick path meandered from the street to the front doors, which were an imposing set of arched mahogany stunners. Underneath a magnolia tree on the front lawn was a fountain crafted from a copper sugar kettle. On the other side of the lawn was a scrolled wooden sign with gilded lettering: "Creve Plantation."

Tom remembered holding hands with Charlotte as he walked up the brick path. He felt her warm skin between his fingers. The window of *their* room glowed.

"Tom, are you okay?"

He squinted and the moment stretched on. "Sure." His words were slow and ambling, and Lena couldn't guess which direction they were wandering.

"It's Creve Plantation," she explained. "Isn't it beautiful?"

"It is…but…"

Tom searched for a response. He took his eyes off the manor and let them feast upon Lena Melendez. How could he tell her what this place had meant to him? After all these years, it still left a dull pain in his arms. When the pain didn't spread into his chest, he knew he'd be okay. He didn't have any desire to tell Lena about Charlotte. His strongest instinct was to protect Lena in every way possible.

"It's nice, but it's not my style," Tom whispered.

Lena wondered what drew him to Creve Plantation. A story was there, but he wasn't going to tell it, and she didn't need to know it. She had secrets, too, and some would never be revealed. Tom was complicated, and that suited her fine.

He leaned over and kissed her cheek. Their faces lingered near each other, waiting for the answer to an unasked question. Tom wanted her, but he refused to let their first real kiss be in front of Creve.

They drove on for another mile before spying, through tall thin pine trees, the Church of Our Lady of Good Hope. It was a white, wooden building with a bell tower on top. Cedar shingles clung casually onto its steep, gabled roof. The pine forest surrounding the church was dark and soothing. Haze, mist, and tiny raindrops shrouded the structure.

Tom stopped the car when he saw it. Now *this*, this was worth a pause. It looked like a place God would live. Once in the parking lot, Tom gripped the steering wheel. Lena touched his sleeve then got out of the car, so he let go and followed her.

He placed his hand on the small of her back, and they crunched their way across the shell parking lot, then through the side door. The church was lit only by circular candelabras over the center aisle, each candle inside a glass hurricane. The sun was hiding; the church shimmered with uncommon brilliance. Stained glass windows were propped outward with sticks. The twittering of forest menagerie and the murmur of humid wind mixed freely within the room. A bank of candles lit up the corner, underneath a statue of the Virgin Mary. Over the altar, a simple wooden crucifix hung.

Tom knelt in front of Mary, bowing his head. Lena lit a tall candle in front of him. One of the smaller votives wouldn't burn as long as this prayer would be needed. When he was finished, they walked across the creaking wooden floorboards and into the front pew. They were so close to the altar that Tom thought he might soon see Father Fenn or his grade school classmates or that pretty girl with the upturned brown eyes.

"I *need* to stay here, Lena," Tom whispered, staring up at the crucifix.

"We can stay here as long as you want."

Tom turned his head to her and said, green eyes begging, "I mean here in Priory, Lena. Not just here in church."

She closed her eyes in an effort to stop herself from wanting him in such a powerful way. The church filled with warm bodies and hot breezes. Tom couldn't recall ever being so comfortable in his sweat.

As the opening song began, Tom continued, only slightly louder, "It's just that…" He swallowed. "I don't want to be lost again. I've been lost for a long time already."

Lena linked pinkies with him on the pew railing. "Me, too."

Father Abelli took his place in front of the altar. He looked at Lena and Tom and grinned. He stretched out his arms. His garments hung majestically.

"We gather here today," Father Abelli started, "as neighbors. All of us. Some from far away, keeping eye on a storm. Some from Priory, going through our daily routines. But in God's House, in this magnificent structure, we are one family." Father's voice was meek and comforting. "We're a family that loves, nourishes, and forgives." Father looked at Tom. "Yes, we forgive others, and we must forgive ourselves. Let us pray…"

Father Abelli folded his hands in front of his slight body and began Mass. Tom was an apostle again, back in the inner circle, a youth within breathing distance of an inspirational priest. And then it dawned on Tom: he had to take ownership for his schism with the Church. If Tom hated Mass with Father McMann so much, he should have wandered all around New Orleans, or Louisiana, or maybe even the whole United States, to find a place where God could be found.

Maybe God had forced Tom's hand.

During his homily, Father Abelli walked among the pews and told a story about Mother Teresa, about sacrifices and self-denial. Tom listened. When Father

Abelli smiled at the altar boy's mistakes, Tom admired him.

But Tom's mind couldn't find a resting place. It bounced around in confusion. Could Father Abelli know his secret? Where was Katrina? Where was his family? What should he do about Lena? There were so many wrong moves he could make. Considering his history, he didn't trust himself to get anything right.

During Mass, a few phrases cut through his fog and buried themselves. Phrases like "Lord, I am not worthy to receive you, but only say the words and I shall be healed…"

When everyone filed into the center aisle to take communion, Tom searched the crowd for familiar faces but didn't recognize anyone. He wondered whether he should stay in the pew. Father Abelli motioned for him to come forward, so he did.

After Mass, Lena and Tom stopped at the back of church. It was a somber but chatty crowd. People talked about the storm and how destructive it looked.

Father Abelli approached, "I'm so glad you both came."

"I didn't know if I should…" Tom baited.

"I know," Father said, extending his hand. "I know how hard it must be for you to be here, but God will help you through this."

The invisible grip holding Tom's neck softened as he shook Father's hand. "Thanks." Tom didn't care who had ratted him out. It was a relief not to have to explain it himself.

When they left Our Lady of Good Hope, Tom looked at the pine forest and then over at the car. Lena pulled him into the forest for a walk, and he wished he had his camera.

Pinecones decorated their path, wind swayed the branches, and leaves whispered secrets. Our Lady followed them with protective eyes.

CHAPTER THIRTY-FIVE

Charles woke to a pounding headache. Inside his brain were images of Pass Christian in his rearview mirror as he'd left town. His eyelids were heavy so he kept them closed. The leather underneath the bare parts of his skin was sticky. His mouth was glued shut. Air streamed in through cracked windows. Birds chirped and a thin layer of moisture covered him. Must be morning.

He felt paralyzed.

Several questions arose, and Charles hoped to remember the answers.

Where was he? Had he driven to Priory to meet up with his parents? That seemed unlikely.

What day was it?

He remembered the endless crawl of cars leaving town, but not much after that. His body felt bruised, like he'd been in a fistfight. Charles opened his eyes. He was sitting in front of a pawnshop.

Suddenly, he remembered unlocking the safe.

PRIORY, LOUISIANA

Mornin', Y'all

Sunday, August 28, 2005

"Mornin', Y'all. This is Melody Melançon and you're listening to WPRY 90.5, bringing you and your mama up-to-date on the latest in Priory.

I know I'm not telling you something y'all don't already know, but that Katrina is up to no good. She has doubled in size, y'all. I did not think that was possible. And last I checked, she was already nearing a Category 5. She's the worst kind of monster: whipped into a frenzy and in a hurry. Worse than that old swamp monster my granddaddy used to talk about.

I'm scared for New Orleans, y'all, and for Southern Mississippi. We have so many friends down there. Unless Katrina turns, it doesn't look good. I've been a nervous wreck, eating and watching TV nonstop. I've been pacing the floors. Jasper, my sweet red Lab, has been matching me step for step. That dog is awesome. Best companion ever. Next to Randy, of course.

People of Priory, I love y'all. I have heard so many stories about folks opening up their homes to distant cousins and long-lost friends. Throwing blankets on sofas and daybeds. I am proud to walk the same cobbled stones of Main with you.

If anyone knows of someone who's displaced and in need of shelter—and if you have no place to put 'em—please contact the Priory CVB. They are working overtime to make sure that no one is alone during this difficult time. Bless their CVB hearts.

That's it for now. But remember, if you're not listening to *Mornin', Y'all*—where you can hear personalized hurricane coverage in the same broadcast as a recipe for jambalaya—you might as well be living in California."

PRIORY, LOUISIANA

CHAPTER THIRTY-SIX

The call for a mandatory evacuation came Sunday morning in the Big Easy, just hours before Hurricane Katrina slammed ashore. It was too late, though. Everyone who had intended upon evacuating had fled already. The stragglers either couldn't or wouldn't budge.

Lafitte and Mary Bell served a comforting breakfast of scrambled eggs, grits, and fresh fruit. With such a wide array of age groups in the house, breakfast was served in shifts as people arose. All conversation focused on the storm.

Mary Bell opened the antique armoire in the parlor to expose the hidden television set, a flat-screen that was used during Bowl games, Triple Crown races, the Meeting of the Courts on Fat Tuesday, and threatening storms. Bands of rain fell softly in Priory, and the wind shook raindrops from the trees. Guests were drawn to the parlor in the hopes of learning more about their own fates.

Ria Legrange huddled in a corner of the dining room and tried to connect with loved ones via her cell phone. She tried her son Charles, her cousin Vera, and the ladies from her garden club. Sometimes the phone emitted a strange series of beeps after she hit "Send." Other times, it gave a fast busy or just dropped the call altogether. She didn't understand that phone, even on a clear day. Now it was operating as if she'd left the handset out in the storm. Oh, where was Charles? Just thinking of him made the energy drain from her body.

Ria sat next to Victor in matching Queen Anne chairs. He reached over and took her hand, a hand that felt more frail than it had the last time he'd held it. How long had it been since they'd last held hands? Victor couldn't recall, but it had been a very long time, indeed. And if he was honest with himself, he would have to admit that hers had not been the last hand he'd caressed.

Ria couldn't stop staring at the TV. Her eyes were glossed over. As beautiful as she still was, he noticed that her face had become drawn and hollow. Her hands were spotted and arthritic. And what about him? He barely recognized himself some days if he got too close to his bathroom mirror or saw a photograph of himself taken in unflattering light.

He noticed, for the first time in years, that Ria was aging. They both were. Victor closed his eyes and tilted his head back to release the tension in his neck. Then he sat upright as the afternoon on the Gulf Coast fell apart. Victor hoped they wouldn't see their stately Spanish tile roof being blown away one terra-cotta wave at a time. He didn't know if Ria would be able to handle it.

The college girls, Lucy and Becca, were sitting cross-legged on the parlor rug, scarfing down leftover beignets, licking their powdered-sugar coated fingers, and guzzling bottles of water. Their silky hair was bundled on top of their heads, and they were wearing the teeniest of shorts and t-shirts. They were barefoot, wiggling manicured toes. Since both their families were up East, this storm was fascinating but not personally threatening. They were empathetic but not distraught.

The young father, Tad, stood with his hands on his hips, not believing the Category 5 images exploding onto the screen. His wife and kids had gone upstairs for a nap, but Tad stayed downstairs where he bit his fingernails, watched TV, and pondered the fate of the work-in-progress renovation of their Uptown home in New Orleans. He tried to keep his eyes off Lucy's fantastic legs, but he hadn't seen legs like hers in a really long time.

The screen door creaked, and all eyes welcomed the diversion. An elderly woman and her aged mother entered the foyer. The eldest of the two was wheeling an oxygen tank with a clear tube resting under each nostril. Both women were sprinkled with tiny, sparkling raindrops. Mary Bell didn't know what to do. She told the curly-haired women The Retreat was full, but she would certainly figure something out.

Mary Bell contemplated giving the ladies her room, but she hesitated. Even though she shared her home with many people, it would have been unbearable to give up her own space.

Becca called over her shoulder, tilting her glossy hair upward, barely taking her eyes off the TV, "They can have our room."

Lucy's blonde mane nodded.

Their easy generosity warmed Mary Bell. "Are y'all sure?"

"Totally," they replied in unison.

Mary Bell walked gratefully toward them and leaned over. "Y'all are so sweet to do this." She spoke in hushed tones, so as not to make the elderly women feel more indebted than they already would. "I could put you on the screened porch out back or on these sofas or…"

"Whatever…" Lucy said, her silky voice entrancing even to Mary Bell. The girls didn't care where they slept. It wouldn't be the first time they had crashed on someone else's floor.

Mary Bell kept checking the front door. Any moment, she hoped Henry would appear. She couldn't stop thinking about him, about what a calm ship he would be in this storm. She couldn't stop thinking about him, period.

But Henry's veterinary office had become a makeshift hurricane animal shelter, and he was up to his ears in furry creatures: dogs, cats, rabbits, a chinchilla, and a nutria. The animals were pacing and panting, whining and scratching. At least they were inside, though. Henry knew how the dead animal count of most storms added up in a gruesome and grisly way. These creatures didn't know it, but they were the lucky ones.

PRIORY, LOUISIANA

CHAPTER THIRTY-SEVEN

Darkness fell upon The Retreat. News cycles grew repetitive. They wouldn't know much more until daylight. Everyone headed reluctantly to their rooms because there had already been too much wind, conjecture and gloom.

Lucy and Becca decided that sleeping on the back porch might be fun, but Lafitte wasn't crazy about it. Even though Priory was a safe town, he liked to err on the side of caution. He couldn't handle it if anything happened to these two girls on his watch.

He couldn't find any nice way to tell them "no," so he set up two cots under the ceiling fan. They looked like they were having a slumber party, not escaping a storm. Their effortless charm hung in the air like jasmine.

In the waning afternoon, they'd wandered over to the grocery and bought some beer, which was now in a cooler between their two cots. Becca turned on a porch lamp and turned off the overhead lights. They sat cross-legged on their makeshift beds and un-screwed a couple of longnecks.

"Are you sure y'all want to sleep out here?" Lafitte asked. "I could set you up real comfortable in the parlor."

"We're fine," Becca said, "this is perfect."

It was muggy outside, but the ceiling fan was helping spread the humidity around so it wouldn't settle too long upon their supple skin.

"Okay, then," he said, heading for the door.

"Lafitte," Lucy purred, "why don't you have a beer with us before you go in?"

In another lifetime, Lafitte would have jumped at the chance. He was a guardian here, not a partier, so he was hesitant. "Nah, I've got a lot to do, but thanks anyway."

"Oh, come on," Becca joined in. "One beer won't stop you from doing your work."

It had been a long time since a woman had asked Lafitte to join her for a beer, especially women who looked like these girls. The answer was surprisingly easy.

He went into the backyard, brought in an Adirondack chair, and placed it at the foot of their beds. The coeds perked up, and Lafitte settled in. Becca handed him a cold bottle. At first, they all drank and made small talk about the storm, but Lafitte was a mysterious figure and the girls were not shy.

Becca was the first one to pry. "Hey, Lafitte, I hope you don't mind me asking, but how'd you get the eye patch?"

Most people tried to pretend they weren't staring at his patch, and almost no one asked him about it, so it was flattering to be the object of such direct questioning.

"I was in the war in Vietnam," he said, "and caught some shrapnel in my eye." The coldness of the beer tightened his throat.

The girls made big eyes at each other, just like they'd done when Mary Bell had told them about Bob's cheese fries. Then Lucy asked the question that only children were comfortable asking: "Do they call you Lafitte 'cause you look like a pirate?"

Lafitte's triangular smile appeared. "Yeah, 'cause I look like a pirate." He chuckled. "It's a name my kid brother gave me. He was in the war, too. He came to the military hospital while I was recovering." Lafitte used his singular vision to look into the shaft of the bottle. "He said everyone in 'Nam would fear the pirate Jean Lafitte."

Becca followed up, "What's your real name?"

He looked up to the spinning blades. "Closely guarded secret. Pirate code, you know?"

When he stopped talking, the smile slid from his face. The girls didn't know to ask, and Lafitte didn't volunteer to tell, that his brother had been fatally shot two days after the nickname-visit. Two days. For months after his brother's death, Lafitte looked for him in every wet field. It had to be a mistake. Bodies were sometimes unrecognizable. Parts missing, whole faces blasted away. Lafitte would know his own brother, though. He'd recognize the freckle on his brother's earlobe or the scar on his brow bone. The military didn't have to be right. Maybe it was someone else who'd bought it. They hadn't produced a body yet.

The military wasn't wrong, though, and this realization hit Lafitte one dark night when he was soaked to the bone, exhausted and hungry. Grieving descended upon him. Edward Joseph Barnes stopped looking for his brother and began calling himself Lafitte. He became a bitter, bloodied pirate who exacted revenge on anyone that came into his path: even the innocent, pleading for mercy in an unrecognizable language.

"What happened after the War?" Becca asked, her words cutting through Lafitte's trance. She was a history major, and here was a living testimonial to an infamous time.

Crickets jingled beyond the screens. "After that, I was lost…"

The girls were silent.

"For months, I stayed in my house, curtains drawn, living like a bum. One day, Mary Bell's parents knocked on my door. Said they were desperate for help around The Retreat."

"And the rest is history?" Becca wondered.

"No, I didn't come right away. After everything I'd done in the War, I didn't trust myself. Didn't think I deserved a new start…"

Lafitte was surprised by his own honesty. He'd never had this conversation with anyone. Why now? With total strangers?

Lucy flung her legs over the end of her cot, rose, and walked over to him. She squatted in front of him and touched his hand.

"Everyone deserves a new start, Lafitte." Lafitte thought that in this dimmed lighting, with that sexy voice, Lucy could be mistaken for a young Marilyn Monroe.

Becca smiled at her friend's outgoing nature.

"The Bateau's saved my life." Lafitte grinned, nodded, and finished his beer. These were two sweet girls. After a round of good nights, Lucy flipped off the lamp and crawled back into her cot. The erstwhile pirate went inside to finish his chores. A couple hours later, he was exhausted, but there was still one job left to do.

PRIORY, LOUISIANA

When he was sure the women were asleep, he snuck back out to the porch and slept upright in the wooden chair. Since his new start, he had vowed to be a protector of the vulnerable. He had reparation to make. It would take a lifetime to undo a season of wrongs.

CHAPTER THIRTY-EIGHT

Tom's cell phone rang late Sunday night, and he almost fell off Lena's sofa trying to find it. He pressed the green button when he saw it was his parents.

"Mom?"

"Oh, Tom, thank God. I've been trying to reach you but these darn cell lines are overloaded. How are you and Mimi doing?"

Tom's ears were hot, and his heart thumped higher in his chest than it normally did. "Ma, I don't know what you're talkin' about. I don't have Mimi."

"You don't?"

"I don't."

"Where are you?"

Tom hesitated. "In Priory. Are y'all in Natchez?"

"We are, honey, but where's Mimi?"

Panic set in across invisible waves. "Ma, I haven't spoken to Mimi since I left last Sunday," Tom said, hoping for an explanation. His mother was too silent. "What's goin' on?"

Sylvia whimpered and then managed to utter, "Mimi told me you called her…and were going to help her evacuate."

Tom sat up and then leaned over, resting his heavy elbows on his knees, trying to stay calm. "Why would she say that?" Tom asked, but he feared he already knew the answer.

His mother's voice was wavering. "I don't know, Tom, but have you seen the storm? It's huge."

Tom knew. He and Lena were glued to the television set on Sunday night, hypnotized by the

PRIORY, LOUISIANA

storm racing toward the watery border between Louisiana and Mississippi.

"Shit," Tom said. "Mom, don't panic. New Orleans is gonna be on the weak side of the storm, so she should be okay. She'll probably lose power for a couple of days, that's all. I'll go home as soon as they let everybody back in."

Sylvia wished she had never given up smoking thirty years ago. She really needed a cigarette. She tried not to panic. There was nothing they could do. New Orleans had been placed inside a locked cage, and there was no easy way to get back in.

PRIORY, LOUISIANA

Mornin', Y'all   Monday, August 29, 2005

"*Mornin', Y'all*. This is Melody Melançon and you're listening to WPRY 90.5, bringing you and your mama up-to-date on the latest in Priory.

The storm came ashore this morning, y'all, on the border between Loo-siana and Mississippi. It's still too early to know anything for certain, but I am not liking what I'm hearing. I'm not repeating it neither 'cause my sources are not reliable—close your ears Cousin Allie—so I'll wait until I see it on the news. But Katrina came ashore as a Category 3 or 4, and that is not good, my friends.

I can't even talk about food this morning, y'all. I feel sick to my stomach. I left the house this morning without so much as a small bowl of grits. Randy couldn't eat neither. We were a sorry lot.

I'm going to light some candles at Our Lady of Good Hope right this very instant. If anyone else is so inclined, I will bring a pocket full of $1 bills. Y'all can meet me there. Candles are on me.

Father Abelli, unlock the doors. We are heading your way.

That's it for now. But remember, if you're not listening to *Mornin', Y'all*, you might as well be living in Antarctica."

PRIORY, LOUISIANA

CHAPTER THIRTY-NINE

Mimi woke early Monday morning in dull light. The digital clock was dark. Her nightlight was off. Still in yesterday's clothes, she rose from the chair and arched her back, resting her hands on her hips. Things within her popped.

She flipped up the light switch. Nothing. The house was bloated with stagnant air. The wind howled outside. Torrents of water pounded against her windows so fiercely that she couldn't see beyond their timid sills. It was coming at the house from all directions. There was little to do but wait.

Although she had initially felt brave about staying, there was a sensation creeping throughout her body that felt more like fear. She picked up the flashlight lantern then dropped it. Picked it up and dropped it again. Finally, she steadied herself, picked it up and turned the black and yellow flashlight on. It reminded her of a firefly.

Excluding closets, the powder room was the only room without windows, so she went in. Closing the door, she felt an unwelcome sense of dread. She sat on top of the toilet and examined the wallpaper with her flashlight. The damask pattern mimicked long, exaggerated faces, droopy eyes, and curly moustaches.

An unlikely sanctuary, she thought. She sat there for hours, praying. She wondered if Sylvia and Richard were okay. *I should've gone to Natchez.*

She couldn't shake thoughts of Thomas. Where was he? Would he come save her? At this point, she hoped not. He could die trying to save her.

Mimi sat upright. *Nothing's goin' to happen to me. This'll just be a good story.*

Trying to drown out the loud cracks that sounded like the roof being ripped apart, Mimi sang songs suited for a hurricane, songs from Pat O'Brien's dueling piano bar. First, she sang, "Sarah, Sarah, sittin' in a Chevrolet. Sarah, Sarah, sittin' in a Chevrolet. All day long, she sits and shifts. All day long, she shifts and sits. Sarah, Sarah, sittin' in a Chevrolet…" It was followed by "Oh, I wish I was in Dixie. Hooray, hooray. In Dixie land, I'll take my stand, to live and die in Dixie…" Several other songs followed suit until she was bored by the sound of her own voice and tired of trying to out-sing the screaming winds.

At one point during the day, she took an excursion to the kitchen to grab a box of cereal and another bottle of water. It was frighteningly dark for daytime. She promptly returned to the safety of the bathroom.

After the winds died down a bit, Mimi ventured into the front room to discover that she could now see out her window to the street. It was late in the day and although it was raining, the worst appeared to be over. Her whole neighborhood lay behind a curtain of dusk and raindrops, but she had a flashlight. Hopefully, the batteries would last.

She grinned, winked at Dirk, and went to the kitchen to open a can of Blue Runner red beans. After eating them with a silver spoon, she chased them with a lukewarm shot of whiskey.

Mimi's house was stifling. The winds continued to lose their power, so she cracked some windows. She wriggled into her nightgown and slid under a solitary sheet, tossing the blanket and duvet onto her bench as if she were tossing off her worries.

Mimi fell fast asleep Monday night, glad to have the storm behind her.

PRIORY, LOUISIANA

CHAPTER FORTY

While Mimi was riding out the hurricane in her Lakeview bathroom on Monday, Mary Bell, Lafitte, and their guests were huddled at The Retreat. Mary Bell decided to serve all meals, instead of just breakfast, since no one could pry themselves away from the television.

Lena and Tom went to The Retreat early in the morning to see what they could do to help. Mary Bell's face broke into a grateful grin when she saw them. After a round of hugs, they all got to work. The Retreat was a busy, fidgety place that day. Guests were spellbound as palm trees swayed wildly on the television, bending like characters in a Seussian windstorm.

Tom had trouble watching it, but he was also drawn to it. It was the same gripping, hypnotic feeling that overcame him when he watched the New Orleans Fair Grounds in flames. In 1993, newscasters broke into nighttime television and said that the racetrack grandstand was on fire. Tom jumped on his bike and peddled as fast as he could. Long before he reached it, he saw the flickering beacon of fire illuminate the dark sky. The towering white wooden structure was being devoured by hungry flames. He wondered if the rising heat might melt the stars.

Now, he had trouble taking his eyes off Katrina.

Trying to stay sane, he forced himself away from the television. He took on a variety of odd jobs around The Retreat, including clumsy attempts at bed-making and kitchen-cleaning. Where was Mimi? He was racking his brain, imagining the possibilities. The phone lines in New Orleans were shot. He was frustratingly disconnected from her.

Walking through the sitting room, Tom spotted the elderly women. Their eyes were out of focus, and their hands were tapping. The one with the oxygen tank was about Mimi's age. Her daughter was somewhere around his mother's age.

"Hey, ladies," Tom said.

The women looked up. The blue eyes of the elder lady flashed above her plastic tubes. He squatted by her chair, reached up, and held her hand. "Where y'all from?"

The daughter, who couldn't have been younger than fifty, answered, "Slidell."

Tom turned away from them to look at the TV. Slidell, Louisiana. A direct hit. The eye wall was passing right over it.

"Shit," he said feebly. "Unbelievable, huh?"

A gas station overhang was ripped to shreds and disappeared into the wild wreckage.

"I'm from New Orleans," he added. "Probably not much better."

Tom wanted to summon up the courage he'd known when he was Father Tom. He wanted to say something comforting or profound. Something about how God had a plan for all of us. How maybe something good could come out of so much destruction. Without the black shirt, though, he couldn't channel the same voice of conviction. He figured no one would want to hear what came out of his mouth.

The ladies watched the hurricane with a continued sense of disbelief. Was this really happening or was this some horrible dream that visited the elderly when they nodded off? If this was not a dream, their entire life's belongings were in Katrina's path.

When a Cat 4 or 5 passed over your city, it wasn't hard to guess what the general devastation would look like: roofs off, trees down, water rising. It was extremely difficult, though, to guess the minute details of your own personal devastation: which furniture was not salvageable, which photos were ruined, which neighbors had drowned.

On a street a few blocks from The Retreat, Henry Shane walked a sheepdog in the morning drizzle. He, Doc Gainard, one assistant, and a couple of volunteers were exhausted. The veterinary office had never housed so many animals before. The stress manifested itself within the animals in different ways. A dachshund wouldn't stop shivering. A tabby cat sat atop a carpeted pole and wouldn't leave it. This sheepdog had been barking and pacing incessantly. Vet and dog both needed exercise.

Henry had taken the Laurelle's two Yorkies to his house. They were so small and sweet, and Olivia had been calling him constantly to check on them. Even with an infant at her breast and a toddler at her feet, she missed her dogs. She missed the way they'd give her endless amounts of snuggling in exchange for nothing more than gentle rubbing behind their ears or an occasional apple treat. Olivia had had the dogs longer than she'd had the children, and being away from them—even just across town—was torture.

After all the animals were tended, Henry went to The Retreat. He opened the creaky screen door and pulled his hooded rain slicker off. Mary Bell spotted him from across the room and nearly dropped a pitcher of ice water, setting it down so quickly. She ran over and threw her arms around his neck. He arched his back like he was trying to uproot a tree and left her feet dangling above the ground.

"Everything's going be okay, honey," he assured her. "It'll be okay." He rubbed her slender back.

"How are the animals?"

"They'll be alright. They're a little stressed, but everybody is. They'll be fine."

"Things are not going well around here," Mary Bell said, turning her eyes toward the parlor. "I don't see any way the Legrange's home could still be standing." She reduced her voice to a whisper. "It looks like the Mississippi Coast was wiped out, and their home is right on the beach."

Henry rubbed his tired eyes with his fingers.

"I don't know what to say," Mary Bell continued. "I called my parents in North Carolina. They're coming back."

Henry kissed her nose. She melted in his arms, wishing she could stay within them all day, but there was so much to be done. He left her and went into the kitchen to help. When he brought a plate of finger sandwiches into the dining room, he almost ran into Tom.

"Tom?" Henry guessed.

"Yeah…"

"Henry Shane." Henry extended his hand and they shook. "I'm Mary Bell's …"

"I know."

The two men sized each other up.

"Just so you know," Henry continued, "she's totally in your corner."

Tom gave half a smile. "She's really something, you know? You're one lucky guy."

"Yeah, I know," Henry said in earnest. "Hey, looks like you may be lucky, too, huh? Seems like New Orleans dodged the bullet again…"

"Yeah, I guess so…"

Even though the hurricane was coming ashore to the east of New Orleans, and Tom's hometown was on the weak side of the storm, he still worried. Mimi wasn't getting any younger. It must be sweltering in their house with no air conditioning. What if she had medical problems? What if she suffered heat stroke?

Tom looked over to the TV set in time to witness the roof peel off the Superdome and the windows shatter on the Hyatt next door. Everyone in the room was stunned. Tom inched closer to the TV set. He forgot he was holding a glass of water until he almost dropped it.

"Damn," Becca said, never believing this would happen. Her parents had stayed at the Hyatt when they'd come in for a Saints game. They'd been on the side of the hotel facing the Dome, the side that was now a wall of glass shards and fluttering drapery.

"We have breaking news," the anchor said, "that one of the levees in New Orleans has been breached. The word is that it's near the Industrial Canal. This is the worst possible scenario for New Orleans. We have reports that a wall of water is pouring in."

No one at The Retreat knew what to say. The patter of rain and voices on TV tempered their silence. On a loveseat, Nichelle and Tamika snuggled together.

Where was Nichelle's sister, Demetra? She hadn't evacuated. For one reason, her family of four wouldn't have fit into Nichelle's small car. Besides, what was the point in evacuating when they had no destination in mind? No way to pay for a hotel room if they found one?

Demetra's finances were pretty pitiful, too, so she planned to either ride out the storm at home in the Ninth Ward or go to the Superdome. With the state of the Superdome worsening and New Orleans filling up with water, Nichelle grew increasingly shaky.

"Oh, my God," Nichelle said. "Jesus, Lord, please help them."

New Orleans was a soup bowl, and they all knew it. For years, graphics depicting the what-ifs of a levee breach had been displayed. Mostly they speculated that water would topple the levees. Invading water would have no way to get back out again. The pumps wouldn't be able to keep up. New Orleans would be doomed. Not many people believed the warning, though. Almost no one, excluding the academic and meteorological communities, thought it could happen to The City That Care Forgot.

Tamika began to pray. She said a series of tiny, short prayers that flew from her soul like invisible birds, folding themselves like origami to slip under the doorway and into the watery sky toward heaven.

This roomful of strangers made her uneasy. She leaned close to her mama and rested her head on a soft shoulder. Through Nichelle's thin shirt and warm skin, Tamika heard her mother's heart skipping beats. At first, it scared her. If her mother was frightened, things must really be bad.

What can I do to help? Tamika wondered. *I'm just a girl, and the storm is so big.*

Then she remembered a time when she and her cousin, Cherry, were walking to the corner grocery. A strange, mangy dog approached and barked at them. Cherry clung to Tamika and hid her face, but Tamika walked steadily forward, ignoring the barking dog. She remembered feeling brave: brave because she wasn't afraid of dogs, brave because Cherry needed her to be strong.

So Tamika reached down and placed her small hand within her mother's. Nichelle squeezed it and gazed down at her daughter's open face.

"Everything's gonna be okay, Mama."

"What makes you think so, baby? I mean, things look pretty bad on the TV."

"Everything's gonna be okay 'cause we're together. And because God is with us."

Tamika sat up straighter. Nichelle rubbed her thumb across the child's fingertips.

Tom took shallow breaths but couldn't form clear thoughts. Lucy pulled him down to the floor with one hand so he wouldn't fall over. He wrapped his arms around his legs to steady himself, leaning against her. Under any other circumstance, leaning against Lucy would have electrified him.

"Shit" was the word Tom chose as his mantra. "Shit, shit, shit." He muttered loud enough for the whole room to hear it, "I think my grandma might still be there…"

Even as he said it, Tom had trouble believing it. Why did that city on the television seem so far away? Was it a tropical wasteland in some equatorial country?

It might as well have been. The images seemed distant and unfamiliar.

Nichelle leaned forward and put a hand on Tom's shoulder. "You from New Orleans, too?"

Tom turned around to face her. "Yeah. Lakeview. How 'bout you?"

"Lower Nine."

Unless she had worked at a house in his neighborhood, she'd have probably never been there. And the only time he'd frequented the Ninth Ward, he was in search of a legendary snowball stand, which he never did find. Their paths might never have crossed before, being that both their neighborhoods had forgotten to integrate.

She had a gentle, round face, though, and Tom instantly liked her. He looked at her timid daughter and smiled weakly before turning back to the TV. There was nothing positive to say. He couldn't convince himself any longer that everything would be alright.

"What's your name?" Lucy asked the guy leaning against her.

"Tom," he said, pulling away from her, looking into her entrancing blue eyes.

"As in the former *Father* Tom?"

He looked back to the TV set. "Yeah. 'Fraid so." Word sure traveled fast in small towns.

Lucy caught Becca's attention and rolled her eyes toward Tom. Then she turned back to him and whispered, "Wow. You must be one crazy dude."

"That is an understatement," he replied.

Mary Bell went to the kitchen where Lena was washing dishes. She tried to speak calmly. "Lena, one of the levees in New Orleans has been breached."

"Where's Tom?"

"The parlor."

Lena hurried to set down a dry plate and then fled to the parlor, hobbling slightly. She saw aerial images of water pouring into the city on the television. Her eyes darted around the room. Tom wasn't there. Through the front window, she spotted him. He was standing on the porch, poking at his cell phone. Tears were streaming from the sky.

Redial. Fast busy. Redial. Fast busy.

When Lena opened the front door, Tom looked up, shot her a look that said, *I wish you could help me but you can't*, and tried again. And again. And again. He stopped dialing, and his phone-hand hung at his side.

Lena went to him and slid her arms under his, pulling him toward her. Tom draped his arms around her and moaned into her shoulder.

There was little to say. After the initial wave of fear and incredulity, Tom and Lena walked over to the hammock and sat together in it, under the sky-blue ceiling. They rocked back and forth and listened to the tapping of rain on pavement. Tom wondered whether God sent messages via Morse Code, using raindrops on any available flat surface. If only he knew Morse Code…

Mary Bell and Lafitte came out to check on them, but Tom was in a state of shock, and Lena wouldn't leave his side while he seemed so frazzled.

"You know, Lena," Tom said, "if I hadn't been away this week, I would've been there. I would've made sure Mimi left."

"Tom, there's no way of knowing what would've happened. If she wanted to stay, she would've stayed." After a moment's silence, she added, "Maybe she *did* leave."

Hypotheticals and second-guessing were frustrating, so they forced themselves to go back into The Retreat. The water level in New Orleans was still rising. The area of concern was centered near the Industrial Canal, miles from Lakeview and Mimi, but edging along Nichelle's Ninth Ward.

Nichelle was fidgeting in her chair. Tamika was rubbing her mama's arm. Lafitte approached Nichelle and asked if she wanted a cup of coffee or something, but she couldn't respond. Her pleading eyes met Lafitte's. In that moment, the two scarred people exchanged a volume of understanding.

"Look," Lafitte said, "if there's anything I can do…"

But as Nichelle returned her attention to the TV and the water invaded her city, her thoughts turned to Tyrell and his treasure-chest coffin. Every floating something was him. In every image, she searched for the chest.

She and Tamika had tried to send him on his way downriver, just a few days ago. Was he trying to come back home now? Was Katrina helping him? Even if the treasure chest wasn't back in New Orleans, had his ashen remains slid out from between the wooden cracks, mixed with surging water, and deposited themselves back in their city? On their street? Inside their apartment? After the water receded, would bits of him become dried upon her furniture? On her floors? In her bedroom?

Nichelle became still, in a frightened, impending doom sort of way. Would he be haunting her apartment for the rest of eternity? A forlorn soul trying to make amends? She wasn't strong enough for that. She'd already told him goodbye. If he was going to haunt that place, she didn't want to be up all night, wondering if every whistling wind was his voice.

The parlor of The Retreat was a ghost town of empty faces.

Mary Bell put her hand on Tom's back. "Hey, y'all have done enough to help us. You and Lena look exhausted. Y'all need some rest."

Lena hoped he would accept the suggestion and, when he did, they walked back to her house, hand-in-hand, rain popping upon their umbrella like acorns, gravel crunching underfoot like broken glass.

"It *is* possible she left with a friend," Tom said. "She and a couple of her blue-haired friends are inseparable."

Branches hovered over them, softening the rain.

"Sure, that's possible," Lena agreed.

"Or, we've got a bazillion neighbors who are always offerin' to help… Maybe she left with one of them."

"She certainly could have…"

Tom knew he was lying to himself. Mimi had hated her last hurricane evacuation. "Total waste of time" had been her words. He was desperate to talk to her, but landlines in New Orleans were down. Mimi didn't even own a cell phone because she had given up her driver's license a couple years back and said the cell phone was nothing but a good waste of whiskey money.

Lena let go of his hand and reached across Tom to take the umbrella and fold it up. She wanted to feel the tepid rain dot her skin. She needed to be part of it.

They walked on. He kept stealing glances at her, but every time he turned his head in her direction, she looked the other way. Was the weight of his suffering too much for her? Rain was gliding down her face and arms. Their clothes were becoming heavy and limp.

In the middle of the street, about a half a block from her house, Tom stopped. He moved toward Lena and pushed the damp auburn hair off her face. Her sagging eyes were sympathetic and weary.

Tom placed his hands on either side of her face, pulled her close, and drew so near to her that only a wet breeze passed between them. Their eyes fluttered in unison, searching for answers, and then he kissed her moist lips.

Their kiss was deep and revealing. It both comforted Tom and compelled him. There was no way to bring himself any nearer to her than he already was. He hoped he wasn't crushing her with his arms, which were now encircling her, trying to dispel a lifetime of searching.

Even though they were in the middle of the street, no cars interrupted them. The road was eerie, soggy, and desolate.

PRIORY, LOUISIANA

CHAPTER FORTY-ONE

Before Tom went to sleep late Monday, newscasters were incredulous. Water was surging into New Orleans. The city was without power. Phone lines were drowned. A poisonous mix of rising sewage, invading salt water, and leaking gas was churning.

Tom wondered whether anyone who had predicted this soup bowl felt vindicated for no longer being the Men Who Cried Wolf. If they did, he hoped never to hear it.

Lena and Tom snuggled on her bed, clothed and overcome with exhaustion. Their sleep came in tattered fragments. In the middle of the night, images flashed inside Tom of his last visit with Mimi. She had hugged his priestly-clad waistline, and her white curls had danced below his eyelashes.

He considered getting up to turn the TV back on, but he didn't want to wake Lena. Because of him, she was exhausted. This week had been crazy for her. There was nothing he could do anyway, no one left to call.

When dawn started breaking, he slid his arm out from underneath her neck and headed for her living room. She felt the warmth of her own body leave with his. A draft slid up against her belly like someone had just torn down one of the walls of her bedroom, so she got up and joined him.

On the TV, the first image he saw was the street sign, Harrison Avenue. Its white letters lay on a royal blue background, hovering inches above the water line.

PRIORY, LOUISIANA

Inches above the water line? How can that be? Tom was confused until the camera panned out to show all of Lakeview underwater, only rooftops and second stories visible. Chills ran through his body.

"Tom," Lena said, trying to figure out his puzzled expression. "Where is that?"

He opened his mouth to speak but nothing came out. It was like a nightmare where he was screaming but had no voice box.

"Is that near your house?"

He blinked and then squinted. "About two blocks away."

A desire rose within him to turn off the television so it would be over. Maybe if he stopped watching it, it would stop happening in the same way some people think they won't get sick if they refuse to see a doctor. Lack of evidence.

"This can't be happenin'," he said. "I don't believe it."

Strength swelled inside her. They couldn't just give up without trying to make a difference. She knew he'd never forgive himself. "Tom, let's go. We'll go to New Orleans."

He turned to her. "Do what?"

"You heard me. Let's go find Mimi."

"The city's shut down. How can we get back in?"

"I doubt anyone's guarding the entrance to the city anymore. They've got much bigger issues than that."

He knew she was right.

"I don't think we have any other choice," Lena continued. "We have to go."

Tom wondered whether he should have gone back home yesterday. *Yesterday.* A day he wished he could have back. He still didn't know whether Mimi was in New Orleans or on the road, but his paralysis wouldn't help.

Lena's idea, like most great plans, was so obvious. After brushing his teeth in the bathroom, he came out and grabbed his duffle to change clothes.

"We'll take Airline Highway as far as we can go," he called from her room. "The I-10's gotta be under water." He walked back out saying, "We'll drive as far as we can and then …"

Lena's face had changed from hopeful to horrified. This one-bad-thing on top of another-bad-thing spiral wouldn't stop. The newest images to shock the screen were looters carrying blue jeans and electronics from the shattered storefronts on Canal. They splashed through knee-high water. They were sweaty and wild-eyed.

A shirtless man, pants hanging low on his hips, had a bag full of stuff in one hand and a TV upon his shoulder. *A TV on his shoulder? What the hell?* Tom was trying not to judge anyone since no one could imagine the mindset of a trauma victim but…a TV? Where could he even plug it in? The city was under water. Tom hoped there were essentials like food and water in the bag.

His thoughts switched to Lakeview. The water was higher there—about eight feet or so. They couldn't be looting in eight feet of water, but who knew what other kinds of hell might be breaking loose?

The coverage flipped to a graphic of the canals and bayous in New Orleans. A yellow circle was drawn around the breach in both the Industrial Canal and now, also, in the 17th Street Canal near his home. *That's why Lakeview is flooded.*

Lena hurried to her room, but he followed her. He held her arm, turning her around. "Lena, you can't go with me."

"Why not?"

"It's too dangerous."

"I know," she admitted with some shame, "but I want to be with you."

"Look, I'm not budgin' on this, honey. I've gotta go, and you've gotta stay." Tom went to the kitchen and scribbled his cell phone number on a piece of paper.

"I need you to be here, safe, when I get back. I'll call you as often as I can."

Lena's throat felt like it had a huge pecan stuck in it, and she couldn't swallow. Cell towers were down, and they both knew it. She wouldn't be able to reach him.

"But what…" Lena said, trying to breathe around the obstructing pecan. "What if you don't come back?"

Tom held her and kissed her cheek. "I will come back, Lena. I promise."

Her whole body ached.

In a hurry to be a man of action and not merely a stupefied bystander, he rushed out the front door but noticed he didn't hear footsteps behind him. At the bottom of the steps, he turned around to look back at the house. Lena appeared in the door, loaded with supplies. She hurried down to him, hanging his Secret Agent camera around his neck and shoving a couple rolls of film into his shorts pockets. She gave him a box of granola bars and two bottles of water.

Tom studied her face, trying to memorize her features. He kissed her pink lips then drove away with as much velocity as the green Jeep could muster.

PRIORY, LOUISIANA

CHAPTER FORTY-TWO

The whiskey and red beans combined to knock Mimi out solid Monday night. Tuesday, in the small hours of morning, she had a vivid dream that she was standing by the side of her bed. A blistering, cold wind was rising up from the ground, racing to the sky.

In this dream, her house had no roof. She wondered how high the freezing air would go. It felt like a huge vacuum was sucking all the coldness out of the earth, through her house, and into the heavens. The force of the wind was so strong that her pillows stood on end, cases flapping. The only thing on the bed, next to her pillows, was a pair of brown leather lace-up shoes, the kind she wore when she was a girl. The wind did not move them, not even their laces.

Mimi woke up, startled. A putrid stench filled the oppressive air and attacked her skin, her hair, her nostrils…

An awful, murky soup was consuming her room. Her belongings floated weightlessly around her bed. The water had risen silently, unnoticed, like snow falling on rooftops, accumulating in the vast peacefulness of night, a revelation to people rising at dawn.

She splashed through a knee-deep pond to the front room, but it was a struggle. Rugs, end tables, magazines, newspapers, hairbrushes, and food from the lower shelves of her kitchen pantry were now all bobbing about.

Her first thought was to leave the house, but when she looked out the front window and realized her entire neighborhood was in the same condition, it seemed futile. At least inside the house, in the attic anyway, she could stay dry. She needed to get out of this water. What if it had snakes in it? Rats? Roaches?

She looked frantically around the room, grabbed the silver-framed picture of Dirk in one hand, a small chair in another, and splashed into the hallway to reach for the rope to the attic ladder. The water kept rising. Her nightgown floated up around her waistline.

The attic rope was beyond her grasp, so she placed the chair tenuously underneath it and, still clutching Dirk's handsome photograph, tried to pull herself up onto the chair with one free hand.

Mornin', Y'all *Tuesday, August 30, 2005*

"Mornin', Y'all. This is Melody Melançon and you're listening to WPRY 90.5, bringing you and your mama up-to-date on the latest in Priory.

Y'all, what is going on in New Orleans? Flooding, looting, lawlessness? I knew Katrina looked wicked, but I never pictured all this. I am sick.

Mississippi? Alabama? How is this all possible? I feel like I'm having a nightmare and no one will wake me up.

I need people around me now, y'all, so I will be at the Priory Library at noon. They are letting us take over the place. I'll bring pitchers of lemonade and all my worries.

Won't you come join me? Bring me your tales of old hurricanes. Come tell stories of evacuations and near misses. Anything you want to talk about. Tell me about loved ones who you haven't heard from yet. I will broadcast whatever info you have to help you find them.

Whether you are a citizen of Priory or a visitor, you come sit with me. We need to be together, y'all. Randy and I will be there. So you can bet there will be some food involved. If you have never seen me before, I will be the plump brunette with the pink sundress on. Randy says I look like a piece of bubble gum in it.

That's it for now. But remember, if you're not listening to *Mornin', Y'all*, you might as well...

See you at noon, y'all."

PRIORY, LOUISIANA

CHAPTER FORTY-THREE

For the second morning in a row, Lafitte awoke in the Adirondack chair to the chirping of early birds. Beads of dew moistened his skin. He had slept in his eye patch again, which he didn't normally do, but he didn't want the girls to see him without it. His eye socket was a puckered, scarred dent he couldn't share. Becca's sleeping body was lying on her stomach, one leg atop the sheet. Lucy was on her side, both hands tucked under her head.

Hoping he wouldn't be discovered, Lafitte peeled off the patch, laid it in his lap, and rubbed his head with both hands. He looked at the girls, in the haze of dawn, and thought he remembered a dream from last night. *Was it a dream or was it real?* In his dream—just a momentary image, really—the sultry Lucy had kissed the top of his head.

He smiled, put the patch back on, and went to freshen up. Lucy heard him tiptoeing across the floorboards and opened her eyes in time to see him disappear into the kitchen. She grinned and went back to sleep.

Within the hour, guests started to appear. Mary Bell and Lafitte put out a buffet of biscuits, sausage gravy, and fresh fruit. Without Lena's help, and with guests who were underfoot more than usual, Mary Bell and Lafitte were stretched to their limits. In the kitchen together, they rested against the counter.

"How you holding up, Mary Bell?"

Her eyes looked small and dull. "Okay. A little tired." She arched her back. "How about you?"

"Better than most people around here." Lafitte looked out the window. The girls, with the fewest worries in the household, were still asleep.

Mary Bell nodded. "Yeah, better than most."

Lafitte uncharacteristically opened his arms. She hugged him, relieved by his presence.

"I'm so lucky to have you, Lafitte."

He squeezed her a little tighter and then let go to turn the TV on in the parlor.

Tad and his wife, Olivia, settled into the loveseat. She was holding their baby, asleep in her arms. Their toddler was rolling a truck across the floor, turning the lines of the Oriental rug into makeshift streets.

Nichelle came down, without Tamika, and sat in one of the Queen Anne chairs.

"Morning," she said wearily. Her insides were shaking around within her shell of a body. Sort of like when she overdosed on caffeine.

The TV showed images of ever-rising water, as Tom and Lena had seen. Uptown was still staying dry, so Tad and Olivia felt lucky until reports of fires started. Newscasters couldn't figure out why so many fires had broken out. Maybe it was gas-related. Maybe it was arson.

They broke away from the fires to broadcast sketchy reports of vandalism Uptown. Uptown was perched on some of the highest, driest, most privileged land in the city. There was sludge in the streets, but not enough to get into most homes. Thugs knew they could get out of the water and into some mischief there. Neighbors who'd ridden out the storm called to each other from front porches. Word quickly spread that unsavories were prowling about.

Someone with a hand-held video camera was getting amazing shots of homeowners defending their homesteads. Two guys sat in rocking chairs on their wide front porches, drinking what had to be warm bottled beer. The one man had a baseball cap on and a shotgun across his lap. His comrade wore a fishing cap and a don't-mess-with-me expression.

Nichelle wondered if this was the end of the world: first Tyrell, now this. Was this the beginning of the end of life?

O, God, if this is the end, please bring me and Tamika home.

The Laurelle's baby woke and started crying, first softly, then with vigor. Olivia rose and patted his back, pacing around the room, trying to keep him quiet.

Ria and Victor came downstairs and chatted with Mary Bell by the buffet.

"Have y'all heard anything more about the Mississippi coast?" Ria asked Mary Bell. She imagined Mary Bell answering, *Yes, Aunt Ria. It was all a mistake. A sudden cool front came through and made the storm fall apart.*

The baby wailed even louder. Olivia looked as if she might come undone.

Mary Bell held Ria's hand. "No, Aunt Ria, nothing new." Nothing positive, anyway, was what Mary Bell meant to say.

Ria walked over and sat in the Queen Anne chair next to Nichelle. Victor stood behind Ria and put his hands upon her shoulders. It was the same thing he had done a week ago, as she sat on the iron bench and watched the subtle sunrise. It was the day Ria had pretended life was perfect. Maybe it had been perfect, as perfect as this life gets.

Staring at the frightening images on television, Ria said to Nichelle, "I don't know where my son is."

Nichelle turned her head to look at Ria. The wrinkles under Ria's eyes were full of sorrow.

"Mine's missing, too," Nichelle said. Her own eyes filled and sagged.

"My son's twenty-six years old," Ria added.

Nichelle blinked several times. "Mine was seventeen."

The word "was" sent tears down Nichelle's cheeks. Ria thought of Charles, her only child. She didn't want to lose him. Without him, life would seem meaningless.

"I'm so sorry," Ria whispered.

"I don't know where my sister or my friends are, neither," Nichelle continued, dizzy with anticipation. The storm's heightened suspense was like watching the last minute of a tight basketball game, except that it lasted more than a minute. Way more than a minute. It was endless, really. The tension was grueling.

Lafitte passed through the room and witnessed the quiet conversation between Nichelle and Ria. He marveled at the way searing pain united people. It made him think of his military buddies, the closest friends he'd ever had. They'd saved each other's lives, died in each other's arms, and had forgiven one another for monumental mistakes in judgment. All amidst bombs falling and the earth opening up beneath them.

Olivia paced with the screaming baby and gave Tad dirty looks, but he was entranced by the news. Victor walked over to her and said, "I used to be pretty good with my son when he was little."

Victor's eyes were alert and clear. Olivia passed off the baby. This man, with his upper-class hands and his proper wife, seemed like someone she could trust.

Ria watched her husband as he took the infant. He turned the baby around and lay him chest-down upon his forearm. Cradling the boy, Victor walked toward the front door and out onto the humid porch. He stayed in view of the windows so the mother would have some comfort.

Olivia sat next to Tad but refused to touch him. Her eyes occasionally flickered toward her baby outside, but she was riveted by the images and distracted by her toddler, who was gently rolling his red truck over her tennis shoe. Thank goodness the Yorkies were safe and not stuck back in New Orleans.

Ria went out to the front porch and stood in the doorway. Victor paced the floor, patting the baby on the back, singing a song he used to sing to Charles, "Rock-a-bye your baby with a Dixie melody. When you croon, croon a tune from the heart of Dixie…"

Where did all the years go? Ria wondered. Hadn't she been in love with him once? In a way that made her feel lucky? Seeing him with the baby, she began to remember…

Another band of rain passed over Priory, one of the trailing bands. The air was rich with moisture and floral scents. Waves of bright green foliage swayed behind Victor. When he finished his song, and the little one fell back to sleep, he turned his attention to Ria.

"I'm sorry, honey," he started.

Ria didn't speak.

"I've made so many mistakes, haven't I?"

She wanted to say, "Yes, you certainly have," but what she said surprised even her. "We've both made mistakes, I suppose."

Victor kissed the baby's head.

Upstairs, two rooms were still inhabited by females in distress. In 2D, an elderly woman lay in bed, on her side, facing the window. Within her field of vision was her oxygen tank. Beyond it was a world that was wet and scary and full of uncertainty. Her aging daughter stood over her.

"Ma, do you want me to help you get dressed to go downstairs?"

The role reversal was a challenge to both women's egos.

"Why didn't you leave me there?" her mother asked.

"What do you mean, Ma? I couldn't leave you in the nursing home. They didn't have any way to evacuate everyone. You'd have been stuck there."

"It was my destiny," she said with intensity. "It's my time." Her eyes were as cold and immobile as glass.

Her daughter thought about this for a moment. "If it was your destiny, you'd still be there." She brushed the hair off her mother's forehead and left the room.

In 2B, Tamika lay upon the plush mattress, looking at the ceiling medallion that had so captivated Tom a few days earlier. One of the leaves in its design looked like it had a crucifix in the middle.

She turned onto her side and put an arm under her head. The top drawer of the nightstand was not closed completely. She sat upright and slid the drawer open. Tom's Bible appeared. Using two hands, she lifted the elegant leather book from its wooden home. She placed it near her nose and inhaled. It smelled like wet summer grass.

She didn't want to open the Book because she wouldn't know where to begin. Maybe the act of holding it would be enough.

Dear Jesus, Tamika said, *I don't know what to ask for anymore.*

Over the past few days, she had said so many prayers. In them, she was asking, sometimes quietly begging, for things beyond her control.

Her mind drifted to a story she had read in school. It was about a woman who asked the gods for something and got it. Then, the greedy woman asked for something else and got it. She kept asking and asking until the gods grew tired of her demanding spirit. Nothing was ever good enough for her. Their final act was to take everything away.

With the Bible resting upon her lap, Tamika thought about this and then formed her prayer. *Dear Lord, thank you for keeping us safe.*

CHAPTER FORTY-FOUR

When Tom ran out of dry pavement on Airline, the old state highway became a boat-ramp, disappearing into a new body of water Tom didn't recognize. He parked his Jeep, got out, and tried to take it in, but the panorama was unbelievable. Its vast expanse spread out before him. If he had taken a step forward, his feet would have gotten wet. He was standing on the very edge of the change in worlds. Yet it still looked so far away. So unreal. So quiet.

The silence was broken by an approaching truck motor. A leathered man with a double-billed cotton cap got out of a beat-up old pickup. When he started sliding his pirogue off the back of the truck, Tom went back to his own car, grabbed the granola bars, water, and camera, and ran to the pirogue as it began to float.

"Hey, where you goin'?" Tom yelled.

"Dunno, man, just wanna help," the man said, urgency underlying his thick Cajun accent.

"Can I join you?"

The tanned gent nodded to the boat. Tom stepped in, centering himself upon the flat front bench.

"Name's Jacques Boudin."

"Tom Vaughn."

They shook hands. Jacques took an axe and a lantern out of his pickup and placed them on the floor of the flat-bottomed boat. He cranked the motor, and they journeyed into Orleans Parish. At first, they had to steer around fence pickets, but the fences quickly disappeared into deeper water. The new, rancid lake soon hid all street-level views. An obstacle course emerged consisting of signs, partially clad roofs, sections of interstate, tips of mausoleums, and tree canopies. Unknown debris floated like alligators, eyes visible above the water line.

"I'm trying to find my grandmother," Tom said. "I think she rode out the storm."

"If your grand-mère's lost," Jacques said, tobacco-stained teeth resolute, "we gonna find her."

While Jacques piloted with his left hand, Tom studied Jacques' wedding ring: silver, scratched, bent into a polygon instead of a circle. Jacques' swollen knuckles told Tom they'd never release that ring. After forty-three years of marriage, "some dat were good, some not so good," Jacques would have said the same thing.

The motor's roll announced them, and an above-water population stirred. Stunned people, splayed on their battered roofs, weakly stood and waved filthy hands. Heads and arms popped out of second-story windows. Tom's eyes saw gaping, pleading mouths, but his ears heard only the motor's roar. Were these people saying something or were they mute from lack of hope or nourishment?

As he neared them, cries of desperation crept into his ears and tore at his soul. Tom and Jacques looked at each other. Invisible question marks floated in the air like hummingbirds.

Jacques turned off the motor and yelled in a voice that was loud and sincere, "We'll pass back for y'all soon as we can! Don't give up, y'all! We'll pass right back!"

A woman screamed, "Please! Can't y'all just take one small child?"

Grown men and women cried as Jacques and Tom passed them—some cursing, some moaning. If they started picking people up, they'd never get to Mimi. It was agonizing. How could they refuse these people? Tom contemplated what kind of hell he might be inheriting by passing them up.

Both men drew mental pictures, trying to memorize the whereabouts of all the desperate strandees. It was a puzzle, though, trying to navigate the top layer of New Orleans, to determine the exact location of their boat, or to find their way to Tom's home. Tom had to put the scenery through a special sieve in his mind so he could try to identify the shrouded streets by examining the things that loomed above them. He remembered, clearly, that his burgundy roof matched the red of his door.

"It's over there, that red roof!" Tom pointed. His heart swelled. Jacques pulled up alongside the gutter. Tom jumped out, paced up the incline of peeling shingles, and tied their line to a metal stack. Kneeling down, he put his ear to the roasting asphalt and listened. The scorching sun beat down upon him.

The only sound he heard was the lapping of waves against the house. Tom wished he possessed some sort of superhero powers so Mimi's raspy voice would ring through. Jacques followed him onto the roof and started hacking into it, asphalt shingles flying, black tar paper shredding, slivers of wood splintering, until he had made a hole big enough for Tom to climb into.

Tom grabbed a flashlight, flicked it on, and lowered himself into the attic. It was so oppressively hot, he could barely inhale. He thought he had found yet another gateway to hell, like the one he'd seen in Mary

Bell's side yard, charred into the grassy lawn below his window.

The air in the attic reeked of burnt toast. If Mimi was in here, she couldn't be alive. He dreaded finding Mimi dead. He stayed still but moved his flashlight around in feverish circles, hoping with every fiber in his body that she wasn't here. Except for pink fiberglass, strategic planks, and feathery cobwebs, the attic was empty. Tom glared at the attic door in the center of the room. Dark water was splashing up through its casement.

He lay the flashlight down on a board and crawled over to the horizontal door. He debated opening it. He could barely breathe from the heat and the stench and the fear. His chest felt like it was going to implode.

Everything below him was a watery tomb. If Mimi was in the house, she was dead. To search for her, he'd have to swim through black bacteria-ridden water and Mimi's suspended belongings. And then what? Then, try to put an arm around his dead grandmother's neck, as if he were saving her from a swimming accident, and attempt to lift her up through the attic door?

With his hand, he tried to push the door down, but it wouldn't budge. His body convulsed. Was something wedged up against it? Maybe it was only water. He stood up and stomped on it with his foot. The door gave way, soaking his lower leg in the process.

The square hole filled with lapping water. It was like peering into a fishing hole in an icehouse. Except that this house was boiling, not freezing. And it wasn't fish that might be floating in it. The impossibility of the situation swam through Tom. He was not going into the water. There was no use.

PRIORY, LOUISIANA

Tom worked his way back across the planks, picked up the flashlight, and climbed out onto the roof. He collapsed, pulled his knees to his chest, and examined the endless, destroyed scene. His heart was beating wildly like it was trying to say something.

Jacques turned away from him. Tom's eyes skittered to each floating, mysterious object. What the hell was all this? The watery grave stretched on as far as the eye could see. Its depressing panorama was hard to process.

Below Tom, being disintegrated by toxic water, were all his earthly belongings: his sports trophies, his fraternity regalia, the mahogany chest of drawers from Mimi, his photo of the harlequin windows...

The chance of Mimi also being below him was incomprehensible. Tom closed his eyes to shut it out. The inside of his eyelids grew dark and impenetrable. He had to believe she was somewhere else. Not here.

Someone shouted his name. A woman. Tom's eyes darted from rooftop to rooftop. He wiped his eyes.

"Tom! Over here! Help!"

Out of a second-story window, two doors down, his neighbor, Paula, flailed her arms like the referee at a Saints game.

Tom wiped the sweat from his face onto his shirtsleeve and untied the line, getting back into the boat with Jacques. Paula disappeared into the second story window to gather her husband and little ones. Jacques was a master at the helm and had no problems navigating his way to the window ledge.

After Paula and her krewe settled into the boat, Tom threw his arm around one of Paula's girls and pulled her close. The last time he saw her, she was showing him her fire-ant bites. The itchy pustules seemed so insignificant now.

"Paula," Tom said to his neighbor, trying to be strong in front of the girls, trying to project his cracking voice so it could be heard over the motor, but remaining steady enough not to be too alarming, "have you seen Mimi?"

Paula's eyes, already having cried a river of tears, welled up again. She shook her head and blinked. "I'm sorry, Tom. I haven't…" She was trembling and hunched over. Her voice was thin and uneven.

Tom wondered why his neighbors hadn't evacuated. Then he saw Paula sending some wicked looks in her husband's direction. Trey wouldn't turn his head toward her. He cradled their toddler and turned to face the hot breeze.

Oh, yeah. Trey loved to ride out storms, just like Tom did. He was always hazing people who abandoned their homes. Paula seemed to like this macho grandstanding. Until now.

The boatload forged on, rescuing a young couple a few roofs away. Tom didn't recognize them, but asked if they had seen a white-haired woman. They seemed confused. No, they hadn't seen anyone matching Mimi's description.

Their boat was now full of sobbing, clinging bodies, so they navigated back toward Metairie. Tom's shredded, rust-colored roof faded from view.

The rest of the day was a blur of loading and unloading passengers, trying to remember where all the stranded people were, hacking away with the axe, carrying little ones on top of their shoulders, maneuvering around floating corpses, and passing out their limited stash of granola bars. They contemplated loading dead bodies into the boat, but with so many live people still in need, they decided against it. Still, if one of them were Mimi, Tom would have wanted someone to pull her out of the noxious water.

He looked for Mimi everywhere: on rooftops, in other boats…

Tom lifted his camera off the boat floor. He'd left it underneath his seat, but panicked when he realized that a small amount of water was swishing under his feet. Fortunately, only the bottom of the camera seemed damp, so he wiped it off with his shirt and slid its hemp strap around his neck. He didn't know for sure if any lasting damage had been done, but he decided to take pictures with it anyway.

There was so much to take in. He didn't want it to pass undocumented. His first photo was one of Jacques at the helm: able, wrinkled, generous, alert. Tom took pictures of their passengers that day, too. Portraits of burnt faces, families huddling, tear-stained cheeks. Stealing photos of people in pain hurt more than Tom would have imagined. By immortalizing their pain, he felt like maybe he was contributing to it, or taking advantage of it, or exploiting them for the sake of posterity, or… It was hopeless to try to think in a straight line, but he was compelled to take more and more pictures.

It was so damn hot. Tom thought he was going to pass out on several occasions. He'd get light-headed or dehydrated or overwhelmed by fumes. The water bottles hadn't lasted nearly long enough.

With nighttime descending and their gas tank near empty, they headed back. Throughout their strenuous and disheartening day, they'd been depositing people across the Parish line, under the nearest dry magnolia tree. When he and Jacques returned, all the people they'd saved were gone. Tom hoped maybe they'd walked to safety. Jacques suggested maybe someone had picked them up. In any case, they were better off now than they were inside the wretched swamp.

At the pickup truck, Tom and Jacques hoisted the pirogue back onto its makeshift dock.

"You comin' back tomorrow, Jacques?"

Tom's hands were shaking, and his eyelids were heavy. Jacques recognized his own son's face within Tom's. Tom was almost the same age as T-Jacques and had the same penetrating green eyes. If it were T-Jacques in this mess, Jacques would want a stranger to help him, for sure.

"Yeah, man, I'll be back. Wanna look for your grand-mère some more?"

Tom nodded and shook Jacques' hand. They made plans and exchanged phone numbers. Then, Tom got back in his Jeep.

On his drive back to Priory, the day's faces haunted Tom. He had lived his whole life in New Orleans without noticing that many faces, in such detail. In the unreal squalor and watery filth, Tom had noticed the black hole in everyone's eyes: how it united their plight, how it appealed to his innate decency.

People who Tom might have previously tagged with unkind labels were laid bare before him, their bodies contorted in distress. Mothers were doubled over with despair because they had been separated from their children. Strapping young men cried in fear and disgust at floating dead bodies. Kids were glossy-eyed. Nearly everyone he found was famished and weak.

The thought kept crossing his mind: Did any of this destruction have to do with him pretending to be a priest?

He picked up his cell phone to call his parents but he had no lines. *Could Mimi still be alive?* Tom kept telling himself it was possible. She could have evacuated when the water started rising or left town with a friend. Maybe one day he would see Mimi in her doorway again, sipping an Old Fashioned.

With trembling hands and a drained body, Tom found it challenging to keep his steering under control. His driving was erratic, but it didn't matter. No one was on the road until he got quite a ways from Orleans Parish. By that time, he had settled into a managed rhythm.

He concentrated on the act of driving, like he did when he was drunk. Much effort was expended, even though he had none to spare, on just staying within the lines. On simply maintaining a constant speed. Roadside railings blurred as he sped by. He became obsessed with the word "dead." Without realizing it, he pecked it over and over again onto the steering wheel.

d-e-a-d

Left hand. Three fingers. It took only three fingers to type such an irreversible word.

When he got home to Lena's, she was sitting on the front stoop waiting for him. He walked toward her and collapsed on the first step. He wanted to tell her what he'd seen, but no words would come. Wrapping his arms around her, Tom breathed into her warm hair.

"I didn't find Mimi."

Lena didn't say anything. She just rubbed his back and helped him into the house.

He retreated to the sofa, where sleep and nightmares came and went in fragments with ripped edges. Lena tossed and turned in her bedroom, too. When she finally fell asleep, it was deep and exclusive. She didn't hear Tom creep into her room in the early dawn, didn't feel his soft kiss upon her cheek, didn't see him place two spent rolls of film on her night stand. When Lena woke up, the film was staring at her, and she knew he was gone.

CHAPTER FORTY-FIVE

"Hello?" Grace yelled into the receiver.
"Hey. Is this Grace?"
"Yeah, who's this?"
"My name's Lena Melendez. I'm a friend of Tom Vaughn."

Grace's bronchial laugh contained a couple of coughs. "I love that nut. How is he?"

"He's okay, I guess, but he's in New Orleans right now, looking for his grandmother."

Grace hadn't known Tom was gone, so she'd driven all around Priory the previous day hoping to find him. "What can I do?" she asked, her voice becoming solemn.

"I want to help him, but I don't drive. Would you mind taking me on some errands?"

Using the address from the camera store bag, Grace and Lena drove to Baton Rouge. The streets were so crowded. The city's infrastructure was swollen with evacuees, so the short trip took a long time.

After the pictures were developed and more film was purchased, they got back into the Eldorado. They each opened an envelope. Their hearts hurt. Is this what he had seen yesterday? Is this what he had endured? Agony. Exhaustion. Devastation. Filth. Death.

They traded stacks until they had both seen everything. Then they traded stacks again. It was like reading a complex poem over and over again. No way to comprehend it in just one read-through. By the time they'd finished, Lena and Grace, two strangers, were in tears, united in their grief and in their admiration for the photographer.

They regrouped then went to the grocery for food and water. After driving Lena home, Grace dropped some of Tom's photos off at *The Priory Post*. One of the editors was a high school classmate of hers. Although he was nearing retirement, he hadn't abandoned his position yet. Tom's photos were intense and raw. *The Post* promised to run them the next morning. Grace negotiated Tom's initial fee.

When Tom pulled up in front of Lena's after his second day of boating around New Orleans with Jacques, she was on the porch swing waiting for him. Someone else was sitting with her but he couldn't figure it out in the darkness. The earth seemed like a black hole, except for Lena's front porch. It glowed with the soft luster of a single gas lantern.

When he got out of his car, he recognized Nichelle. It dawned on him that she must've heard of his trips into their abandoned city. The city both of them had fled.

Lena approached and hugged Tom tightly. He kissed her on the cheek and brushed a strand of hair off her forehead. "Still no Mimi," he whispered.

He turned his attention to Nichelle. "Hey," he started. With an overloaded brain, he couldn't remember her name. Only that she was from the Ninth Ward and that she had a young daughter.

"Tom," Lena said quietly, afraid to disturb his unsettled eyes, "you remember Nichelle?"

He forced concentration. "Sure." Her face was familiar, but she seemed to have aged ten years in the last couple days.

Nichelle rose from the bench and smoothed her flowered cotton dress. She inched toward him but remained silent.

Lena continued, "Nichelle and I have been talking about what you've been doing in New Orleans."

Tom saw in the wreckage of Nichelle's face that she needed something.

"I just wanted to ask you…" Nichelle said, timidly. "Have you been to the Ninth Ward?"

He wondered if the truth was called for under these circumstances. It was hard to hide from the destruction, though, having been on round-the-clock news.

"Yeah. I've been there."

She couldn't find the voice to ask her next question, so Tom added, "Both our neighborhoods are under a lot of water."

She already knew, but she appreciated the way he had linked their fates. "You going back tomorrow?" As soon as she'd asked it, her eyes teared over.

He'd been debating that very issue on the drive home. Every muscle in his body was urging him to lie down on the sofa and stay there. Every corner of his subconscious said this was too much to endure.

"Yeah, I'm goin' back tomorrow."

When he said it, Lena reached out to hold on to the porch railing her father had carved.

Nichelle summoned her strength and drew closer to him. She handed him a scrap of paper with an address scrawled on it.

"My sister stayed there to ride out the storm," Nichelle said. "Her name is Demetra. Will you please, please look for her?"

He studied the note and its quiet desperation. It was scratchy and nearly illegible, like the phone number of his mysterious lunch date at the oyster bar less than two weeks ago.

His attention flipped back to that afternoon. At Big Monty's, they'd switched from beer to shots: Jäger Slippers, Irish Car Bombs, Sex on the Beach. They'd gone to her place, which smelled of expensive perfume, making Tom want to puke. She'd stripped her suit off to reveal a black lace bra and panty set that was filled out generously. They'd made out in animalistic fashion, rolling on the bed, biting and teasing. It had been sloppy and frenetic.

Tom remembered flesh and lace. She'd stripped his shirt off and unbuttoned his pants. Then he'd taken her with no regard for what might happen later. He'd made love to a woman who was pretty and friendly and maybe just the slightest bit desperate for someone to cling to. Like a thief who'd tricked his way in the front door, Tom had stolen things from that woman's soul. What he didn't realize at the time was that he'd also left part of himself behind.

Now, in his hand, he held yet another desperate and nearly illegible note. Tom silently swore that this time—this time he would take better care of the woman who'd written it.

He didn't want to make any promises to Nichelle. Didn't want to fill her with false hope. His own dwindling hopes were bad enough. And Tom couldn't explain how difficult it was to navigate even familiar neighborhoods. He couldn't express clearly that the flooded New Orleans didn't at all resemble the pre-Katrina New Orleans.

It didn't look the same or smell the same or feel the same. He and Jacques had to steer around stubs of street signs, if the metal plates came above water at all. Instead of Creole seasoning floating out of windows, the stench of rotting flesh permeated the heavy air. He dreaded going back to this city he didn't recognize, although it had been, until recently, the only place he'd ever wanted to be.

"I'll try," he said. "I can't promise anything, but I'll give it a shot. You have a picture of her?"

Nichelle shook her head and lowered her eyes. She didn't have much of anything. She hadn't brought any of her family photos with her. No reminders of Tyrell or Demetra, no black and white photos of her parents. Nothing.

"Tom," Nichelle said, "I need to tell you something."

He rubbed his hands through his black hair, trying to come to grips with all the mounting misery. When he motioned to the front step so Nichelle could sit down, she declined.

"Last week," she said, "I lost my only son. He was shot dead."

Even though he felt the stab of it, Tom didn't want to hear it. Not just because he couldn't stand any more heartbreak, but because he didn't want it to be true. "I'm sorry."

Nichelle's tears were flowing freely and she gasped in-between sentences. "My daughter and my sister's family are all I have left. If Demetra's not safe, I don't know what I'll do. It's not enough for Tamika to just have me. It's not enough for a young girl…"

The logistics of finding a woman he didn't know in an unfamiliar, flooded part of town were mind-boggling. It was a long shot. He knew instantly he would probably fail her, this woman who did not need more disappointment.

"I'll try to find her. I will. I'll do whatever I can."

"I'm gonna say a prayer for you," Nichelle said. "I know you don't think you can do it, but I got faith in you, Tom."

PRIORY, LOUISIANA

CHAPTER FORTY-SIX

One tension-filled day after the next passed at The Retreat. Everyone stayed as calm and collected as possible. No one yelled at the toddler or gave dirty looks to Olivia when the baby cried. Smiles were forced, if formed at all. Stomachs lurched. Pacing became the norm. But this could not be sustained forever.

Pacing gave way to visiting, and small moments of kindness were exchanged between total strangers. Ria Legrange read books to Tamika. Nichelle squeezed oranges for juice in the kitchen. Tad changed a light bulb on the back porch. Of course, it didn't hurt that Lucy and Becca were out there, thanking him profusely. Olivia spent time visiting her Yorkies at Henry's office. Then she'd volunteer to walk other dogs, too. Everyone had become exhausted from inactivity and dread.

Lafitte couldn't stand the constant stream on the television anymore. It was too much. He couldn't willingly bring any more pain into his psyche, so one day he went into the kitchen to cook a pot of pralines. The sugar boiled brown and gooey. He picked through pecans while standing at the counter. The scent of vanilla wafted through him, reminding him of his childhood. His mother cooked pralines whenever she was sad.

He stirred the pot and turned his thoughts to Lucy. Lucy with the enthusiastic eyes and the fabulous legs, who gave up her room so easily, and who might have kissed him while he slept. It was inappropriate, he knew. He was trying to keep his mind busy. She was way too young for him, and she certainly couldn't be considering him in a romantic way, but it was good to feel that pang again.

One by one, guests filtered into the kitchen, inhaling the intense sugary concoction. Ria sat at the kitchen table and talked about how much her mother loved to make macaroons with a homemade pecan extract, instead of the usual almond extract. Victor leaned against the burled linen press nearby. Tad joined the group, eating pecans off the counter, and said that his grandma crumbled pralines and sprinkled them on top of homemade vanilla ice cream. The elderly ladies rolled in and joined Ria at the table. Lafitte gave them the first pralines that were cool enough to eat.

Mary Bell, Tamika, and Nichelle entered through the swinging door, saw the assembled group, smelled the warm flesh of caramelized nuts, and wondered what all the quiet was about.

"What's up?" Mary Bell asked. Lafitte handed her a praline that was still firming up.

Lucy and Becca came in through the back screen door. They were sweaty and looked like they'd just come back from a run. Lafitte tried not to let his gaze rest too long on Lucy's sinewy body. The girls jumped up to sit on the granite countertop. Lafitte filled some small glasses with milk.

Victor spoke up. "It's been an honor riding out this storm with y'all. Being here with Mary Bell, in a home that's familiar to us, surrounded by caring people like yourselves, well, it's been very comforting. I can't imagine a finer group."

Ria smiled at him.

Mary Bell said, "All I know is: y'all are some of the most amazing people I've ever met. So resilient and kind. I just wish I could do more for you."

Nichelle put an arm around Mary Bell and squeezed her shoulder.

Breaking the mood, Becca said, "Oh, my gosh…" She was sitting next to the small television set suspended under the cabinet. Everyone huddled around it.

A dog was struggling in dark water somewhere in the storm-ravaged wasteland, fighting for its life. To Mary Bell, it appeared to be a Golden Retriever. It tried to swim to a concrete slab of some sort, but it couldn't climb out. The water was swirling and swollen and fast-moving.

"Where's the photographer?" Becca wondered.

"Yeah," Lucy agreed. "And why doesn't he put down the camera and rescue that dog?"

Oh, please save the dog, Mary Bell prayed. *Please save that poor dog.* Her thoughts turned to Henry and the long hours he'd been dedicating to the animals in his care. Henry would save the dog if he could. Her thoughts turned to Tom. Sure, Tom had been out there taking photos, but he would have put down the camera to save a life.

The Golden was whisked under the surface and out of sight. The camera stayed focused on the lapping waves for a few heart-pounding seconds. Then it was refocused to take in a panoramic view of the desolate, watery landscape. Maybe the cameraman had been further away than they thought.

Lafitte turned off the television.

One by one, they put down what morsels remained of their pralines. They thanked Lafitte in a quiet, reverential way. Within a minute, the kitchen was empty.

PRIORY, LOUISIANA

CHAPTER FORTY-SEVEN

Anger and exhaustion rode with Tom into New Orleans the next morning. Most of his aggression was aimed at God.

Why are you doing this? I mean, I really don't get why you let this kind of shit happen. Where's Mimi? Why won't you answer me?

If you are the Father and I am your son, like it says in the Bible, you should answer me. I would answer my child. This is ridiculous. You're totally ignoring me...

Tom wondered again if he himself had been the reason for this storm. Maybe he had wooed disaster and the destruction of New Orleans by recklessly pretending to be a man of God. In a self-centered slice of despair, Tom imagined himself as a magnetic force powerful enough to beckon a hurricane into the world, shattering the lives of loved ones and strangers alike.

I'm not up to this, Tom said. *Don't make me keep doing this. If I'm not gonna find Mimi, you tell me right now so I can make it stop.*

Tom's hands were shaking with exhaustion, fear, and anger. When he met up with Jacques again, he saw that it had taken a toll on both of them. Jacques' eyes were pink and half-closed.

To complicate things, the National Guard was flanking the entrance to Orleans Parish. The two men pled their case to the uniformed soldier, begging to rejoin the melee.

"There's snipers out there," the Guard warned.

Tom and Jacques looked at each other. They hadn't wanted to talk about it, but they'd both seen reports on the news. It hadn't happened to them.

"We've seen nuttin' like that," Jacques assured the Guard.

Armed with a boat and provisions instead of guns and bad intentions, they were allowed to pass.

Jacques agreed to help find Demetra, so they trolled in the general direction of the Ninth Ward. They rescued an old black man with a pasty mouth from a steaming rooftop. The smell of melted tar was sickening, and the man lay so still, they feared the stranger was dead. He hadn't even flinched when their boat approached. Tom felt his skin. It was hot and sweaty. Jacques poured water into the man's mouth, and he spurted to consciousness. They lifted him up and lay him in the boat.

"Sir," Tom said. "Sir, are you alright?"

The man blinked in recognition. Tom put Nichelle's scratchy piece of paper in front of the man's face. "Do you know where this is?"

The rescued man squinted, blinked, and nodded. "Couple doors down," he rasped.

Tom looked to the surrounding rooftops. There was an apartment building that seemed to be a couple doors down, but the open windows were void of faces or arms or signs of life.

"Who you lookin' for?" the old man asked.

"Demetra Jones. You know her?"

The man nodded. Tom's heart raced. "Have you seen her?"

The man shook his head and closed his eyes.

"I'm sorry, sir. Sorry to keep bothering you, but did she live in that apartment building?" Tom pointed to the brick three-story. Two stories were above water.

The man opened his eyes, squinted, nodded, and closed them again.

Tom and Jacques trolled over to the apartment building. Jacques killed the motor and Tom yelled out, "Anybody in there?" Nothing. "Anybody there?"

No answer, except the splashing of their created waves against brick, seeping into missing mortar joints.

"Stay here, Tom," Jacques said.

Jacques tied up to the frame of an open window and climbed in, shrimp boots first. Tom tended to the weak man and prayed for him. It was the first time Tom remembered praying for an individual he didn't know. He'd said prayers before for "poor people" or "homeless people" but never for "this man who might be dying in our boat."

Please don't let him die in this boat. This whole thing sucks, and I know I don't know him, but I can't imagine he deserves to die like this. No one does.

The longer Jacques was gone, the more Tom's ears rang with fear. Finally, Jacques' double-billed cap reappeared.

"Ain't nobody in there," Jacques said, panting. "They must've all gone."

Tom didn't see anyone else on neighboring rooftops. There was no one else to ask. No one named Demetra to rescue.

Another harrowing day in the stifling heat was almost spent, and Tom wondered whether or not he could press on. They'd seen more than one floating body that day, and he had thrown up over the side of the boat. Besides his own vomit, what other volume of human fluids and excrement were stirred into this disgusting bath? His throat was raw, his skin was sunburned, and he had a pounding headache. He began wondering about disgusting things like: why do all the dead bodies seem to be face down?

In the distance, Tom saw a fire light the horizon, almost like a flame rising from an oil refinery stack, except that black smoke billowed skyward. It seemed to be coming from a building in Gentilly, and he wondered whether it was gas-related or man-made. *This place is a God-forsaken mess.* Looking skyward he said aloud, "You have abandoned New Orleans."

Jacques shook his head. "Dat ain't true. He doesn't abandon no one. It's just hard to find Him now and again."

Tom couldn't stop thinking about Mimi. They'd searched for her in every exhausted crowd, on every populated rooftop, in every open window. Each time they saw a white-haired woman, and it wasn't Mimi, he grew more hopeless.

After a couple of days of photography, Tom wondered whether he should have been taking black and white pictures instead of color. Most the pictures were devoid of color anyway. They contained ashen faces, black smoke, pewter sky, graying corpses. Things were shriveled, distorted, shrouded. The humidity even drenched the air with a leaden mist.

In the distance, Tom heard the sound of what seemed to be a million flapping birds. He and Jacques watched helicopters approach. It was the Coast Guard. Tom was relieved they'd finally shown up, but the whoosh of wind off their blades played havoc with

Jacques' small boat. Hot sheets of air swooped down from the 'copters and tossed the pirogue viciously, as if it was being attacked by ocean swells. The stew became impossible to navigate. Tom's ears were buzzing, and his body was deteriorating. Both men agreed: they were finished.

They trolled back to the pickup and loaded the pirogue one last time. The dull scrape of metal on metal sounded like a vault door closing. Before parting ways, the men shared an emotional embrace.

"Keep in touch, you hear?" Jacques said.

Tom nodded. This Cajun was one of the finest men he'd ever met. If Tom wasn't so exhausted, he'd have wanted to go straight to Jacques' house for dinner.

Instead, Tom drove back to Priory. Later, he couldn't recall the drive itself. He couldn't account for the time. When he pulled up in front of Lena's, he was dripping with sweat. Or was it floodwater? Or someone else's sweat? His memory was gone. His thinking had become circular and confusing.

A trio of women—Lena, Nichelle, and Grace—welcomed him back to Priory. Nichelle came down from the porch first. He touched her upper arm. "Not many people left in Lower Nine," he said, defeated. "So sorry."

Nichelle thanked him in a hushed voice, then stepped into the street and walked back toward The Retreat and Tamika. She kicked stones illuminated by moonlight. The moon painted them purple, blue, gray, silver. Concentrating on the act of kicking these stones felt therapeutic. It briefly masked the fear that she might never eat, sleep soundly, or hear her sister's voice again. As Tom watched her walk away, he was heavy with sorrow and a sense of failure.

Grace and Lena were sitting on the top step. He approached them, put one foot on the bottom step, and stayed there. Standing here in the sweet air of Priory, he realized how badly he reeked. It was an unidentifiable stench so he kept his distance.

After giving a few brief details of his journey, Tom asked how everything had gone in Priory while he'd been away. Lena picked *The Priory Post* up off the porch floor and handed it to him. It was then he noticed how grimy his hands and nails were.

He tried to ignore his filth because in smudgy gray ink on flimsy newsprint was a photo he'd taken with his Secret Agent camera. It was above the fold on the front page. A distraught woman clutched her dead infant against her breast. *Was it an ink smudge on the baby's lifeless cheek?* Maybe it was a fly. He couldn't remember. What he did remember clearly was the far-away look on the mother's face. How rigid the baby was. How the woman kept talking to the child, saying everything would be okay.

Tom didn't want to experience success during this unbearable situation. He didn't deserve it. It wasn't his time. His grandmother was still missing. His house was under water. He couldn't find Demetra.

A second picture was just below the fold. It was a woman in a housecoat sitting on her roof, surrounded by littered blackness, her peppery hair a wiry tangle. Hammer in hand and a self-made hole whacked in her patchy roof. This survivor was not afraid to save herself from the forces of nature or ill-intentioned men.

PRIORY, LOUISIANA

"Grace knows someone at *The Post*," Lena said. "They love your work, Tom. They want more."

Tom had plenty more, but he wished he didn't.

Grace rose and walked down the steps, past Tom. She stood in the middle of the road, staring down the path Nichelle had walked, as if Nichelle might change her mind and come back.

"Thanks, Grace," Tom said, summoning every ounce of strength. He felt like he was going to pass out, like he'd had one too many shots of absinthe. It was nearly impossible to stand up straight.

"You're welcome, Padre." Grace flicked her spent cigarette to the ground and blew a stream of smoke from her wrinkled lips. Tom stood next to her and draped an arm across her shoulder.

"Grace," he said wearily, "haven't we lost enough people already?" He flattened the cigarette butt. She smiled and bumped him away with her hip before getting into her Eldorado and driving off.

Lena helped Tom inside. He'd grown weaker and more hunched over each day. He collapsed on the sofa and put his head in her lap. She caressed his forehead, which was ablaze with fever. Tom's eyes were closed, and he began muttering about how this was all his fault. He'd seen Mimi… God was punishing him…

Tom mumbled something about the missing birds, the damned cell phone lines, Katrina taunting him…

Lena slid out from underneath him, covered him with a sheet, and called Doc Wilson. Doc drove over in his chocolate Caddy, doctor's kit in tow. He gave Tom an antibiotic, ibuprofen, and a sleeping pill.

"Don't you worry, now, missy," Doc said. "He'll sleep comfortably for a while, and then I'll check him out good tomorrow."

Lena nodded and forced a smile.

"I don't know who he is," Doc continued, peering over his glasses, "but he must be pretty special if you're taking care of him."

A warm hug was exchanged between the doctor and his long-time patient. When he left, she sat on the edge of the sofa and brushed Tom's matted black hair off his sweaty brow.

"Please don't take him from me," she said, certain Tom wouldn't hear. Even though his body was trying to fight a malicious infection, his soul registered her plea.

PRIORY, LOUISIANA

CHAPTER FORTY-EIGHT

When Hurricane Katrina waved her destructive arms across New Orleans, and the levee along the 17th Street Canal gave up its fight to hold the water at bay, a silent liquid enemy spread through Lakeview.

Mimi positioned a chair under the attic door, splashing murky water. The oily bath and surrounding air temperatures were almost the same. She couldn't tell which parts of her body were submerged and which were not. Everything smelled wrong, sounded wrong, tasted wrong: too sour, too quiet, too bitter.

She pulled herself up onto the chair. Poised like a marble statue in a fountain, with one foot on the chair and the second one in mid-air, Mimi felt the chair slide out from underneath her.

She watched from outside herself as she fell hip-first into the water, hitting the edge of a floating table. Pain shot through her body. Dirk's picture disappeared into the pungent blackness and although she was now dizzy with confusion and heat and fear, she was even more frantic at having lost his face.

"Dirk, where are you?" Salty tears cut through the grime on her terrified cheeks. She tried to keep her head above water while feeling around for the picture frame. Her lower body was immobile, but her hands found the silver frame, and she clutched it to her breast.

The water rose in Mimi's home until it reached her rafters. On that swollen August day, Mimi found Dirk, not just a black-and-white photo of him, in a stream of cold air, hovering high above her home.

PRIORY, LOUISIANA

Mornin', Y'all *Monday, September 5, 2005*

"*Mornin', Y'all.* This is Melody Melançon and you're listening to WPRY 90.5, bringing you and your mama up-to-date on the latest in Priory.

I'm sorry I've been off the air for a few days, y'all. It's a bad time to be out of pocket, but I could not help it. I will explain in a minute.

For those of you who showed up at the Library to talk hurricanes with me, I thank y'all. It helped me to re-center. Y'all always make things better for me. Randy and I truly enjoyed your company. We had a couple dozen people show up. I laughed and I cried. It was the perfect tonic, just like that spoonful of bourbon and orange juice my mama used to give me for a cough.

For those of you who got battered by the hurricane, we are all praying for you. Katrina was even worse than we ever imagined. My stars, it's been so hard to grasp. The Gulf Coast is shredded and New Orleans is still underwater one week later. When will this all end? Only the good and mysterious Lord knows.

As for the past few days, for me, it has been full of sadness of another sort. My beautiful friend, Darla, who was working so hard at battling breast cancer, died of a heart attack the evening after we went to the Library. Doctors say that the chemo weakened her ticker.

I think maybe God was just wanting Darla to be closer to Him. That's His right anyway, you know.

And I can't blame Him. Everyone wanted sweet Darla to be closer to them. But I am missing her something awful.

Y'all will love this, though. Do you know what her family buried Darla in? Upon her head was a white knit cap that had silver flecks in it, crafted by our very own Priory Knitting Circle. And I tell you she looked like an angel in it.

We are all suffering these days, in one way or another, but it will bring us closer and make us stronger. Hang in there, y'all. Do what you can to find comfort.

Randy's at home right now baking me a chocolate pecan pie with some homemade whipped cream. That can't make my sadness go away, but I will love it anyway. And it can't hurt.

That's it for now. But remember, if you're not listening to *Mornin', Y'all*, you might as well be living on Mars."

CHAPTER FORTY-NINE

At The Retreat, guests were making plans for their immediate futures: plans that needed to span future months, not days. Hurricane evacuees usually left home for less than a week before returning. With this storm, normalcy was nowhere in sight.

The coeds were going back East. Schools across the country embraced displaced students, so their parents contacted East Coast colleges, securing them much-appreciated, tuition-free educations at other universities for the semester.

Tad and Olivia made arrangements to rent a house in Baton Rouge, one that allowed small dogs. They wanted to be close enough to New Orleans to return when they could. They'd be grateful to discover later that they had only a few broken windows and some peeling shingles. Most of their renovations and belongings were intact. Their car had been stolen from their driveway, but that seemed like only a nuisance at this point, so they counted themselves lucky.

After many pleading phone calls from Mary Bell, the two elderly women were able to find an assisted living facility in Shreveport to take them in. Lafitte drove them there, relieved nothing had happened to them during their stay at The Retreat. The older woman wasn't looking so good, like she had flat-out given up. No one had ever died on-property. Lafitte didn't want the place to be haunted. His own demons didn't need company.

The Legranges stayed on because it wasn't possible to go back to Pass Christian. According to news reports, the Mississippi Gulf Coast was almost completely destroyed. Bridges were gone. Only a handful of houses survived. Ria and Victor clung to the slim hope that Ria's ancestral home had won the lottery.

Their son, Charles, finally reached them by phone. He was in Jackson, Mississippi, staying with a college buddy. Ria was relieved but worried because he sounded off-kilter. She asked him if he needed money and he said, "No," in a strange tone of voice. *Charles doesn't need money?* He never refused an offer like that. It was hard to process anything these days after spinning through their endless swirl of despair, but at least Charles was safe.

Nichelle and Tamika didn't make any plans. They had nowhere else to go.

CHAPTER FIFTY

Whatever menacing bug had gotten into Tom's system had been exorcised by Doc Wilson, but it had taken a couple of weeks. And lots of drugs. He grew healthier each day until he was finally able to sit up and think clearly.

"Ma?" he asked softly when he finally called his parents.

Sylvia sobbed at the sound of his voice. "Oh, Tom, thank God." She tried to catch her breath, but it was scratchy and wheezy. "I've been trying to reach you forever."

Tom let her cry for a while before he said anything else. He was thinking. Thinking of what to say. He couldn't tell her about his false priesthood. If he told her about his boat trips back home or his desperate attempts to find Mimi, she might lose it.

"I know, Ma. Sorry. I've been sick, but I'm okay."

She sniffled and took a deep breath, then laid her hand upon her chest and tried to talk again. "You're still in Priory?"

"Yeah."

"Tom…have you heard from Mimi?"

His stomach twisted like wet laundry. "No. Have you?"

"No. Your sister posted Mimi's picture on an Internet site for people missing since the storm. We haven't heard anything, though."

"Great idea." Tom was surprised he hadn't thought of that himself, but he hadn't been able to think in a straight line since the storm. "How's Rachel doin'?"

"She's a little frustrated at being so far away from all of us right now. You know, survivor's guilt. She offered to come to Natchez, but getting from D.C. to Mississippi is not that easy. Besides, what's she going to do here?"

"Yeah."

"I told her I thought you were still in Priory and she seemed surprised. Where are you staying, hon?"

He hesitated, but not for long. Cell phone lines were still spotty, and he needed to tell her the truth.

"I met someone, Ma. A woman. She's really sweet."

Sylvia felt a twinge of self-satisfaction. When she heard he'd left town, she'd figured there was a woman involved. It was a relief to know he wasn't alone. "You did? Who is she?"

"Her name's Lena Melendez, and she lives here in Priory. I'm staying with her right now. I guess I'll be here for awhile."

Tom gave his mom the phone number, and the basic depth of his relationship. He was crazy about the girl, but it hadn't gotten very far.

"Y'all are living together? Already?" Her tone was accusatory.

"Not exactly. I'm stayin' at her house."

"Well, I'm so glad you've met someone. I can hardly wait to tell your Father."

"She's the best."

"We've got news, too, hon."

"You do?"

"Yes. Your dad's going to New Orleans to look for Mimi."

Tom couldn't process what she'd just said. His father, a man of many words and few actions, was not the kind of man to remove his white linen suit and trudge about a storm-ravaged wasteland.

"Dad's goin' to New Orleans? Is the water gone?"

"Well, mostly. It's down, anyway. They're still pumping, but Lakeview's reachable. They're being very careful, though, about who they're letting into the city and for how long."

His mom's voice sounded strange now. It was a higher pitch than she usually carried. There was a fake bounce to it that was odd.

She continued, "Your dad wants to get Mimi and bring her back here to Natchez."

Alive or dead? Tom wanted to ask, but he knew she didn't have the answer anymore than he did.

"Is Dad there?" he asked. "Can I talk to him?"

"He's not here right now. He's out walking Bitsy. She's been a nervous wreck. We've never kept her away from home so long. It took us a week to find the dog food she's used to. You know, Natchez is so small…"

Tom looked out Lena's front window. She was pulling weeds from the garden along the walkway. How could life here still look so normal?

His mom went on, "We're going to have to move out of this inn and rent a house. It looks like our stay here will be longer than we—or anyone—anticipated. Maybe that'll be better for Bitsy. I don't know."

Tom wished he could be at his mother's side, to look into her eyes, to see if she was as unstable as she sounded. "So, Dad's headed home? When?"

"As soon as he comes back in from walking the dog. He says he's going to look everywhere for Mimi.

Then he's going to check our house to make sure no one's burnt it to the ground or looted it."

Ahh. Now that makes more sense, Tom thought. *That sounds like Dad.*

Richard Vaughn had been in contact with a neighbor who'd ridden out the storm. The majority of Uptown and the Garden District were high and dry. No one had looted his house, and it hadn't caught on fire, but he wanted to see it for himself. His son wasn't giving him as much credit as he deserved. His primary focus *was* finding his mother-in-law. Mimi had been generous and entertaining and, Richard thought, what more could a man want?

Tom got off the phone and went over to the computer in the corner of Lena's sitting room. He'd been out of it for so long that he'd lost touch with the rest of the world. It didn't take long for him to search and find the picture Rachel had posted of Mimi, a cropped snapshot from the previous Christmas. So far, no one had posted anything below the pictures. Staring at the grainy photo, his pulse began to quicken.

Into the search bar, he typed, "Demetra Jones." He focused on the glowing screen and waited.

While Tom searched for Demetra again—this time in cyberspace—his dad drove one hundred and thirty miles back to New Orleans with dreams of finding Mimi.

Richard followed the very specific orders being broadcast about what proof you had to carry and what hours you had to keep so you didn't get harassed by the National Guard or the NOPD.

The temporary order to allow people back into New Orleans was issued for daylight hours only.

Residents were supposed to gather their belongings and leave again. The electricity had not yet been restored, there were no working phone lines, and no running water.

Richard headed straight for Lakeview, hoping to find Mimi's house empty. By the time he reached Canal Street, it was impossible to drive further. Debris filled the streets: trees, trash, people's belongings, hazards of every imaginable size. Mounds and mounds of unidentifiable muck. It was all baking in the late summer sun into crispy, crusty, mountainous heaps.

He parked his car and walked through a dry, cracked dirt overlay. In some places, it was difficult to discern that there was a street underneath it all. It was a steamy day. His polo shirt was soaked with humidity. Richard, normally calm and cool, could barely stand the sight of it. Lakeview was a barren wasteland. It looked as if it had endured a massive carpet-bombing. If Mimi were not still missing, he would've turned around and left.

Each house was devastated in its own way. One brick home was sliced horizontally in two and stacked unevenly back upon itself. A battered shrimp boat had settled in someone's front yard. Windows were shattered; rooftops were missing; trees were uprooted. Pieces of brown grass and filth were dried upon the sides of buildings up to the water line, just above the first floors, at the gutter-line on ranches.

The smell singed his nostrils as if he had placed his face above a burning flame.

The devastation was overwhelming. It was more severe than he had imagined. TV hadn't relayed the full impact. It couldn't. Destruction tied itself around Richard Vaughn's ankle like a sandbag.

When he reached Mimi's, he saw the axe-hacked roof. His heart leapt in his chest. Could she have escaped? She was a salty old girl. Maybe she had persevered.

He summoned every ounce of adrenaline in his body and kicked open Mimi's water-swollen, rust-colored door. The stench shrieked out, stabbed at his lungs, and made his innards convulse. Although he had never experienced it before, he felt certain that it was the odor of rotting flesh. He turned away from it and doubled over.

After regaining his composure, and saying a quick prayer, Richard turned again toward the house. He crossed the threshold and gasped. He felt like he was choking on the thick air. Furniture had been completely rearranged. Most of it had fallen apart after sitting in a poisonous bath for too long. Pictures were missing from the walls. The ceiling and walls were covered in spotty mildew. Sheetrock was peeling in some places, completely absent in others. The floor was warped and buckled.

But the odor. The odor Richard smelled that day would haunt him for the rest of his life. It seeped into his pores, became one with his flesh, and would forever refuse to leave him. It crept up on him later while he was doing mundane, daily tasks: driving to work, watching a Saints game, walking in Audubon Park. The resurfacing stench would send him into a bout of depression or a momentary despair. Even taking a long, hot shower could sometimes not rid him of the smell. There was no way to wash it away from the place it had become lodged.

Richard stumbled out of the Lakeview home and heaved onto a pile of broken glass and desiccated mush. He struggled, hinged forward at the waist, to the half-missing curb for cleaner air. Cleaner air was nowhere to be found.

Goddammit, Richard thought. He didn't want to go back in. He didn't want to push around all that filth and look for Mimi. If she was in there, what state of matter would her body be in by now?

He grabbed a big branch from the front lawn. A rat ran out from underneath it and into a pile of branches nearby. Richard glared at the rat with contempt before trudging into the house. Using the termite-eaten branch, he pushed around parts of decomposed cabinets, molded fabric, and morphed items he could not identify. He willed his feet to move forward, willed his arms to work against his soul.

He used that massive foe—the odor of Mimi's remains—to find her. What was left of her was under the disintegrated china cabinet. Richard's throat closed up. Tears poured from his already swollen eyes.

Goddammit.

An unbroken crystal goblet, filthy but whole, lay next to her. How could such a delicate thing have been spared when Mimi had been wasted? Richard picked it up, glared at it, then hurled it across the room. It shattered against the mildewed wall and cascaded into the rubble.

Now that he knew Mimi's fate, how was he going to tell Sylvia? What was he going to do with Mimi?

He wished answers fell from the sky like rain.

PRIORY, LOUISIANA

CHAPTER FIFTY-ONE

Mary Bell approached Nichelle in the dining room the day after everyone else left. It was quiet in The Retreat now: a sad, uneasy quiet.

"Any news about Demetra?"

"No, no news. Still no answer on her cell." Nichelle poured a glass of orange juice for Tamika.

"I know the towers in New Orleans are overloaded or underwater or both…" Mary Bell said, "but I hear that every once in awhile, someone gets through."

Nichelle nodded.

Just then, there was a rap on the front windowpane. Tom was standing there, grinning widely, pressing a piece of paper against the glass, chest-high.

Goose bumps rose up Nichelle's legs from her ankles to her ample thighs. "Oh, my God." She looked at Tamika, and then slowly stood up to cross the room. She hoped to see Demetra's face on that piece of paper. Instead, when she reached the window, she saw a picture of herself.

Tom pulled the paper away from the glass and walked in the front door.

"It's not Demetra?" she asked him shakily.

"No, Nichelle, it's you."

She looked confused until she read the print under her photo. "Missing: Nichelle Taylor. Please, please, please, look for my sister. I can't find her nowhere. Last seen leaving New Orleans. If you have any info, contact me at the Red Cross shelter in Houston at the number below. Many, many thanks. Demetra Jones."

Nichelle hugged Tom as hard as she could until they were both laughing like kids.

The next few weeks passed quickly. After Demetra and Nichelle had enjoyed a tearful, long conversation, Nichelle had been granted one evening of sound sleep. If she hadn't been dreaming so much about Tyrell in the following days, she might have been able to hope for more uninterrupted slumber. But she was grateful to get what she could. And grateful to know that she and Tamika were not alone in this world.

Uncertain about how long she'd be staying at The Retreat, Nichelle began helping with light chores. She didn't want to feel like a freeloader. Mary Bell and Lafitte were as kind to them as the days were long, and they deserved some help in return.

One morning, Nichelle was sweeping the front porch and humming a song from church, using a swishing broom against the wooden floor as her instrument. It was a soothing, transcendent moment that she tucked inside herself.

She stopped sweeping and humming, and turned her attention to the front yard where Tamika was jumping rope with a neighbor girl. Tamika's numerous braids danced in the air like the weightless arms of a sea anemone.

Mother and daughter had been through so much turmoil, but here was a moment of unexpected serenity and beauty. If only she knew what to do about the future. She couldn't return to New Orleans. It was a mess. In the Ninth Ward, there was still no electricity or running water.

The screen door creaked, and Henry came outside.

"Morning, Nichelle."

"Mornin'."

Henry looked out to the front lawn and smiled at Tamika. She was good at jumping rope, and she looked like a child should: happy and carefree. Even if her happiness was only fleeting, maybe that was a good start. If she could string enough happy moments together, Henry thought, things might be okay.

"We're still so busy at the hospital these days," he said. "Overwhelmed, really."

Over the swooshing of the broom, he continued, "Looks like we might have some of these animals for a long time. People who can't go home are wanting to leave their pets with us indefinitely. Sure could use some help."

She stopped sweeping and looked at him.

"Know anybody I might hire?" he asked, turning his focus again toward Tamika and the neighbor girl.

Nichelle's dark eyes followed his.

"Father Abelli says they've got room for Tamika if you've got a mind to send her to Catholic school. Said he wouldn't charge you anything, either, 'til you get on your feet."

"A job, huh?"

Henry nodded.

"And a school?"

"A great little school," he answered.

Her cheeks grew rosy buds. "Well, praise the Lord."

"I don't know how long we'll need you," he said. "At some point, people will get settled and come back to get their pets. Could be temporary."

She thought about that briefly. "I understand," she said. "Temporary's all I got. We're just passing through *this* world, Henry."

He held out his hand, but Nichelle answered with a sweaty kiss on the cheek.

CHAPTER FIFTY-TWO

Ria tried not to obsess about her Gulf-front home. She was grateful, she kept saying, just to be alive. They were both relieved Charles had fled to safety. And even though there was a strong chance her family home had been destroyed, they hadn't shed tears over it. An odd detachment had crept into them. They found the television images to be disconnected from their world. The pictures were too rectangular, too flat, too big-budget-movie-ish to belong to them.

Mary Bell's parents returned to Priory. It was a welcome diversion for Ria and Victor. The old friends took walks together, made lavish dinners, and hoped for the best.

One night, sitting underneath the magnolia in the Bateau's backyard, the four old friends sipped cocktails and watched the sky dim, become psychedelic, then darken. In the heat of the evening, they reminisced about days gone by: double dates, trips to North Carolina, the birth of their children.

When the laughter died down and the crickets had the air to themselves, it was hard to keep up the charade.

Marcel Bateau broke the silence, trying to keep the mood festive. "I've got an interesting tidbit for y'all."

Faces opened. Marcel pulled his pants up higher on his belly and rubbed his balding head. "I think y'all will find this very interesting indeed, especially you, darlin'." He winked at Mary Bell's mother.

"What is it, Marcel?" Gigi wanted to know.

He continued, cheeks filling and emptying like bagpipes. "I was paid a polite visit today by a certain handsome veterinarian."

"They're a lovely couple," Ria said. "He's been doting on her since we came to town. What did he say?"

Marcel attempted to lean forward in his chair. Pretending to whisper in a voice that could've been heard in the next parish, he said, "He asked for my permission to propose."

Ria touched Gigi's arm. Victor grinned and shook his friend's hand, "Congrats, old man."

"Thank you, thank you."

Gigi and Ria embraced and held the pose, letting love and concern flow between their pressed cheeks. Gigi's sparkling eyes met her husband's.

"Marcel," Gigi said, her dyed black hair reflecting moonlight, "do you think you should've told us?"

Marcel lifted his crystal glass and said, "If ever there was a time when we needed good news, this is it."

"Yes, this is it," Ria agreed.

She and Victor looked at each other with an underlying pain that was hard to mask. They tried to put on a celebratory air for their friends, but their eyes were too darkened with the smear of loss and worry to make it look realistic. Charles' own future engagement seemed to be in some otherworldly time zone, not pending and fortunate like Mary Bell's.

It was hard not to be envious of the Bateau's good fortune and intact house.

The friends rose from their chairs, clinked glassware, and took a cool sip before heading for the comfort of the air-conditioned house.

"Now, don't forget," Marcel said, "this is our little secret. Mary Bell mustn't know. He wants to surprise her…"

They walked through the back screen door.

Marcel continued his story, even as they were placing crystal on the granite counter. "Victor, do you know what Henry's last question to me was?"

Victor smiled. He never knew what was coming next from Marcel. "No, what?"

"He said, 'Mr. Bateau, if Mary Bell and I marry, what would you like me to call you?'"

Victor waited for the answer.

Marcel replied, "I said, '*Sir*, would be nice.'"

The old friends laughed and headed up the intricately carved staircase. Within the week, Henry was on one knee in Priory's Rose Garden.

CHAPTER FIFTY-THREE

When people were finally allowed to return to The Pass, Ria and Victor made plans to meet Charles at home. It was hard to get to Pass Christian, though. Bridges were wiped out, roads were debris-filled, and the closer they got to water, the worse things were.

At first, they saw common but depressing hurricane sites: roofs off, trees down, windows shattered. As they got closer to the Gulf, whole homes were gone. Chunks of concrete and errant bricks were commonplace.

The beach road appeared on the horizon. They were still at least half a mile from it, but there weren't any homes blocking their view.

Ria gasped. Goose bumps crawled up her legs, burrowed under the skin on her back, and pricked her forearms. Her throat swelled. Tears filled her eyes.

The dread that had been building within them surfaced. There were no homes left on their stretch of the Gulf. Not a single one. It was unbelievable. News reports had been hard to grasp. Pictures in the newspaper were impossible to identify.

Now, in person, it was terrifying. How could so many homes and businesses just disappear? Did they disintegrate? Did they evaporate? No. Shredded wreckage littered every inch of ground, and in that rubble were remnants of people's lives.

It would have been hard for visitors to guide their way with no buildings as landmarks, but the Legranges had driven these roads many times.

PRIORY, LOUISIANA

When they saw Charles' car sitting in front of an empty lot, there was no doubt. It was parked in front of their brick walkway, next to a few puzzled steps, and a naked foundation.

Where had everything else gone? The family photographs? The leaded doors? The heirloom rugs? The antiques? Everything had vanished. Nature had looted their home in an unrepentant fashion, strewing tiny, indistinguishable pieces of it about the coastline for miles. Maybe some of it had even gotten caught up into the swirling twister of the hurricane and landed in other states, in people's backyards, or out to sea.

When they got out of their car and saw their stately oaks, as dry and lifeless as if they had been infested by termites, they braced each other. It would never be the same in their lifetimes. Even if the house could be rebuilt, the oaks were two hundred years old. It would be generations from now before this land grew oaks so magnificent.

Tears flowed in torrents, stinging their eyelids like a swarm of bees. Ria gasped for air, as if Katrina had reappeared and was trying to drown her.

Victor helped her sit down on the steps, putting his arm around her. She had always been strong, so able to handle all of life's challenges. Now she needed him, for the first time in ages.

Charles had been watching them from his car, uncertain what he might say. He had rehearsed different versions of the same speech over the past few weeks. Each one hopelessly inadequate.

He walked over and huddled with them, grieving over their collective loss. Charles backed away, trembling. His parents sat on the Steps To Nowhere.

"Mom, I'm sorry about the house. Houses, I should say. Mine's gone, too."

Ria raised her eyes to him.

He continued, "I know how much you loved this place. I wish there was something I could do."

"Thanks, hon," she said, suddenly trying to suck the tears back in. She instantly wanted to console Charles for the loss of the home he would never be able to inherit.

Charles put his hands into the pockets of his khaki shorts. "I don't know how to say this," Charles said, trembling. His face was contorting in a way that frightened his mother. Victor kept his hand on Ria's back. Charles' brow was furrowed. The outer edges of his eyes sagged.

"I have something for you," Charles said.

He went to his car and retrieved the writer's journal his parents had given him. Its pages were wavy. Ria's heart leapt. Empty pages didn't possess that much bulk.

She opened the cover. Charles' handwriting was unmistakable:

It was in my childhood home, a home that smelled of peach muffins, reflected salty waves, and entertained Gulf breezes, that I betrayed my mother.

Ria's eyes darted up to his. The journal was full of his handwriting. She wanted to read the rest, but didn't even understand the beginning. Tremors ran down the left side of her body, and she briefly thought she might be having a heart attack.

Charles reached into his pocket and came out with a fist. His mom held her hand open under his. He lowered the strand of pearls into hers like the pooling of a waterfall.

Her mother's pearls. She'd recognize them anywhere. Ria had worn them to Charles' christening. She gasped.

Victor spoke for her. "Charles, where did you get these?"

"From the attic safe."

Ria looked over her shoulder at the empty foundation. She needed the visual reminder that it was gone. She tried to imagine the exact space in the air where the safe would have been.

"I took them from the attic safe," he repeated.

"Safe" didn't seem like such an appropriate word for that device anymore, considering its complete disappearance from their property.

She turned her face back toward his.

"Charles, you saved them," Ria said, her voice softening.

"No, Mom, it wasn't like that."

Ria didn't want to guess the circumstances.

Charles refused to be a hero. "I stole them, Mom, to sell at a pawn shop."

Victor was furious but kept it in check. How could he do this to them after everything they had given him?

"Charles," Ria said, staring at her mother's pearls, "you *didn't* sell them. And now, they're all I have left of hers." Turning her red eyes up again to her son, she reiterated, "You saved them."

A lump thickened in Charles' throat. "I took more than that."

Ria's eyes grew large and hopeful. "You did?"

"I did," Charles said, with such sadness in his voice that Ria's upper lids grew heavy.

She couldn't speak, couldn't ask the unimaginable.

"Charles, what…" Victor began.

"I had a few drinks the day I left here. I know it's not a good excuse. I… I sold a bunch of stuff because I'd already spent everything you gave me, and I didn't want to ask for more."

No one comforted him.

"I'm sorry."

No one absolved him.

The lapping of the Gulf waves wasn't as soothing as it used to be.

The threesome looked out to the water, wondering where the sense was in all this. Wondering how one storm could rearrange their world.

Ria put on her mother's pearls, clutched the journal to her chest, and turned her eyes to the Gulf.

CHAPTER FIFTY-FOUR

"Son, I'm sorry to have to tell you, but Mimi is dead."

Tom had suspected it, but hearing his father say the words was a necessary conclusion. It had been hard to dismiss the very real possibility after standing in his blistering attic, staring into the watery abyss of their home.

"I figured she was," Tom said solemnly. "I went there, Dad."

Tom poured the whole story out to his father, in an uncharacteristically open fashion. He told about meeting Jacques, riding in the boat, hacking away the roof, and staring into the hole. He talked about rescuing the neighbors, snapping photos, and recovering from the infection. He told his father that he had fallen in love in Priory.

It was more than he had ever revealed to his dad before, but Tom couldn't seem to stop the flow. In some ways, reliving the experience was horrible and exasperating. It was also therapeutic and liberating. During this conversation, Richard was quiet. By the time Tom was finished, an uncomfortable silence set in.

"Dad?"

His dad didn't say anything. Then Tom heard sniffling. Then all-out crying. He'd never seen or heard his father cry before. Never.

"Dad, are you okay?"

After regaining his composure, Richard said, "You sound so much older…so much older than the last time I saw you."

Tom didn't know what to say.

"Thank you," his dad added, "for trying to find her."

"I should have gone back before the storm."

"No. I should have insisted she come with us."

Tom rubbed his eyes with his fingertips. A long pause followed.

"I love you, son." The simple sentence caught Tom off-guard. He leaned his head back to rest it on the sofa cushion.

"Love you, too, Dad."

Tom and Richard ended their conversation. The younger Vaughn curled up on the sofa and fell asleep. His entire being was heavy with fatigue. Each heartfelt conversation, long walk, or new image of devastation exhausted Tom as if he'd run the Crescent City Classic. Doc Wilson said he was lucky to be alive. Doc said that many people who'd caught infections post-storm had died. Although he was weak, at least Tom was still alive.

He kept mulling over the finality of Mimi's death. His anger at losing her wouldn't fall away. It built upon itself like a forest fire until it could no longer be contained. God had abandoned him in his hour of need, and he was angry.

One day, he stormed the steps of the rectory behind Our Lady of Good Hope. The gentle Father Abelli opened the door.

"Do you believe in God?" Tom questioned.

Father knew better than to respond.

"I mean *really* believe in Him, even when all signs point to his non-existence…"

"Why don't you come in?"

"No. I don't think I will."

Tom turned and walked out into the woods, the same woods where he had found solace with Lena. Now, instead of enjoying their shaded paths, they heightened his dark mood. He kept wishing for a bench to sit on.

That night, he called Jacques.

"Hey, man, how ya doin'?" Jacques asked.

Tom didn't hesitate. He wanted the telling of it to be over. "My grandma's dead, Jacques. My father found her. She was in the house."

Silence. Wrenched guts. Tom's heart beat so loudly he heard it in his own eardrum.

"Aw, man. I'm really sorry 'bout dat."

"Yeah, I knew there was a good chance she was gone, but I still have trouble believin' it."

Tom lay on the sofa, drained. "Anyway, thanks for your help, Jacques. I want you to know how much I appreciate…"

"Yeah, man, I know. I'm just sorry it didn't turn out some other way. Listen, man, you wanna pass by tomorrow and have my wife cook up a big ole pot o' jambalaya? The family'd all love to meet you."

Tom tried to envision the energy required in doing that one simple thing. "Can I take a rain check? I'm not quite ready for that. I haven't been feelin' great lately. Have you been okay since you got back?"

"The body's fine, but the soul's kinda weary."

"Yeah."

"You keep in touch, you hear?"

"Will do."

The next day, the former Father Tom reappeared on Father Abelli's doorstep. This time, he didn't say anything. He wanted to say something, wanted to complain about God's lack of respect for his grandmother, His total disinterest in human suffering, His absence from Tom's life, but he couldn't, so he turned to leave.

Wait," Father said, grabbing his arm.

Tom felt exhausted.

"Why don't you come in so we can be angry about this together?"

After he reluctantly crossed the threshold, Tom stayed for more than an hour. Father had taken two beers from the fridge, and they'd both downed a few swigs, before Tom's conversation flowed in a one-way stream toward Father Abelli. His sentences were bitter and choppy.

"Father, I think I brought this storm on myself…"

"You know I was pretendin' to be a priest…"

"I left my grandmother in New Orleans by herself…"

"How could God allow this to happen?"

"How could I have done this?"

"If there's a reason for everything, what could it possibly be? How could He destroy so many people?"

The gentle priest didn't pretend to know any answers. He listened with sadness and offered cold beer. Father marveled at Tom's faith, which was in crisis but alive. Francis Abelli had doubted his own faith many times.

When he was younger, Francis had been taught that the world suffered so it could share in Christ's suffering on the cross. This train of thought always led him back to some essential questions:

Was it necessary for Jesus to be humiliated and then murdered?

What about John the Baptist? If you were Christ, wouldn't you save your own cousin from a beheading? Why were so many of Jesus' followers killed or imprisoned?

Wouldn't the miracles of Jesus have been enough to prove God's love to the world? Couldn't He then have ascended into heaven without the bloody drama?

If Francis couldn't understand the thought process behind Jesus' life and death, how could he understand the molestation of children or the starvation of the poor?

Francis struggled with uncertainty. Then, one Good Friday, when he was venerating the cross, his clouds of confusion parted.

Of course. He'd had it all backwards.

Man's suffering has always existed. We don't suffer so we can share in the crucifixion of Christ. That wouldn't make sense. People suffered long before Jesus came to this world.

Christ came to share in *our* agony. To feel our sorrow. He wanted to experience human frailty. He wanted us to know that he understands what it feels like to be hungry, tormented, stripped naked.

Francis Abelli placed his faith in a compassionate God, in the One who sent his Son to this earth, because life offers no explanations. God wanted to feel our pain, so He came to experience it for Himself. And then he promised that we would one day overcome all our suffering.

Francis hoped he would see God face-to-face and ask Him why life had to be so thorny. Until then, he prayed with conviction, "Thy will be done…"

Francis and Tom said the prayer together. God wouldn't care that they had beer on their breath.

PRIORY, LOUISIANA

Mornin', Y'all   Wednesday, October 12, 2005

"Mornin', Y'all. This is Melody Melançon and you're listening to WPRY 90.5, bringing you and your mama up-to-date on the latest in Priory.

There have been so many sad stories from the hurricanes, y'all. But once in awhile, I hear something awesome. Yesterday, my friend Teeny called me with the best evacuation story I have heard yet. Her niece was leaving New Orleans before the storm—with her gorgeous husband of two years—when the baby she was carrying decided to come into this world. I kid you not. And hubby's panicking, saying, 'Hold on, honey. Don't you have this baby in the car on the I-10. Please do not have this baby right now, hon.'

And guess what, y'all? Teeny's niece said, plain as Doris Day, 'Hon, this baby is coming whether you like it or not.'

The way Teeny tells it: they were inching along the I-10 anyway, so he just put the car in park, got out in the rain, and waved his arms around like a madman, hollering as loud as he could to the massive sea of cars around him, 'My wife is having a baby! Help! Please!'

Some elderly lady—a retired nurse—splashed on over and birthed that baby in the backseat of their car. Right there on the leather seats. Can you believe that?

But wait. There's more. Y'all will never guess what they called the sweet little girl. Her name is Sunshine. Teeny says that the cute hubby was singing Governor Davis' "You Are My Sunshine" the whole way to the

Baton Rouge Medical Center with his exhausted wife and screaming new baby girl in the back seat.

And as if that wasn't enough, y'all will never guess where the retired nurse was from. No, not Priory. She was from Missouri. Bless her Midwestern heart. I promise to never make fun of your boot-heeled state ever again.

I tell you, I laughed and cried when I heard Teeny's story. It truly wore me out. I am emotionally exhausted, y'all. Exhausted and hungry. I hope Randy is making something good tonight. I could go for some cold crabmeat salad. You listening, Randy?

Congrats, Teeny. Congrats, lovely niece of Teeny and her gorgeous husband. Thanks, Miss Elderly Missouri Nurse. Welcome to the world, Sunshine.

One more thing: There's a fundraiser called Pennies for Pets over at Doc Gainard's veterinary office tomorrow afternoon. They'll be selling homemade pet treats for your favorite furries. You can put your name on a waiting list, too, to adopt one of the cute abandoned creatures if they never get reclaimed. I can only tell you from my love affair with Jasper that a dog is truly a blessing from above.

That's it for now. But remember, if you're not listening to *Mornin', Y'all*—especially with me giving you stories about babies birthed on the I-10 in the middle of a hurricane evacuation—you might as well be living on Jupiter."

PRIORY, LOUISIANA

CHAPTER FIFTY-FIVE

On a clear October day, with slanted sunlight promising a new season, Tom and Lena drove to Natchez. Tom's palms were slick, and Lena fidgeted with her black dress.

Mimi would've hated being buried in Natchez, Tom thought. But this was Sylvia's loss, too, so he knew it had to be his mother's decision. Their small family mausoleum in New Orleans had been damaged in the storm, and they had no idea how long the restoration would take. Sylvia needed to put her mother to rest. But not beside Dirk?

Tom promised himself that one day he would move Mimi. He didn't know when that day would come or how it would happen, but Tom wouldn't leave Mimi in Mississippi. He glanced over at Lena, who was twirling auburn hair around her finger. It looked so pretty hanging loose and wavy around her shoulders.

He took one hand off the steering wheel and reached for her. "You okay?"

She nodded and squeezed his hand. Cool green pines blurred by them on the neutral ground.

Tom summoned his courage. "Lena, I know this might sound crazy, but I think the storm may have been my fault." Dotted lines on the interstate approached and disappeared. "You know, pretendin' to be a priest and all. You think that's possible?"

Lena thought about it for a minute. "I heard some people saying that it was the gambling on the Gulf Coast that summoned the storm. It's too hard to think like that. Only God knows why He sent it. Maybe He didn't send it at all. Maybe He lets nature do its own thing."

He took his eyes off the road for a moment to look at her. Her right hand was clutching the door handle as if the wind might rip it off its hinges. Tom slowed down. He'd already promised himself he'd never drink and drive again. Now it appeared he might have to curtail his speeding, too.

When they arrived at the funeral home parking lot, he parked the car, leaned over, and kissed the smooth skin beneath her earlobe. "Thanks for bein' here," he whispered.

Lena looked into his green eyes. "I'd go anywhere for you."

Their desire had been lurking below the surface for weeks. During that time, Tom hadn't done more than kiss her, but he'd become quite the tease. He kissed her face, her neck, her eyes. She knew that one day things would progress, but she was enjoying every moment of their slow romance.

Tom had been in a state of limbo, floating on a watery sea, trying to lower his anchor and settle down, but he was still bobbing around.

They got out of the car and walked, hand in hand, into a meticulous brick building. Tom introduced Lena to his parents and his sister, Rachel, who'd flown in from D.C. They exchanged hugs and tears and lingered near the doorway, not wanting to broach the stale room. Tom stared at the closed mahogany casket, so alone in the middle of the dark room. The wood was familiar, like the wood of his chest-of-drawers. His dad said it was gone now, disintegrated.

His parents walked forward slowly, so slowly. As if it would be too dangerous to get so near death.

Tom was drawn to it, though. He went straight to Mimi's casket and her photo resting atop its lacquered dome. Her eyes were twinkling, even in this dim lighting.

Rubbing the slick wood, as if polishing a family heirloom, Tom felt the rest of the world slide away. He was small again, like on Mary Bell's front porch. It was comforting in a way, but also sad. And lonely. He temporarily forgot about Lena and the rest of his family. A dark mist shrouded everyone else from view. It was just Tom and Mimi now.

"Goodbye, Mimi," he said. "You were the best friend I ever had."

Invisible pins pricked his skin. Sweat and sorrow seeped from his pores. He wiped his face with both of his palms then dried them on his pants. Tom composed himself, reached into his suit pocket and took out a deck of playing cards, placing them next to her beautiful photo.

The room was stuffy and warm. The intense aroma of Stargazer Lilies perfumed the air. He kissed his fingertips, picked up her picture frame, and rubbed her flabby cheek with the kiss.

Then he knelt down in front of the casket, and Lena joined him, sliding her hand under his on the velvet rail, dispelling the dark mist.

Lena wished she'd met Mimi. Tom had told so many stories about her, and Lena imagined how much she'd be missed. That kind of profound loss was all too familiar to Lena. Just being in a funeral home again made her feel like she might faint. She rubbed his back and prayed for the right words to comfort him.

When the ceremony was over, they all had dinner and got to know each other a little better. Although Tom worried that Lena might be dismissed by Sylvia because she was a housekeeper, and because Lena was not from a family of any known prominence, this was not the case.

Sylvia, while discovering a few things about the unpredictable world, had replaced her sometimes-critical streak with a new openness. Her pretentiousness had been tempered by a fog of uncertainty and pain. She was kind to Lena because she saw on Tom's face what she had been hearing in his voice lately: her son was in love.

Rachel, usually the epitome of self-confidence and energy, was visibly worn. She was going to New Orleans with her parents to clear out Mimi's house, a job Tom couldn't bring himself to do.

"If you find anything of mine," Tom said, "pitch it."

Sylvia promised herself she'd find something of his to save. She wouldn't pitch anything that was still whole.

At dinner, Tom felt a warmth for his parents he hadn't felt in a long time. When Tom excused himself to the restroom, Sylvia followed him. Outside of everyone else's sight, she tugged on her son's sleeve. He turned to face his mom, a mother who had recently been orphaned. She seemed smaller now. Smaller and more frail.

Sylvia slipped her hand into the pocket of Tom's jacket and inserted a tiny box. He patted the fabric of his pocket like he was searching for missing keys.

"She would want you to have it," his mom whispered, fresh tears welling. "She loved you so much."

He knew immediately that it was a ring box, but he didn't want to take it out of his pocket. Instead, he just put his arms out, letting his mom fall into them. She cried into his shoulder.

"She loved all of us," he said.

Tom pushed her back to look at her. At first she seemed broken, but then Sylvia laughed through her tears. "Everyone except Father McMann."

She would be alright, this mother of his. *This* was the mother who'd raised him, who'd made him banana splits and hemmed his pants and sang him to sleep. He'd forgotten how full her heart could be. He'd forgotten that she could make jokes even when her soul was weary.

When dinner was over, they walked back to their cars. The days were getting shorter and dusk was upon them. A noisy flock of starlings circled overhead before vanishing into the piney woods nearby. It was time for the seasons to change. A welcome, stable environment had settled upon the South.

"How long y'all stayin' in Natchez, Ma?" Tom wondered.

"Oh, I don't know, hon. Things are still so crazy in New Orleans. We're going to keep the house here for a while. Rachel can't take a lot of time off. She's got to get back to Washington so we're going to clean out Mimi's house tomorrow."

Tom turned to his father.

"Sorry I can't help, Dad," Tom said. "I just can't…"

"I know," his dad replied. "Besides, I hear you're pretty busy these days." Richard smiled at Lena.

Lena grinned. Laugh lines blended with tiny scars, softening them.

"Being a photographer is solid work, Tom," Richard said. "I think it suits you. Besides, we've got enough computer geniuses in this world."

Tom's cheeks stung. With the uttering of that small sentence, Richard gave Tom permission to let so much angst fall away. After shaking his father's hand, he kissed his mother and sister goodbye.

On the way back to Priory, images of giving the ring to Lena consumed him. His body burned with desire. He wanted to take Lena home, give her the tiny box, and begin the rest of their crazy lives together.

As the highway passed under the car, he pondered how absent he'd been from his own life lately. Mimi would've chastised him for it.

Tom wanted to live in Priory, but he also wondered if he might someday go back to New Orleans to help chronicle the recovery. He'd need to bring with him lots of film and a willingness to feel the sorrow.

He also wanted to go see Father Abelli and thank him, wanted to call Jacques and meet his Cajun kin, wanted to find his own displaced New Orleans buddies, and he wanted to go back to Bob's to rebuild some relationships.

"Lena," Tom said, glancing over at her, suddenly noticing a freckle on her cheekbone he hadn't remembered.

"Yes?"

"Would it bother you if I still went by Bob's now and then and had a beer or two, not more, with the guys?"

"Of course not."

"You know," he said, "I think I've got more stupid Boudreaux jokes they haven't heard."

"I'm sure you do."

CHAPTER FIFTY-SIX

By the time Tom and Lena arrived at home late that night, the harvest moon had risen over their Southern sky. In a violet cottage, in a cypress-infused home, Tom approached the woman he loved.

He raised his hands as if he were being robbed. She mirrored him and intertwined fingers. He pulled her forward and kissed her, slowly and passionately, wanting to taste every delicious part of her.

Lena's body slumped against his. Tom slid his hands down to her lower back and pulled her up against him. He stopped kissing her and brushed the wavy hair away from her face.

"Lena," he said seriously. "You are the best thing that's ever happened to me."

She grinned.

"And I know I'm far from perfect," he said into the softness of the room. "I'm a mess, really, if you want the truth of it."

Lena didn't think he was a mess. When she looked at him, she saw hope and promise.

Tom reached into his coat pocket and withdrew the ring box.

"If you marry me, baby," he said, "I will do my best to deserve you."

Without opening the box, he held it up between them. Pulling her near with one arm, he kissed her again, deeply, longingly. "Will you marry me, Lena Melendez?"

She pressed her forehead against his and blinked. A tear landed on the velvet box.

PRIORY, LOUISIANA

"I'll take that as a *yes*."

Tom opened the box and was newly amazed at how perfect Mimi's ring was. It was platinum with an oval diamond in the middle and smaller diamonds encircling it. He pictured Grandpa Dirk putting it on his spirited grandmother. Their black and white wedding picture decorated his thoughts.

Mimi, I promise I'll move you someday so you can be by Grandpa D. You won't be stuck in Mississippi.

Lena admired the ring. "Where did you get this?"

"It was Mimi's. My mom gave it to me today."

She took a step backwards and sat on the sofa's edge. "Oh, Tom… I don't know what to say."

Tom knelt on the floor in front of her. "Say 'yes.'"

He raised her left hand to his lips and kissed the bare expanse of skin on her ring finger. Then he slid the ring into place.

"Tom Vaughn, I would be so proud to be your wife." She ran her hands through his thick black hair.

He'd never heard anything more achingly beautiful. He stood and pulled her up, hugging her, lifting her off the ground, twirling her in a circle all around the intimate room.

"Baby, you are gorgeous," he said into her ear. Her familiar orange scent filled his lungs.

Lena's chest heaved with desire. "You really love me," she marveled.

"I really do."

Love. It was more painful and more promising than Tom had ever imagined.

He held her close to his heart and tapped on her back: l-o-v-e. It was a word that took two hands to type.

PRIORY, LOUISIANA

An owl's hooting entered through an open window and circled them. Nearby, in a busy swamp, green tree frogs moaned. Moonlight shone through lace curtains into their simple country home, casting pieces of silver upon Tom and Lena. The night air in Priory was clear and still.

ABOUT THE AUTHOR

Pat Kogos is a writer of fiction, poetry and nonfiction. She was born and raised in St. Louis, lived in New Orleans for twenty years, then moved back to her hometown. Pat's writing combines her affection for both her Southern and Midwestern roots.

After receiving her Bachelor's at Loyola University in New Orleans, Pat earned an MFA in Writing at Lindenwood University in St. Charles, Missouri.

She has been both a Finalist and a Semi-Finalist in the Faulkner-Wisdom Creative Writing Competition.

Although Pat is thrilled to be back home, she's proud of her continued ties to Louisiana, including her husband Sam's highly regarded Creole and Cajun eatery, Riverbend Restaurant & Bar in St. Louis.

Pat lives in the Gateway to the West with her husband, two creative teenagers, and one adorable Yorkie.

Photograph by Heather-Lynne Photography, LLC, St. Louis, MO